Shadowland

Also by Pam Leonard:

Death's Imperfect Witness (Midwest Book Awards finalist, 2010)

Where Echoes Die

For more information about the author go to
http://www.pamleonard.com/

SHADOWLAND

Pam Leonard

North Star Press of St. Cloud, Inc.
St. Cloud, Minnesota

Printed in the United States
by Sentinel Printing, St. Cloud, Minnesota

Published by
North Star Press of St. Cloud, Inc.
P.O. Box 451
St. Cloud, Minnesota 56302

www.northstarpress.com   Facebook - North Star Press

For Kati and David

Acknowledgments

As always, I begin with family. Thank you, Bill, for your faith in me—you add muscle to my dreams. A special thank you to David for orchestrating the video and photographic support of my work, and for those hours and hours we spent together creating my new website—bless your generous heart! Another big thanks to Kati and Matt for your voiceover work on the Shadowland video trailer—you guys rock! Mom, thank you for your ceaseless support and encouragement—it's always appreciated. And to all of you, thanks for the inspiration—everything that I do is with you in mind.

Dear friend, Sue Halena, once again you have my gratitude for so generously sharing another weekend in review of my manuscript—having trusted and honest feedback is priceless!

To Merle Sykora and Tom Olson, thank you both for sharing Splashing Rock with us, and for your continued friendship and support.

To Patrick Arden Wood, I offer my heartfelt gratitude for sharing your knowledge of the homeless, and for steering me toward additional resources on Ojibwe spirituality—your support and encouragement throughout this effort was greatly appreciated.

My friends Kirsten A.S. Mebust and Kate Stanley, thank you for the stimulating spiritual discussions—you both know how much they meant! And to Joe Olivieri, thank you for stepping up to help.

Finally, Uncle LeRoy, it's with a wink and a nudge that I thank you for sharing your love of all things unique, inventive, and architecturally personalized! It's how we roll.

"It is the glory of God to conceal things, but the glory of kings is to search things out."

—Proverbs Ch. 25, vs. 2

CHAPTER ONE

BELIEVE ME WHEN *I* TELL YOU *I* COULD NEVER KILL A MAN . . .
Zoe recognized the song—Alison Krauss, singing as a man—words that hung like smoke in the bar. Zoe smiled into her glass—*That's what you think, Alison.*

---

*BELIEVE ME WHEN *I* TELL YOU *I* COULD NEVER KILL A MAN . . .*
Grace felt the bar fall silent. The words didn't echo exactly, but she heard nothing else for several moments afterwards. Bracing her back firmly to the wall, Grace thought hard about what people could and couldn't do.

SOMETHING PASSED THROUGH THE BAR WITHIN a momentary interruption in background conversation that, while barely perceptible, seemed unnatural. Zoe was sure it happened—not just in her imagination—and there had to be forty, maybe fifty people in the place. What were the odds they'd all stop talking—even for five seconds?

GRACE *HAD* DONE THE MATH, actually picked up a calculator and crunched the numbers once. In the presence of any fifty people in this Minneapolis bar there'd be at least two who, unlike Alison, had a real knowledge of what people could and couldn't do. The rest only thought they did.

ZOE STUDIED THE FACES AROUND HER.
Following the most frequent direction of their gazes led to a woman with jet-black hair at the far end of the bar. She sat back-to-wall, the only stool

positioned to allow it. Zoe always noticed those things—protective zones, escape routes, hiding places—and risked staring as she drank.

Looking over the rim of her glass, Zoe was struck not merely by the degree to which this lady was pulling at her drink, but by how much just didn't add up. The woman's face was lined in a pattern of hard knocks, but her body looked ten years younger, fit even. And the black-haired woman didn't slump. Even though her expression was one of exhaustion, she remained alert—never turning to avoid any intersecting glances. Her face read aggression. Her position at the bar read defense.

Zoe continued to watch as the woman emptied her glass, got the bartender's attention by slamming it down, and then signaled for another.

After pouring the woman's drink, the bartender made his way back toward Zoe. He didn't even try to hide the grimace after seeing her reach into her pocket for some Swedish Fish.

"You want some more beer to go with that candy?" He winced—apparently the combination didn't appeal to him.

"Yeah, another would be good." Zoe held out her hand. "Want one?"

He smiled, and declined.

Zoe smiled back, but in a way she now had to practice. Modifying her reckless come-get-me smile wasn't easy, especially when her awareness of it barely registered—it had been habit, and wildly successful, for so long. But now she had a real lover. Someone she was expected to be faithful to—someone she *wanted* to be faithful to. And promises. Suddenly, at age thirty-two, there was someone who felt possessive about her, and someone whom she claimed as hers. Lifestyle modifications.

As she sized up the bartender, it *did* register that this could be hard.

"You're Dr. Lawrence, aren't you?"

"Guilty," it was the first word that came to mind—Kaj wouldn't have liked the way she'd been looking at this guy. "Why?"

"You're reputation precedes you."

Zoe smiled again, and worried it was the wrong kind. "Care to explain?"

"Ah, the cops who hang out here—they know you. They talk."

"About what?"

"Depends on who's talking."

"Ray Perry?"

"He's not over you."

"Tell me something I don't know."

"Jack..."

"...Would like to kill me. You must be new here."

"Part time. Just started a month ago. And..."

"...I'll take another, thanks."

GRACE RECONSIDERED A FAMILIAR QUESTION AFTER downing half the refill. The answers, the reasons, all collided in her head. They were slippery and hard to pin down—as always, coated with booze—but one of them stuck, right alongside other stuff she couldn't ignore. The glass stopped halfway from bar-top to pale, chapped lips—her eyes looking through it. *I know*, she answered her accusers, her mouth actually forming the words.

Her fingers tightened around the glass and her arm moved again. She coughed as what was left of the drink burned her throat. Slamming the empty down—just one more—she looked around at all the faces, severe in their judgment, sweeping her into their communal consciousness.

They weren't any different from her, not really—just luckier, nothing else. They sure as hell were lucky to have her around.

In fact, ninety-six percent fucking *owed* her.

Fortunately, the other four percent didn't know that yet.

ZOE FELT HERSELF JUMP AT THE SOUND OF THE GLASS nearly shattering, and returned to her study of the drinking woman. The lady was dressed for action. She wasn't in some sort of frilly, low-cut dress or high heels. Her clothes were a little unusual, almost hippy-like—Bohemian?—but if this woman had to run, she could. If she had to fight, she could. Zoe noticed things like that, too, and looked down at her own t-shirt, hoodie, jeans, and running shoes. "Hmm."

The sudden hand on her shoulder turned Zoe's face up toward shadowed eyes under a hat pulled low—and she laughed.

"Kelly! What, or should I ask *who*, are you hiding from?"

He sat down beside her and whispered, "Order me a beer."

"Riiight. And why can't you order it yourself?"

He signaled for her to look above the bar—at a photo. It was his face . . . with a big, red "X" drawn over it and "30 days" written on his forehead.

"What the hell?" Zoe tilted the brim of his hat back to better see him.

"Don't." He repositioned the hat. "And don't ask me why. I can't exactly remember. But I think it had something to do with a frozen pizza."

Zoe laughed hard, and drew a look from the bartender.

"Zoe, cut it out," he said in ventriloquist mode. "I just need a beer, that's all."

She slid her own beer in his direction and signaled for another. "Did it involve this bartender?"

"No, but if he looks at that picture he'll have to kick me out. I'm temporarily banished. It's only been two weeks, so tone it down, will ya?"

"Kelly, you should have told me this when I called. We could easily have met for lunch somewhere else."

"Yeah, well, I sort of forgot. It was one of those 'memorable' nights you can't quite remember. Know what I mean?"

Zoe smiled, "No doubt. What kind of pizza you want? I'm hungry."

"Whatever you're going with. Why out so early?"

"I stayed up all night with a patient. Everything about the guy was labile. He needed babysitting."

"That's not unusual."

"Nope. But I wasn't supposed to be on call last night. I was on the night before. So the incoming on-call team sprung me early."

"And the patient?"

Zoe only stared into the fresh beer in front of her.

"Didn't make it? Sorry."

"No, it's not that. He made it—through the two nights I made him my biggest priority. But Minneapolis General's incomings are merciless on the call-night teams. Don't get me wrong—not complaining. That's how we learn. But the on-call team can't possibly spend the time required to really understand how he responds. So I stayed."

"Well then, that's good!"

"Except that I can't stay awake another night, and he's still not stable."

"Up three days and two nights?"

"Yep."

"Well you wouldn't be doing him any good by staying. Not in your condition. You look ready to fall asleep right here."

"That's what the attending said when he kicked me out."

Trying for a smile, Zoe crumpled under a sudden coughing paroxysm that had the bartender looking at her with concern and the bar falling unnaturally silent again. Kelly patted her back vigorously, keeping his head tilted away from the stare of the bartender until Zoe's fit was over.

As she worked to catch her breath Kelly reached over and drew the hoodie tight around Zoe's shoulders. He was as close to a father figure as Zoe had, and never shied from acting the part. "How long you had that cough?"

"It's only been two weeks. What kind of pizza?"

"Only?"

"I'm tired, though—have to admit. The cough's been keeping me up at night, even when I'm not on call. So things aren't sharp, you know? Now what kind? I'm hungry."

"A Doyle's Habit okay with you?"

Zoe called to the bartender, "Make it a Doyle's Habit over here." She looked back at Kelly, "You know, I took care of him once."

"Who?"

"Doyle."

"Before or after his last overdose?"

"Before. He died on a different service."

Kelly was staring at her. He touched her forehead. "How long you had that fever?"

"What fever?"

"Aw come on. You're a damn doctor. You should know when you're sick."

Zoe looked around the bar—thickheaded, but working it over. Her gaze went from the man in the corner, typing furiously on a laptop computer, over to the little boy hopping excitedly next to a woman at his table—his mother maybe? The boy looked to be about five, jumping up and down, succeeding in getting everyone's attention except for his mother's. Instead, the woman appeared to look right through him. To Zoe, the boy's antics seemed hard to ignore—but no matter how fast he hopped, his mother didn't react. No matter that his chanting climbed to piercing decibels, she seemed immune. How could anyone not respond to his song and dance? But just as she thought it was impossible, Zoe's attention was diverted—her focus swinging from the urban opera taking place in the aisle over to the door as it opened.

A young man, using one hand to hold up threadbare pants and the other to pull tangled dirty locks of hair away from his eyes, was the first to enter. November chill was evident in his posture—a folding in on oneself that happens during the colder Minnesota months. On his heels was a teenager who, unlike the tentative entry of the homeless man, announced himself energetically. The teen was almost dancing to attract the attention of the bartender who'd instantly locked onto the problem of the street-person. Zoe thought she recognized the homeless guy—almost sure she'd taken care of him once in the hospital—but redirected her attention to the teen.

He looked at her briefly—more like through her—but then yelled, "He's gonna jump! Come on!" Pointing outside and up, the kid moved to the window.

Zoe bolted for the door, along with almost everyone else in the bar. Seeing a shadow pass over the pavement had her expecting to see a body on the asphalt. But instead she looked from an empty street up toward the buildings. Nothing. No body, no jumper.

A tree full of argument brought her gaze to where the crows perched, barking their alarms. With nothing else to see from inside the window, curiosity pulled Zoe, Kelly, and the bartender farther out on the sidewalk for a better look. Most of the other diners followed—only to witness crows lifting for another tree.

As they returned to their places, Zoe and Kelly scanned the bar for a kid who wasn't there anymore—then rested their gazes on the opened, empty till.

"Oh, shit." Kelly got up to leave. "This is all I need. I was never here."

Neither was the kid, the drinking woman, or the homeless guy. Neither were half the customers, some of whom, at a minimum, had managed to skip out on their tabs.

But one left the hard way. His body was discovered outside the rear entry to the bar.

TWO HOURS LATER, ZOE'S CALL TO KAJ WENT unanswered so she left him a text.

As an attending physician in the Emergency Department, she knew there were plenty of moments when he couldn't even look at his cellphone. She knew it first hand because she'd been an Emergency Medicine resident-physician training under him up until last summer, when she'd switched to Internal Medicine. Though it was a surprise to her and to everyone who thought they knew her, she'd felt the need for long-term relationships with her patients. And so far, the decision seemed to have been a good one. It was rewarding, and the intensive care units were full of the adrenaline-packed action she loved about the ER.

There were some who speculated that the switch had something to do with the romantic relationship that developed between Zoe and Dr. Kaj Parker. But in reality, that was what made it hard as hell—because she'd loved working with him. They were a good team.

"BZ ENUF DAY 4 ME. ENDED ON A SUPREMELY WEIRD NOTE. HOW BOUT U? MET UR NEW STAFF DOC THIS AM. WE NEED 2 TALK ABOUT THAT. SHE HAS AN INTERESTING TAKE ON U. FA! NM. HEADING HOME."

Zoe mounted her bike and got less than a block before her cell beeped.

"OK. C U THERE. BUT WHAT DOES FA MEAN? & NM? LUV U. GOT 2 RUN. BZ HERE."

Zoe laughed. There were only five years separating their ages, but it was an eternity when it came to texting.

"CONSIDER FA 2 B A SOUND EFFECT. NM MEANS NEVER MIND. I'LL TRY U AGAIN L8R." She hit send and replaced the phone in her pocket while returning her attention to the trip home . . . and to why she'd been of such little help to Ray. Her cloudy take on events in the bar had made her a piss-poor witness, and even Ray had urged her to go home and "take care of that cough."

Probably the tenth time she'd heard that in a four-hour period—and it might even be true. But on her way home the image of the dead man nagged.

Zoe had looked over the crime scene before the cops arrived. She knew how to analyze it safely, and how to preserve it by keeping everyone else at bay. The skull over his temple was fractured, a triangular chunk piercing his brain, and the orbital bones and eye socket on that side were caved in. Scanning the wall next to the body, it was evident that the blow to the head had been both the first and fatal wound. But he'd been beaten after being felled. There were wounds all over his body, including obviously broken arm bones. They didn't look to be defensive wounds, they'd been broken where he lay—probably after his death. Although the crowd that gathered around him was abuzz with a jumper theory, Zoe was certain his death had nothing to do with high places.

CHAPTER TWO

KAJ'S ARM CIRCLED HER WAIST AS SHE SURFACED.

"What time is it?"

Kaj turned to look. "About five."

"You must have gotten off early."

"It's 5:00 A.M, darling."

"A.M.?"

"Yes, and you haven't moved all night except to cough—incessantly."

Zoe rubbed furiously at her eyes, hoping to clear the fog. "I got home at about 3:00 P.M. That puts my little 'nap' at twelve hours. I can't remember the last time I slept that long—and dammit, I still feel tired."

"Come with me."

"Where?"

"Here," he pulled her on top of him.

Zoe laughed, and leaned in to kiss him. "Now where?"

"A ride."

WHEN ZOE EMERGED FROM THE SHOWER SHE FOUND Kaj waiting with two fresh cups of coffee.

"This should help. So, tell me about this 'weird note' your day ended on. I should also hear about my new colleague and her 'take' on me. Your text piqued my curiosity."

Zoe grinned and reached for a towel. "I stopped for lunch at that dive with the good pizza. You know, the one that doesn't know if it wants to be a diner or a bar? Angie's. That's when all hell broke loose."

Kaj offered her coffee after she was done toweling off, sat down, and then patted his lap. "All hell broke loose?"

Zoe sat, drank deeply, and then continued. "Upshot is they found a dead body behind the place—freshly dead. Theory among the diners was that he jumped . . . landing head-first."

9

"And you're not buying it?"

"No way. He was beaten with something—something that wasn't there anymore. Ray agrees."

"Ray was there?"

"He was called in. Showed up after all the hoopla." In Zoe's former life as a cop, Ray had been her partner—and her lover. While Ray and Kaj had come to tolerate each other—mainly out of necessity when a serial killer threatened Zoe's life and their cooperation was crucial to finding her—there was still an edge to their relationship. She always pictured alpha wolves circling each other, waiting for the chance to attack—but then again, that was their problem, not hers.

Kaj nodded. "It's been a while since I've seen Detective Perry."

"Bar-league hockey starts soon. We'll both be seeing a lot of him."

"Perfect place to cross paths." His smile looked demonic.

"Don't get any ideas. Besides, I've got my own issues with your new colleague."

"Connie?"

"Yes. Dr. Sayre." Zoe emphasized the title.

"And what's that all about?"

"She's hot for you." Zoe grinned.

"Excuse me?"

"Well, who isn't?—and I suppose it's my cross to bear." She paused to let him roll his eyes. "Anyway, she let it slip when I came down to collect a patient a couple days ago. The ER was hopping, but apparently she's a little slow on the uptake."

"Well that can't be. I'm open about us—we're no secret. And believe me, she's not stupid. In fact she's quite amazing in the ER."

"Hmm." Zoe focused on the cool blue of Kaj's eyes. "That puts a whole new spin on things."

"You must have misunderstood, that's all."

"Yeah, guess it must be me." Zoe set down her coffee and turned in his lap, repositioning her legs to straddle him. "And of course there's the fact that you're simply irresistible to anyone." He managed to laugh, even as Zoe felt his breath quicken and his muscles tighten. In one smooth move Zoe slipped over him, around him, whispering, "But does she play hockey?"

Pam Leonard

THE MAN DIED OVERNIGHT.

Zoe looked at the resident's note. She could picture the code he'd run, and knew that by then there'd have been no hope. But then again, that was the whole point of her long vigil—to babysit, to prevent a code—because there'd be no way he'd survive the trauma of one. She should have stayed—found a way around the attending's admonition. She'd done it before.

"When?"

"Just before you got here." The nurse was still writing up her own notes after the event.

…Or should have come in early. Instead she'd been home getting laid. "Fuck!"

The nurse glanced up.

"What was he like overnight?"

The nurse looked back toward her notes as she answered, "There were a lot of phone calls."

"Did he respond?"

"Who? The patient?"

"You know what I mean."

"He usually sent his intern."

"And?"

"And I kept calling—until he finally showed up at the code."

"Goddammit!"

This time the nurse looked at her square on. "Sucks, doesn't it?"

OUT OF FRUSTRATION, ZOE FOUND HERSELF in the ER—where Kaj now listened patiently.

"Damn it, Kaj, I have to do something!"

"Settle down. Let's go in here and talk." They slipped into an empty ER cube. "From what I hear, it was a crazy night—we sent the medicine service far too many admits. The resident was probably so busy he simply couldn't respond and did the next best thing by sending his intern."

"But…"

"…And you have to consider the possibility that your patient wasn't going to make it anyway, Zoe. He'd been on the edge for three days and nights. Ready to crash that entire time. It was heroic, what you did, but not sustainable. I looked at the record after you called me. Zoe, he wasn't going to make it ..."

"No ..."

"... He was never coming off that ventilator. His heart couldn't possibly recover from that degree of insult. He couldn't be sustained on dialysis but for brief, non-productive periods. All his organs were failing. The real surprise is that he lasted as long as he did. Zoe, the intern did everything appropriately."

"Not like I ..."

As Zoe started to protest again, he added, "And if he'd had family, I venture a guess they'd have asked to end his suffering."

That stopped her. She couldn't win—first guilty for not being there, and now guilty for having stayed ... all while looking for someone else to blame. "Aw, fuck."

Kaj smiled, and wrapped her in his arms. "But I love that about you."

"What, that I cuss like a sailor, or that I'm an idiot about most things?"

"That you care."

Her eyes filled, "But he was such a nice guy."

"I know, Zoe."

"A really nice guy."

"Of course he was. Most of them are. And mostly you help them."

"Maybe I'm just experiencing the dark side of my switch to Internal Medicine. In the ER, I got to know a lot of the repeaters, but not quite this well."

"Knowing him well, you'd have come to the same conclusion, soon enough."

"And let him go?"

"Listen, I get it—how hard it is not to keep trying. We face that in the ER regularly. You know that. It feels like failure. But, yes, you'd have done that for him."

The curtain flew open as Dr. Sayre entered. "Kaj, they told me I could find you in here." She stopped upon seeing the embracing couple. "Sorry. Am I interrupting something?"

Zoe looked at the barely disguised smirk on the woman's pale-pink lips— a shade that matched her pale-pink nails. A shade that, Zoe had to admit, she liked.

Kaj whispered in Zoe's ear, "See? Now be nice."

Zoe brushed her eyes against Kaj's shirt before letting go of their embrace. She put a hand over his shoulder to cover the damp spot that remained, and then turned to leave. "See you later, Kaj. Connie." Zoe nodded, and walked out. She'd be goddamned if she was going let this woman see her cry, ever—about any fucking thing.

"ZOE," RAY HELD OUT A PHOTO, "you recall this woman in the bar?"

Zoe ignored her nagging beeper as they both stood in a fourth floor hospital hallway, "Of course. That's the woman I told you about. She's practically all I remember. She was the hook in the whole song and dance. I was so goddamned tired that everything else is a blur. But she stood out for some reason."

"Well, we can't find her."

"As in suspiciously?"

"Dunno. Apparently she's a bit of a loner, so I don't know if it's unusual for her to be gone. Neighbors don't have much to say about her. All I know is that she never returned home last night. We tried her place several times during the night. Might not be a big deal, except that I want to talk to her."

"What was she in for?" The photo was an old mug shot.

"Assaulting an officer."

"Huh?'

"It was nothing. No one got hurt. Feisty, that's all. She was on the receiving end of a domestic assault and refused to cooperate."

"So?"

"So . . . she decided to get physical with the officer sent to question her, and he had to take her down. The whole thing was dropped."

"Funny. I remember thinking that she was fit—and ready for action. Guess she's impulsive, too. Best be careful when you find her, Ray," Zoe said through a laugh.

"Powers of observation . . ."

But her laugh turned into a cough, and wouldn't stop. Her eyes watered as she gasped for breath and she held up a hand signaling for patience from Ray. Zoe paced as her fit continued. Finally it settled and she sat, exhausted, breathing deep to recover.

"...Indicate that you need to see a doctor about that cough."

"My attending right now just happens to be one of the pulmonary specialists—and he agrees with you. I've got a two-o'clock appointment that he insisted upon during rounds this morning. Wouldn't take no for an answer. I suppose it didn't help that one of my med students was actually wearing a facemask to avoid catching what I have. Guy looked like an idiot—but it kind of forced the attending's hand, I suppose."

"As it should! Keep the appointment, Zoe"

"Why wouldn't I?"

"Zoe, I know you. Keep the damn appointment. And if you see this lady again, let me know." He turned to leave.

"Wait. What's her name? And tell me where you are with the dead body. Homicide? Or accident?"

"Homicide. No doubt. But you already knew that. The blood spatter and velocity characteristics place the point of convergence at about six feet above the ground. He didn't jump, unless the ground jumped up to meet him. Blunt trauma to the head, while standing."

"Any leads?"

"Leads? Not so much. He was seen in the bar just before the commotion with the kid. Other than that, no one seems to have any idea who he was—or simply won't say. That is, among the bar patrons who didn't skip out. I'm still working to track the others down. Got some leads there, but it takes time. I'm not worried though, we'll get one of them to talk. Probably just means he was into something no one wants any part of."

"Wish I could remember more. I'll keep trying. Her name?"

"Grace Prescott. She lives above the head shop on Hennepin—the near Northeast side. Now take care of that cough."

"Yeah, I've heard that more than a few times today. But I will."

Zoe watched Ray's back as he headed away. Then she turned to jump down the stairs toward Kelly's office. His day job was as head of maintenance at Minneapolis General, a job he'd finagled in order to work his second job—which was keeping an eye on Zoe. As a former cop, he'd been on scene at Zoe's horrendous ordeal. He knew she'd witnessed the murder of her entire family, and that she'd been tortured by the men responsible—the very same men who'd caused the death of his wife and kids.

While Zoe had eventually managed to kill one of them—in a calculated ambush—
he wanted the other. But after a long and unsuccessful manhunt, sticking with Zoe
had seemed to be his only hope of finding the clearly obsessed man—a man who
Kelly predicted would come back for her. About that, he'd been right.

They both still hoped that last summer's encounter with that very same
man had resulted in his death—but despite Lucy's aim, they never did find his
body after it fell into deep water in the Wilderness Area north of Duluth. But
fifteen-year-old Lucy had hit him, and the blood trail had been significant. Their
hope seemed justified.

"KELLY. YOU MISSED OUT ON ALL THE FUN—leaving before they found the body."

"What body?"

"Good question. So far, no one admits to knowing him. Dead by blunt
trauma to the head. Found behind the bar, just outside the entrance. Fresh kill.
Problem is, half the patrons left during the commotion about the missing money
from the till. Including you!" she grinned.

"So?"

"So, you're a witness. I am, too, but I was so tired I can't recall things I'd normally
notice. I'm not much help. They could use your input, though. I didn't mention you
were there, but you'd better check in with Ray. What do you remember?"

"Zoe, I was wearing that damn hat pulled low and wasn't making eye
contact with any-fucking-one—the idea being that I didn't want to be noticed.
Ring any kind of bell with you?"

"So you didn't see much?"

"Nothing. My few minutes in there, I was totally focused on you . . . and
hiding my face."

"Okay, I guess I see what you mean. But if you think of anything, let me
know. Or talk to Ray."

"Of course." He paused. "You're sweating. Still got that fever?"

"Apparently." She held up a hand to stop him. "I've got an appointment
about it this afternoon."

"DEEP BREATHS."

Zoe kept trying, but whenever she breathed deeply, the ribs on her left side hurt like hell and she'd start coughing again.

Her attending brought up the chest x-ray on screen. He turned it towards her.

"No, way. Is that really mine? Check the name."

"It's yours, Dr. Lawrence. I double-checked. Care to make a diagnosis?"

"Aw, fuck."

"Excuse me?"

"I mean, pneumonia."

"Yes, and one that I'm barely willing to send you home with."

"You mean I can't stay and work?"

"Would you tell that to a patient?"

Zoe wanted to fight this. "Well . . ."

"Would you?"

"No. I suppose not."

"Right. And my instincts tell me to keep you here as a patient . . ."

"Absolutely not."

". . . But, as I guessed that would be your reaction, we'll start the antibiotics here and I'll send you home with more—as well as something for that cough so you can get some uninterrupted sleep."

"But . . ."

"No arguments. If you weren't otherwise so fit, I'd have to insist that you stay. But I know it'd be a losing battle, so let's just get you started on antibiotics and then home—right away."

ZOE MADE A STOP AT THE PHARMACY to pick up her medicine and then swung through the ER to inform Kaj.

She found them together, discussing a patient. Connie stood close, too close. It was an intimate distance—one that Zoe was familiar with. She'd also tossed her white coat over a chair and if Kaj hadn't already noticed her shrink-wrapped jeans, he wasn't all man.

Zoe was sick, tired, and angry—and for a moment, she weighed whether to simply say fuck 'em both or to go down swinging. Instead she coughed, felt a metallic taste in her mouth, and grabbed a Kleenex in which to expel the blood.

Both Connie and Kaj looked up to see her toss the tissue in the garbage and walk toward them. The pain in her side had her wincing.

"I've been cut loose. Sick. See you later."

"What? The cough?"

"Yep. Apparently it's pneumonia. My attending basically ordered me to go home and rest. Just wanted to let you know." But really, she wished she hadn't come down to the ER at all.

"I'll be over as soon as I get off."

"Don't bother. I just need to sleep." She sent Connie a look that was meant to remind her of what she and Kaj did at night when they weren't sleeping. But Connie Dr. Pink Sayre didn't seem impressed. Instead she looked back toward Kaj as if Zoe were already history. When Zoe slumped in another coughing paroxysm she was sure that Connie had lengthened to her full height in response. Fit, clearly athletic, just the way Kaj liked them. *Some competition I am*, Zoe thought. Sweaty, coughing up blood, doubled over with pleuritic chest pain.

Kaj reached out to her, but she waved him off. "I have to get home— doctor's orders. In fact I've been given several days off. Adding the weekend, I'll get six whole days of rest. He wouldn't take no for an answer and threatened to hospitalize me if I continued arguing," her last word caught on the hard "g" and was lost in another coughing fit.

"And I can imagine you tried." Kaj's look was a serious one, while Connie only registered a tolerant smile. "He did the right thing. Why don't you stay at my place instead?"

Zoe looked first at Kaj, who seemed clueless about what was really happening, and then at Connie. "No, we'd never get any sleep."

One little jab, she thought, the only one she had any strength for at the moment. But apparently it meant she was of a mind to go down swinging—later, she decided, when she felt up to it.

As she turned to leave there was little doubt in her mind that this woman was a threat. It wasn't just Zoe's fever, the ever-present anxiety, or her obsessive distrust of happiness. Dr. Connie Sayre was already moving in on Kaj—and he didn't see it. Or did he?

Chapter Three

Z OE'S EYES SNAPPED OPEN AND SHE REACHED instinctively for a gun she no longer routinely carried. Swinging upright in bed, her sense of an unfamiliar presence in the room had been correct.

But Lucy looked as shocked as Zoe, and jumped up from her seat by the window.

"It's just me!" Lucy was backing away.

Zoe slumped back down in bed. "Sorry, Lucy. You startled me."

"It was kinda the other way around."

Zoe smiled. "What are you doing here?"

"Kaj gave me a key and said I'm your nurse for the next several days. He said to tell you—and I'm supposed to quote him here—that 'you'll get your sleep this way, but you'll also be taken care of.' And he said to tell you that he insists. I'm a little uncomfortable saying this part, but he also said to tell you 'there'll be no arguments.'"

"He did, did he?" and her laughter turned again to coughing.

"Can I help you with anything? He said companionship would do, if you didn't want help. But he strongly encouraged me to try and give you a hand. I'd appreciate the chance to tell him I did."

"What about your school work?"

"I do it online. It doesn't take long that way. In fact, I've got most of this week's work done already. What little I have left can be done while you sleep. It won't take me long at all."

Zoe thought for a moment. "Okay. Maybe there are a few things you can help me with. I may have six days off, but I'm sure as hell not going to sit around the whole time. You sure you don't have much to do this week?"

"No. Just a couple more hours worth."

The coughing paroxysm that followed was the worst yet, and had Lucy hovering. Zoe grabbed for some tissue and expelled bright-red blood into it.

Lucy's eyes grew big. "That doesn't look good."

"It's nothing. How long have you been here?"

"Kaj dropped me off last night and I slept in the guest room. Been sitting here since sunrise."

"Did I cough much during the night?"

"Nope. In fact you slept like a baby. Made me think this gig was going to be too easy."

"Too easy, eh?" Smiling, Zoe rolled over and looked at the two medicine bottles. "Don't worry, I'm sure to find a way to make things difficult." The antibiotics were a must-take—no question. And it looked like the opiate for her cough had worked, too. She'd only planned on taking it at night, but this coughing had gone on for too long and had her exhausted. Suppressing it during the day was also a must—especially with the stabbing pleuritic chest pain she was now experiencing with each cough.

"Okay, Lucy. One more question. Did you get your driver's license?"

"Yep. Pushpa lent me her car for the driver's training and test."

Pushpa was an elderly resident of the retirement "commune" where the freshly sixteen-year-old Lucy lived and, usually, worked.

And Kaj was one slippery son-of-a-bitch.

After their recently shared life-and-death experience, he'd known that Zoe and Lucy would both feel beholden to each other—a relationship he hoped to cultivate. It was a near-death encounter with a madman for them both. And both had thought of themselves as saving the other. The deal had apparently been sealed—and here was the proof.

Zoe swore at Kaj under her breath and sat up in bed, suddenly feeling energized by the possibilities. "Why don't you go and grab me a glass of water and let's plan our day."

THE CAR FULL OF FRESH PRODUCE AND SWEET TREATS made its way slowly down the side street.

"I like taking the smaller roads. I don't get as nervous."

Zoe opened her eyes. "Lucy. Are you kidding me? You drove that SUV between here and Duluth during our ordeal—and that was before you even had a license! What, exactly, is there for you to be nervous about?"

"Well, that was an emergency."

"It seems that this is, too. I mean, why else would I be allowing all that healthy food into my house?" Zoe reached into the back seat for some candy corn. "You want some?"

"Not while I'm driving. Maybe later."

Zoe chuckled. "Since when did you become such a stickler for the rules?"

Lucy kept her eyes on the road. "Since I realized there was such a thing as following them."

Zoe paused in silence, thinking about the kid's hard life—she still didn't have all the details, only a rough idea. Finally, she said, "Yeah, I guess you never had that side of things modeled very well."

"Nope." Lucy sounded very matter-of-fact, and it made Zoe grateful. She'd never been very good with kids, and since the death of Zoe's brother when they were both kids, Lucy was the first one she'd connected with in any meaningful way.

Zoe should have dropped it right there, but instead she asked, "What do you remember about your parents?" Must be the medication, she thought, while realizing it was too late to take back the question.

"Too much," Lucy answered, "and not enough."

"What?"

"I remember the awful things they did, and their deaths. But I also remember loving them," again, matter-of-fact, stoic—the same way she'd been about losing Poppy, a beloved resident of the commune who'd died recently.

Zoe was quiet, the opiate coursing through her as she remembered. She, too, had experienced the awful truth of loving someone and being left behind. She, too, had witnessed her own parents' deaths. And she, too, had grown hard and cold afterward—self-sufficient, distant, mistrustful. But their encounter with the man who would have killed them both had brought the unlikely pair together. In fact, if Kaj had had his way, he and Zoe would have found a way to adopt Lucy on the spot. Zoe knew better, though—better than to disrupt Lucy's life, or her own. Both were navigating each day by working hard and looking inward in small, manageable bits. This wasn't like quitting an addiction, where it was better to change everything about your life, giving up all your "fix" frames of reference. Instead, both Zoe and Lucy needed to hang on to as much normalcy as possible.

With Zoe, that meant work, and her new relationship with Kaj—indeed her first real relationship with a man that hadn't begun and ended primarily around the purpose of casual coupling. While she'd come close with Ray, it hadn't been the same. And in the end it had been Ray's need for intimacy that scared her off.

In Lucy's case, she'd found "family" at "1219"—the old-folks commune. Sara, the home's supervisor, was like a second mother to her—a good and loving one. And Sara's son, Walt, was like a brother—a slightly quirky, some would even say autistic brother—to whom Lucy was good and loving. Lucy was learning lessons that Zoe couldn't possibly teach her. And she was getting her high school degree online. All good.

It was better this way.

But Zoe asked anyway, "What did you love about them?"

Zoe felt the car briefly accelerate, then overcompensate by slowing below the limit. She shook her head, "Sorry. Stupid thing to ask."

"Yeah. Kind of."

They drove on in silence.

Finally Lucy said, "I remember loving the painting."

"What painting?"

"It was the painting of a dog-soldier on his war pony."

"Where was it?"

"In our house, before all the shit went down."

"What happened to it?"

"They pawned it. Wasn't even ours, really—I think they stole it to begin with. It probably had nothing to do with us anyway. My mom was Ojib—the painting was of a Sioux warrior. Still, it was this huge, beautiful idea that we came from something bigger than our crappy little house with the meth stink—that we shared something noble, I guess. Like it symbolized my connection to strength, not just the weakness in my parents—and honestly, whenever I looked at it, I felt powerful.

"I remember reading the artist's description of the painting, over and over. He'd written it on the back. It fascinated me." Lucy's face flushed red. "I guess it all sounds kind of stupid."

"Of course it doesn't. What do you know of your ancestry?"

"Not much. I wish I knew more."

"Lucy?"

"Yeah?"

"I'm part Ojib, too."

"You?" Lucy turned to look at Zoe.

"Hey! Watch the road! Not half, like you—but some."

Lucy turned again, for a briefer look. "Yeah, I should have seen that."

"You see it in me?"

"Your hair . . . and your cheekbones. I used to think you just had a Scandinavian face, like most everyone else here—especially with those iced blue eyes of yours. But I see it now." Lucy smiled broadly.

"What?"

"You're beautiful, is what."

Zoe smiled, too, and hoped Lucy saw that in herself as well.

LUCY SLAMMED ON THE BRAKES—stopping for a panicked man at the curb.

And to Zoe, it was an immediate assessment—her impression of him. A recognition born of too many nights spent working in ERs—a homeless vet, in camouflage clothing, thin and wasted, his only reliable friend would be this dog on the sidewalk. Everyone was giving the two a wide berth as they scooted by.

Zoe jumped out and told Lucy to park the car.

"I don't know what happened! He was sick, and then he just passed out! You gotta help him!" He grabbed at her arm, pulling Zoe toward the dog.

She looked from his frantic face to the limp figure on the ground lying next to a water dish, and then stooped to examine it.

The small dog was without obvious injury. She felt for a pulse—figuring the neck was a good place to start. There was nothing. Then she put her hand over the tiny dog's mouth. No air movement, no warmth. She felt over its chest— no sign of anything beating or moving within. Zoe wasn't sure how to do CPR on a dog, especially one so small, but remembered something from a book she'd read as a child.

Lifting the dog by its back feet, she swung it like a helicopter rotor all while keeping one eye on camo guy—who now looked like he wanted to kill her.

The man's lunge toward her was interrupted by the dog's sudden yelp, and Zoe brought the tiny black creature to her chest. It was breathing. Amazing what getting blood and oxygen to the brain could accomplish, Zoe thought. Then she risked looking at the man.

This time he looked ready to cry. He reached for the dog and brought it to his neck, leaning into it as you would a lover. When he closed his eyes in fur, a few tears actually escaped. He *was* crying.

Zoe's next move was a mystery even to her. "Ah...looks like he's okay. What happened?"

The young man opened his eyes slowly and stared at her as she tried to read him. His face was filled with emotion, but she couldn't tell what kind—and he didn't seem capable of recognizing just how uncomfortable that was making her.

Finally, after what felt like minutes, he spoke. "It's been a rough day."

"Yeah, maybe for both of you." Zoe scanned the man, estimating his weight at maybe 110, 120 pounds, max. "Well, um, maybe he's got some type of cardiac arrhythmia or something. Listen, I'm no vet, but you should probably have him seen by one, eh?" Of course she knew that he wouldn't...or more correctly, couldn't.

He didn't answer the question, but pressured her instead, "What's your name?"

"Zoe. Zoe Lawrence."

He reached out his hand. "Pleased to meet you, ma'am. You look familiar."

"So do you. Go ahead and call me Zoe. And your name?"

"Wolf."

She almost didn't ask. "Is that all? No last name?"

"It's the only name I want anymore. They gave it to me."

"They? Meaning?"

"The only ones who count. My guys, from Iraq."

"Oh, I see." She thought she did anyway.

"But now you count, too. You ever need anything, I'm your man."

"Why...thank you...Wolf." *I guess.* And that he had anything to give was hard to imagine. "So what's the dog's name?"

"Thor."

Zoe puffed air into her cheeks to keep from smiling, and then she couldn't help it, "Kind of figured the God of Thunder would be a little bigger."

He laughed—and that was a good sign. Not so far gone he couldn't laugh at a lame joke. Just then, Lucy came skidding to a stop at Zoe's side.

Zoe asked, "Want some food, Wolf?"

He looked at the dog.

"We'll take him along—feed him, too."

"No one will let me in." He looked down at his own clothing.

Zoe smiled. "No, probably not with a dog."

He raised his eyes to hers—they were smiling.

"So we hit the McDonald's drive-thru if we have to. You can manage that, can't you, Lucy?"

"Sure as shit."

"Hop in, Wolf. Bring Thor."

"He was in rough shape."

"Yep."

"I don't blame him for not letting you find him a place to sleep, though."

"Me neither. But I had to try. Besides he claims he's got one."

"All that food you bought—I hope no one takes it off him."

"They better not try. He's got my number."

"He won't use it."

"Yeah, I know. But again, I had to try."

"Why were you asking him all those questions about Angie's?"

"Because I think he was there the other day—when they found the dead guy. And I'm pretty sure I took care of him in the ER—quick trip to detox, probably."

"Yeah, Jack was over visiting Sara and he told us all about the murder."

Jack was Ray's partner, a homicide detective, and traditionally wary of Zoe. He'd been downright hateful toward her when she and Ray had been an item, arguing that Zoe treated him poorly—and of course, he'd been right.

But they'd come to an understanding of sorts. On his side, it'd happened after he discovered details about Zoe's past—about the torture she'd endured at the hands of the two maniacs who'd killed her parents. It put things in perspective for him.

On Zoe's side, she'd seen something human in him when he'd helped her home after a night of overdrinking in remembrance of those same nasty details.

The two of them had cemented the deal over a shared concern for Sara, Walt, and Lucy. But they also shared a history, one that still shadowed them—and it was habit to give each other shit. Yet Jack was Sara's new lover and, Zoe had to admit, she approved of him as a father figure to Lucy.

"Well, he didn't exactly say he wasn't there. Only that he couldn't remember. Which makes him pretty useless as a witness anyhow. So I guess it doesn't matter in the end."

"Do you believe him?"

"Oh, I suppose I can believe that he doesn't remember—if he'd been drinking. But I'm almost certain it was him I saw." Zoe kept pulling healthful groceries out of the bags. "Here they are—my Swedish Fish. Can you finish unloading this shit? I'm going to lay down a few minutes. You actually know what to do with this stuff?"

"Sara's been teaching me. Trust me, you'll be glad to eat it. And Kaj will be happy to know that I've done my job," she grinned. "Go lie down. Then maybe I can finally feel like I'm doing something useful here."

Zoe grabbed the candy, a sports drink, and both medicine bottles—then walked away thinking about how much Lucy had matured from the loner street-kid she'd first encountered. She called behind her as she made her way into the bedroom, "Take your time, I'm going down for the count. Maybe an hour or two?"

"Sounds good. Go sleep!" Lucy called back.

INNER CRIME CIRCLES ARE A CURIOUS LOT. They function as if in their own universe. The boss is the center of that universe, and his minions are like fractals, imperfect little offshoots—similar but not identical, more vulnerable, and certainly not at the center. Mostly, they earn their keep—forming an insulating buffer. Less often, they screw up and require babysitting. But in general, at least they're loyal.

On occasion, however, their loyalty is questioned—and when that happens, a good boss has to know when to cut them loose. A sacrifice has to be made. Every boss has to do it once in a while. Every boss even looks forward to the opportunity now and then. It serves several purposes. One is to set an example—an unfortunate, but necessary one. It keeps the rest in line. Second—at least for this particular boss, it was pleasurable.

But someone had beaten him to it. He'd been considering what to do with Jeb. Up until now, Jeb had proven worthwhile, despite his obvious flaw—a tendency to damage the boss's property. But some damn motherfucker had beaten him to it.

Now he had to wonder what in the hell that meant. Was Jeb's death some kind of a message to him? He couldn't see how. Everything had been quiet lately—property moving easily through his system. New and used models were all moving well. The supply wasn't drying up—no problem there. No new competition to worry about. And customers willing to pay at all price points. Business was prospering. And, importantly, there had been no follow-up threats or demands. No one seemed to want anything from him.

So then it might be that this was all about Jeb. In his own reckless way, he'd gotten mixed up in something—something that had nothing to do with the boss. In which case, they'd saved him the trouble.

But the boss didn't like the idea that someone from outside had acted upon his universe—or even that Jeb might have links to another universe. Being at the center of one's own domain, didn't mean that a good boss wouldn't recognize that others existed. It would be just plain dumb not to.

And now there was another problem. The commotion that day had scattered the horses. Another one was missing.

ZOE TOOK THE ANTIBIOTICS, BUT HELD OFF on the opiate until the cough became bad enough that Lucy looked in on her.

Red tissues littered the floor.

"Yeah, I know. I'll take it right now." Zoe used the last of the drink to wash down the pill then laid back into her pillow and thought.

When she looked toward one wall, she thought about Angie's. When she turned her head toward the door, she thought about Lucy's Ojibwe heritage. Looking at the ceiling brought on images of Connie in her pale pink lipstick and nail polish, and then about the dead man behind the bar—about his brain showing through. Flipping on her side and seeing the tissues, she thought about the color red, and the walls of her home after the shootings. They'd been red, too.

Zoe kept tossing in bed, looking from one trapezoid to another —first a wall, then the ceiling, followed by a patch of light on the floor, until finally she forced her eyes shut.

THE DREAM LEFT HER SOAKED IN SWEAT. But then again, maybe it was the fever.

It also brought her back to Angie's—and into a clearer picture of one small detail.

In the nightmare there were distortions, and seemingly random, unrelated insertions. For instance in her dream, it was the Rex Bar, in Duluth. Big Wave Dave and the Ripples were playing and the child jumping up and down to get his mother's attention was suddenly Garrison Keillor in his trademark red shoes—dancing like an addict.

And that was the point. Dancing like an addict. They could be slippery, manipulative, and even entertaining—anything necessary to get what they wanted. Correction—to get what they needed. There'd been dancing in that bar—the little kid, the teenager, even Grace—the drinking woman. There'd been drama. And what about the guy in the corner, tapping on his laptop keys?

But it was in picturing the child—alongside the bizarre image of a dancing humorist—that she had the small insight. The kid wasn't trying to gain his mother's attention; he was trying to entertain someone. But not the mom—instead it was the man walking toward the mother and child—the man who'd been killed. He'd been facing away from Zoe as he walked, just before Wolf and the teenager had made their entrance.

And in Zoe's memory, the mom wasn't looking at the child at all … she was watching the man approach. Fearfully? Maybe. But it was the kid Zoe had focused on. What was in the kid's eyes? Zoe tried for a clear picture.

She remembered the kid's eyes being focused on the man.

They were frantic. Yes, that was it. And that's why she thought of an addict. He was using his only power to get the man's attention away from his mother—creating a comical scene, one he hoped would produce laughter, one that would ease the tension—forestalling the argument?

That must be why she'd inserted Garrison Keillor into her dream. The kid was trying to make the man laugh, to change his mind, to protect his mother.

It suddenly seemed very important to track down the mother and child. She reached for her cell and dialed Ray.

"HOW YOU DOING, KIDDO?' Jack gave Lucy's shoulders a squeeze as he walked into the kitchen.

"Quieter here," she smiled.

"Yeah, I bet. At least Zoe doesn't snore," Ray said, having first hand knowledge.

"No shit. At home, some of the residents snore loud enough it wakes you through the walls—and then when Luke hears it, he starts snoring."

"Luke?" Zoe asked.

"The household African gray."

"Oh, yeah, the parrot. Almost forgot. He's quite accurate in his mimicry," and she started coughing. "Sorry, I'm due for a pill. Hang on." Zoe swallowed an opiate and washed it down with her beer.

"Not entirely quiet, though?" Jack asked Lucy.

"As long as she keeps taking those pills, she sleeps fine."

"Well, boys, I'd offer you a beer, but since you're on duty, how about lunch instead? And don't worry, Lucy prepared it, not me. It should be fine."

Both men sat down as Zoe told them of her recollection. And by the end of their meal it was decided that Zoe would work with an artist to reconstruct the faces of both mother and child as neither one had remained in the bar after the commotion.

"Bartender's been of no help whatsoever." Jack leaned back in his chair—full from the meal. "That was great, Lucy. Sara would be proud."

"Yeah, and Sara would be prouder still if you'd demonstrate your cooking skills on her," Lucy replied.

"Have I been slacking off?" he grinned.

"Ya think?" Lucy stayed seated. "Bus your own dishes, pal."

Jack laughed and got up to carry everyone's plates to the dishwasher. Zoe laughed too—reassured by the easy banter between them—until it stimulated another coughing fit that had her doubling over from the pain in her ribs. "Pill evidently hasn't kicked in yet," she said at the end.

Ray continued, "Bartenders are supposed to be observant. You'd think I could get more out of the guy."

"Doesn't surprise me. He said he was new." But Zoe had to admit that it did seem odd.

Jack returned to stand behind his chair, ready to leave.

Ray rose, too, giving Zoe's shoulder a squeeze. "You need a lift, Zoe?" he asked.

"Nope, got myself a chauffer. Kaj set it up." Zoe turned to Lucy, "Think you can get me downtown this afternoon?"

"No sweat, Zoe."

THE FINAL ARTIST RENDERINGS WERE JUST OKAY—not great, but okay. She'd been dull the day of the murder—owing to fatigue—and was now off her game because of pneumonia, a fever, and the medication required in order to quiet her cough. But still, she tried her best to contribute something useful.

"Lucy, next stop is Angie's."

"Yes, ma'am."

"You're still driving, kiddo. They arrest people for driving in my condition."

"This is great! It's good driving experience, and the best way to treat pneumonia—ever. I thought we'd be stuck at your place with the heat turned up and a humidifier or something."

"If anyone asks . . . that's all we've been doing."

Lucy grinned, "Gotcha. We've been home the whole time."

THE SAME BARTENDER WAS THERE. Zoe looked around to see if she recognized anyone else from the other day, but no one clicked.

"Beer for me, and a Cherry Coke for the kid," Zoe told him as they took seats at the bar.

He looked curiously at Lucy, but his eyes clearly recognized Zoe.

"So did you figure out who emptied the till?"

"Nope." He set down their drinks.

"Did it have anything to do with the dead guy out back?"

"Not that I know of, but the boss doesn't tell me everything."

"Recognize anyone in here? You know, someone who might have been here that day?"

"Nope. Still new at this."

"Yeah, but you knew who I was. Remember?"

"So?"

"So, you pay attention. I know you do."

"I pick up on some things. But like I said, I'm new."

"What's your name?"

"Why?"

"Easier than calling you 'bartender' every time I want a refill."

"Yeah, well, it's Josh."

Zoe noticed the small tattoo. It looked to have been homemade. On the inside of his wrist the word "pissed" was poorly scribed.

Lucy whispered to Zoe when he walked away. "Did you see those scars?"

"Yep. Good eye, Lucy. And he's good at hiding them. Where've you seen those before?"

"My folks use to pick at 'crank bugs' all the time. Made me wonder why they liked using. Anything that could make me hallucinate bugs crawling on my skin, I didn't need to pay for."

"Smart kid." Then Zoe called to Josh, "Where'd you work before you started here?"

He walked back toward them. "What is this—the third degree?"

"Maybe. Just wondering if you've left your old habits behind?"

"What?"

Zoe nodded toward his scars. "Hey, no offense man, but those are crank craters."

"Listen, I'm clean." He showed her his skin. "These are scars, yeah, but they're old. Nothing fresh."

"Well, apparently you've been smart enough to stay out of jail, or Ray would have been all over that."

"Never been inside—and I plan to keep it that way."

"Is that why you won't cooperate?"

"With what?"

Zoe gave him her most disapproving look. "Josh. You don't really want to do that now do you? Not in front of the kid. Be a good role model."

"Yeah, well," he looked briefly at Lucy. "I'd just rather not get involved. Besides, I don't actually know anything. It's not like I'm withholding information."

"But you are. You owe someone, or what?"

"No!"

"Is that why you cleaned out the till?"

Lucy elbowed Zoe. Zoe ignored her.

"No! I didn't!"

"How about the dead guy? Know him?"

"I don't have to keep talking to you."

"No, you don't. So, does your boss know that you roll hard?"

"Used to! I don't anymore!"

Although she believed him—his body was in excellent condition, except for those few scars and the silly tattoo—why tip her hand? "So then, you think your boss'll care that it's 'old damage'?"

"Okay, so maybe I did sort of recognize the dead guy."

"Why don't you clue me in and we'll call it my memory flashback."

He studied her a moment. "Shit. What I overheard those cops say about you is right."

"And what's that?"

"That you were good in interview."

"Nice try. But don't even think of distracting me."

He smiled. His teeth were good. His body was fit. In fact, Zoe remembered noticing his body the other day—thinking it wasn't half bad. He wasn't using anymore, and probably hadn't used for quite a while. Just long enough to get shitfaced to the point of allowing someone to carve a meth addict nickname on his wrist . . . and long enough to experience crank bugs.

"Okay, so maybe I only knew him enough to say that he hangs with a lady that was in here that day. She had a kid with her."

"Maybe you knew them well enough to know that they weren't getting along?"

"Hey, isn't that a leading question?"

"Just answer it."

"Yeah, they argued—both times I saw 'em in here."

"Now listen carefully, Josh ... do you know their names or where they live? A lot's riding on your answer."

"Do you believe me?"

Zoe looked at Lucy. "What do you think, kid? Do we believe him?"

Lucy looked at Zoe with uncertainty.

"It's okay, kid. Be honest."

"Yeah, I believe him."

Zoe smiled at Josh, "Okay then. She's a good judge of character. We'll operate on that premise. Now answer."

"You'll leave me out of this, then?"

"I'll try."

He set his mouth in a tight line, but then opened it, "I only knew her name because the guy was yelling it the first time I saw them in here. It was a pretty big argument. I swear I would've called the cops, but they both left right after they turned up the volume. I'd say they were old pros at it."

"And?"

"Her name was Christie. Or in his terms ... Fucking Whore Christie."

"Hey, watch the kid here."

"Sorry. Just trying for detail."

Zoe grinned.

"So, we're good?"

"Good as gold, Josh."

"Because I need this job."

"We're good. Don't worry. But if you think of anything else ... here's my number, and I'll leave you out of it if I can."

Zoe put a twenty on the bar.

"SHIT, ZOE! THAT WAS AWESOME!"

"You were weren't half-bad in there either. Knew when to keep quiet, and you had him pegged, didn't you?"

"Yeah, I saw the tattoo."

"You believed him, then?"

"I did. You told me to be honest."

Zoe smiled. "When partners work a suspect together, they don't always mean what they say."

"Well, did I get it wrong? Cuz, I don't think so."

"Nope. I'd say you got it right. Is that why you elbowed me?"

"Yeah, I thought you were making a mistake. I've seen too many meth-heads—and he just didn't feel like one."

"You're right. But that doesn't mean he's not useful to me. He's got more of a memory than he's letting on."

"So you were just working him? You think he knows more?"

"Correction, we were working him. And, yes, he knows more. It's just that he may not realize it yet. We have to figure out the right questions first. But for now, let's work with what we have."

"How? All we have is the name Christie."

"No, Lucy. We have a lot more than that. We have 'Fucking Whore Christie.' There's a big difference."

"You think she's turning?"

Zoe only smiled.

IT TOOK ALL OF TWO MINUTES FOR THE CALL TO COME IN. The boss's crew was loyal—and observant. Someone had jacked the new bartender for information. The kid they didn't recognize, and she only seemed along for the ride, but the woman was another matter. In fact, the bartender himself had dropped the dime on her—after a little convincing. Convincing that had lasted all of two minutes.

"THIS DAMN FEVER HAS ME ALL FOGGY, but at least my cough's temporarily tamed."

"Seems to me you're pretty sharp. That was fun in the bar."

"Crap, I'm burning up right now."

"You know what? When Walt gets a fever, he's better."

"What do you mean, 'better'?"

"Well, that tic in his little finger stops, and he actually wants to cuddle. I mean normally, he never wants to touch at all. And he even talks more . . . like a lot. He gets all chatty. It's kinda fun, actually. Sara's noticed it too, because she doesn't give him any Tylenol. I think she likes it when he gets that way."

"Hmm. No shit?"

"Hey, watch the kid!" she grinned.

Zoe laughed and looked down the street, "You're no kid."

"Thanks."

"I think I'm going to have to ask one of the neurologists about that fever stuff. It's pretty interesting. But in my case, it's not exactly making me better."

"Well, like I said, you kicked ass in that bar."

"Thanks, kid. Now where'd we park the car?"

THE CONVINCING PART HAD ONLY BEGUN. The boss was already in his car, headed in to finish the job. Josh had been an easy mark—at least according to Jeb. It was Jeb who'd done the deal. He'd called the new guy, Josh, an asset—one that would pay off big when the time came. Called him a guy with connections, and needs—needs that outweighed everything else. Perfect for the job.

Well the boss didn't much care what Josh's needs were—it could be drugs, it could be women—because he had access to all of it. In fact he didn't much care about the guy at all. All he cared about was getting something out of his investment.

And that was about to happen.

ZOE LEANED HER HEAD AGAINST THE GLASS and watched the buildings pass at a crawl.

The cool of the car window on her forehead felt good, but the snail's pace was irritating. "Lucy, you go any slower, they'll arrest us for going in reverse."

"I just want to be careful. I'm new at this."

"Yeah, and I want to get there before sundown."

"Okay, I'll try."

Lucy pressed on the accelerator, but not so you'd notice. "Well now that's a whole lot better." Zoe rolled her eyes. "Wake me when we get there."

"If I can find it."

"I gave you good directions. You'll find it." Zoe closed her eyes. "And when we get there, you stay in the car. Leave this one to me."

"What, you think I haven't seen a homeless camp before?"

"I just don't want you seeing any more of 'em. Besides, I'm not sure what I'll be getting into. I'd rather not take the chance with you."

"Pretty weird road trip, but … whatever."

"Atta girl."

Zoe's eyes opened at the sound of a honking horn. "What'd you do?"

"Me? It wasn't me. It was that kid up there. Jumped in front of that car, then slid across the hood and across the street."

Zoe locked onto the teenager—the same one who'd come into the bar. "Lucy, stay with the car!" Zoe opened the door and joined the traffic in one fluid move. Before closing the door she shouted into the car, "And try to keep up!"

LUCY GRINNED AND GRIPPED THE WHEEL with determination, "Fucking A. Best road trip ever." She paused the car at the entrance to an alley both runners had disappeared into and could see that it ended in a brick wall. It became quickly obvious that neither the kid, nor Zoe, saw that too-tall barrier as any sort of impediment.

First the kid launched into the air and hit the wall of the adjacent building with one foot as if he intended to run up the sheer face of the building. Instead he pushed off and grabbed the top of the thick wall, pulling himself over and disappearing.

Lucy stayed where she was, until unexpectedly witnessing Zoe duplicate the move.

"Oh, crap. Now where?" Lucy hit the accelerator and, at a speed Zoe would have admired, made her way around the block. The front of her car dipped at the next stop sign and she looked toward her right to see the two runners disappear into another alley—the distance between them hadn't changed.

This time instead of turning to follow, she anticipated their path and squealed tires as she broke from the intersection. She looked right again at the next intersection, where all she saw was Zoe darting in between two buildings.

"Keep up, Lucy." she mouthed, and then darted through the intersection ahead of the driver who had the right-of-way. It earned her a honk and glare, but she was determined to get to the next intersection first.

At that point it was apparent that Zoe had somehow managed to close some distance. The kid looked back at her then turned right—in the direction of an overpass. Lucy turned right to follow and found herself caught behind two cars stopped to allow the runners a path in front of them. She watched Zoe mimic the kid's vault across the hood of the lead car using one hand to ease her movement. It was a graceful move, requiring nothing but one hand in contact with the car. Both broke at a run when their feet hit the ground. What Lucy watched was beautiful—she couldn't help thinking it.

The kid's next move was to navigate an opening in a thick cement wall by diving into it. There was barely enough height to allow for a push off with his hands and an almost simultaneous tuck of his legs before emerging on the other side—already vertical and ready to land.

Lucy could see Zoe hesitate, gauging what the kid had just done—probably doing the move in her head and doubting her ability to match the kid's agility. But as Zoe approached the thick cement wall, she used the opening as a step—leaping up instead of through it. Zoe caught the top of the thick cement wall and swung her legs up to a standing position on top of the wall. From there, Lucy could see Zoe take off in what looked like a standing long jump. Problem was, she was jumping into a drop-off of about ten feet—maybe more.

Zoe landed in short grass on the toes of her feet and immediately dropped into a roll, jumping up at the end and continuing the all out run. To Lucy, it looked like a judo move, and it fucking impressed her. But she was also losing them, as the drivers ahead of her also seemed impressed—enough to stop and stare. Lucy leaned on the horn and got the finger in return … but she did make the cars move.

"Getting damn good at this car shit," she grinned and nodded. "Yep, home in bed. Humidifier," and this time Lucy stomped on the accelerator.

After pulling even with the cement barrier of the overpass she pulled over, got out of the car and peered over the edge. The two were still running, but they were caught between the freeway and a sound barrier. If they kept running in that direction there would be only one way to emerge back into the city's maze. Lucy returned to the car and pulled out, shooting for the next overpass.

"I WOULDA HAD HIM. HE LOST ME WHEN he vaulted from that rooftop." Zoe pointed toward a flat roof with a small wall around its edge. "I couldn't see what was on the other side in time to make the jump." She looked at Lucy, white-knuckled in the driver's seat, "Aw, relax. I'm not *completely* crazy you know."

Lucy's mouth still hung open—her face aimed out the front window.

"Hey, kiddo! You did good—keeping up and all that. What's with the face?"

Lucy turned her head toward Zoe, "That was fucking awesome!"

"Yeah. Brings back memories. But I guess, truth be told, I didn't have the wind going up those steps to the roof. I'd never have kept up. The kid had me beat. Even started coughing on the way up. Where are those damn pills anyway?" Zoe dug around in her pockets. "Thank God. Here they are." She swallowed one dry.

"So, Lucy, I've been thinking…"

"When? While you were running?"

Zoe laughed, but said, "Yes."

"You're scary."

"…About the interest you have in your heritage."

"You had time to think about that during the chase?"

"Yeah. My mind works that way. Anyhow, I have a friend—he used to teach at the Heart of the Earth Survival School."

"What's that?"

"It was a school emphasizing Native American culture—used to be in Dinkytown. I think it folded, but I could still hook you up with him. He'd be willing to teach you a few things—that is, if you're interested. He's a great guy. What do you think?"

"Really? No shit?"

"No shit. I know some stuff, but not enough to teach you anything of value. You need an elder."

"An elder. Now that sounds cool."

"Yeah, someone with a vast amount of patience, and very little ego."

"So … like, the opposite of a teenager?" Lucy grinned.

"Exactly. Consider it done then. I'll make the arrangements. Now, what in the hell were we doing before that interruption?"

"Wait. What about the kid? Are we giving up?"

"Nope. We'll find him—now that we have a link. And now I know why he was pointing to the rooftop that day."

"Why?"

"Probably had a buddy doing a trick."

"A trick?"

"Yeah. The kid's a Traceur."

Lucy pulled the centers of her eyebrows up in confusion.

"A Traceur is a practitioner of Parkour."

"Keep going. I'm still lost."

"Tell you what, I'm not up to visiting the homeless camp today. Let's call it a day and get some food."

"Where to?"

"Back to Angie's. There's more info to get there. Especially now."

"Why especially now?"

"Because we have a link to the kid."

"Zoe, just lay it all out for me. Quit making me feel stupid."

Zoe smiled at Lucy's look of irritation. "You're sounding more like my old partner every minute. Ever think about being a cop?"

"Zoe."

"Okay. We know the kid's a Traceur—but not a legit one. He uses his skills to make escapes. The kid's a thief. I'm pretty sure he was the one who emptied the till. Created a diversion—had us all looking up and out—then grabbed it and ran. Clever kid. On the rooftop, he ditched a woman's wallet he was carrying—it made me pause. He dropped it there on purpose, knowing I'd stop for it. Perfect storm. An unknown jump, my coughing fit coming up the stairs, and the wallet he presumed I was after."

"Still don't see the link, Zoe."

Zoe grinned, "Can't shake you, can I? Okay, we'll find him either on YouTube—showing off his apeshit moves—or through the community of Traceurs. We'll get him."

"What's Parkour?"

"It's a discipline involving movement through ones environment by way of the most efficient paths—through climbing, jumping, vaulting, rolling, and of course, running. The goal is to be as fast and efficient as possible, without getting hurt."

"Like after that jump, when I saw you roll?"

"Exactly. It was a way of protecting myself from a flat-footed, dangerous landing by transferring the energy of my movement into the roll, instead of into my knees or ankles. You've got to land on your toes, then immediately bend your knees, tuck and roll. Roll as many times as you need. If your momentum continues to carry you through another roll, you go with it—because that momentum needs to be dissipated."

Lucy nodded in understanding. "I've been studying physics for school—makes sense. But it looked like a Judo roll."

"In essence, it was. Parkour borrows from other disciplines. Tell you what, tonight when we're at home nursing this frickin' cough, we'll look up all the details of the art, and then we'll go hunting online for our little thief."

"Sounds like fun."

"First, we eat. Take that street, instead." Zoe pointed to the road that would send them by Kaj's building—the one in which he had his penthouse condo. She looked up to see the lights on. "He's home," she said, before stopping herself from letting it slip.

"What? Who?"

"Nothing. Just drive. That pill is starting to get to me, and my breathing's getting a little rough. I might need to lie down for a while. Let's skip Angie's for now and go home instead." Zoe reached for her cell—grateful for the several missed calls and messages.

Lucy added, for emphasis, "That was apeshit awesome, Zoe."

"Thanks, but I didn't catch the guy," Zoe said as she preoccupied herself with the phone's messages.

"How'd you learn to do stuff like that?"

The messages were all from Kaj, and it made her feel foolish about her paranoia over Dr. Pink. Foolish but not forgiving –– *the bitch.*

"I learned from kids like him. Or more accurately from chasing kids like him. You see it, you do it—even if it's on the run. So I graduated by catching kids like him."

"Which way now? There's road construction."

"Cut over to Franklin. You can find it from there."

"Okay."

There was a theme to his texts—"HOW R U FEELING? HOW'S THE COUGH? U & LUCY DOING OK?" and the one voicemail was similar—"Hard day at work. Connie and I had to take a multi-vehicle accident together, all stabilization room cases—and all critical. Worst one didn't make it. Heading home for a drink. Let me know if it's okay to come see you tonight. I promise to be good," and Zoe could almost see him grin as he spoke the words.

So it was okay, she thought—he was okay. Everything seemed normal—except that he wasn't knocking down the fucking door to see her. And he'd made a point of mentioning Dr. Fucking Pink—as *Connie, together.*

She ran that idea through again, thinking it best to stay sane. *Stupid, Zoe—you're being very stupid, and very jealous.* After all, she was the one who'd asked for time and space to heal. Besides, it had just been one ridiculous day.

"Zoe, we're home."

Zoe looked up from her phone, surprised they'd arrived so quickly. "Good driving today, Lucy. Let's get inside, eat, and formulate a game plan for tomorrow. Any leftovers from that great lunch of yours?"

"Nope. The guys polished it off. But we're stocked up on groceries. Just give me half an hour and I'll have us happy."

"Holler for me. I'll be down for the count."

THE MEDICATION WAS SWAMPING HER—but at least she wasn't coughing.

Tomorrow, she decided, would include a trip to the two homeless camps nearest Angie's—at least the two she was familiar with—and, she reckoned, another drop-in at Angie's. Everyone she needed to find had been there that day—including the witnesses, the thief, the dead guy, and most likely his murderer. Odds were they lived close since, although it was better than a mere bar, Angie's wasn't exactly a destination restaurant. And odds were if they lived close, most would be back. Besides, if nothing else, Josh had more to offer. She was sure of it.

It felt as though she were merging with the bed—that moment just before sleep. But she was forgetting something. What?

"The prostitute," she said softly, from the edge of sleep. "Gotta track her down, too." And she decided that tomorrow would be a good day to hook Lucy up with her Ojibwe friend. In reality, homeless camps and prostitutes were nothing new to Lucy, but Zoe thought it best to keep them something old.

STILL SHE COULDN'T FALL ASLEEP. "WHAT ELSE?" She rolled to her side, facing the empty spot on her left. "Ah."

Zoe reached for her cell and texted, "BEEN RESTING ALL DAY. APPRECIATE THE PEACE & QUIET. NEED IT. LUCY & I R DOING GR8 2GETHER. THANX 4 SETTING THAT UP. GOING 2 SLEEP 4 THE NITE."

Zoe knew he liked the idea that she was hitting it off with Lucy—he thought it healthy for both of them. And Zoe had to admit that Lucy had proven to be a pretty good sidekick before, and was doing so again.

CHAPTER FOUR

S O, THE DIFFERENCE BETWEEN PARKOUR and Free Running is that Free Runners like to show off?"

"That's how I see it. Others might disagree. But you see, Free Runners use all this gymnastic shit, stuff you and I don't know anything about. Makes them elitist to my way of thinking. But Parkours, well they're just trying to get from point A to point B in the fastest, most efficient way possible—without getting hurt. Simple. Accessible to folks like you and me and, to our Ojibwe ancestors, I suppose it would have been the logical and utilitarian thing to do."

Lucy seemed to like that, and she nodded in agreement. "I've been chased before, but it was nothing like jumping between rooftops."

"Well, did you get away?"

"The hardest race I ever ran was last year when that serial murderer guy was chasing me."

Zoe smiled. "And you got away. That makes you a Traceur—or more accurately a Traceuse."

"Traceuse?"

"A female Parkour practitioner. The terms have French roots, and the French have all those feminine and masculine rules. But speaking as someone with French-Canadian roots, I'll just stick with the wine and cheese—and one term for a Parkour practitioner, Traceur."

"Cool. I get that."

"And do you know where Traceur comes from?"

"Clearly I don't," Lucy said, irritated. "You're making me feel stupid again."

Zoe laughed. "Sorry—old habits, kid. I had to act all alpha with the cops in those days—you know, keep them on their toes so they didn't have any openings to give me shit for being female. It was damn exhausting, but I got pretty good at it. Anyway, Traceur comes from 'disappearing without a trace.'" She grinned at Lucy, "Something you were pretty good at."

Lucy looked busted, and redirected the conversation, "Breakfast?"

"Yeah, I'm starving. What'd you make?"

"Eggs with fried onions, and bagels with cream cheese and honey."

"Coffee?"

"Just started it. Here's some juice until it's done."

"This nursemaid thing's working out pretty well—for me."

"Me, too! That was righteous yesterday!"

Zoe grinned and nodded. "Yeah, yeah it was. But today, you're going to meet Phillip—the Ojibwe elder I told you about."

Lucy fidgeted nervously with the coffee mugs, almost dropping one. "Anything I should know about first? Like, is there a special way to act?"

Zoe hid a grin behind the rim of her juice glass. "Just be yourself. If you don't, he'll know it. He'll see right through you. So while I know you've had to play games to protect yourself in the past—best not do it with him."

"Okay. I wasn't planning on it."

"Yeah, but you and I both know how easy it is to slip into those old ways when you feel insecure, or threatened. Brain ruts, I call them—default mode."

"He's going to threaten me?"

"No, of course not. But it may feel that way. So don't let your mind play those tricks—and be kind."

"Kind?"

"There's rarely an excuse not to be kind. But then again, I talk a good game, don't I?—and hardly ever live up to it."

Lucy smiled—and Zoe knew it to be a forgiving smile. After all, Lucy had been on the receiving end of Zoe's lapses in kindness before, and had been required to earn Zoe's trust and friendship—while Lucy had never placed any conditions whatsoever on their relationship. It was Lucy who could teach kindness.

"Sorry," was all Zoe could say. She stuffed her mouth full of eggs.

"Here's the coffee. Milk?"

"Yep, thanks."

"So, when do we go?"

"I'm not going."

"But . . ."

"… Two reasons. First, I'm tired. I need to stay home and rest. Yesterday kind of took it out of me. And two, this is something you need to do alone—that is if you're serious about it." Zoe stirred the milk in her coffee and locked eyes with Lucy, "I told him you were."

"I am! But I'm a little scared, too."

"Kiddo, think about what you've been through. Not much should scare you anymore."

Lucy smiled at the realization, and puffed up—filling her lungs and straightening her back.

Zoe noticed and added, "But don't get too full of yourself either. If there's one thing I know, it's that the Ojibwe spiritual tradition is full of cautionary tales for anyone who gets too bigheaded—even their gods. They don't much care for that sort of thing."

Lucy looked even more terrified. "I'll screw up, I know I will."

"Well, of course you will. Really? Did you expect you wouldn't?"

"No, I suppose not, but …"

"The other thing I know about the Ojibwe is that they're a forgiving people—I mean think about it."

Lucy nodded. "Yeah, I guess I get your point."

"And often they show forgiveness through a sizeable sense of humor. Does that calm you down?"

"Maybe," but to Zoe, Lucy didn't look too sure.

"…And humor exists because of our imperfections. Thank God we have humor. It requires a slightly skewed, asymmetrical view of things, don't you think?"

Lucy tilted her head, like dogs frequently do.

Zoe only laughed. "So it's all right to screw up. If nothing else, it'll give us something to laugh about later. Now after breakfast, take my car. I've written down the directions for you. His place isn't far."

"But what about that Traceur kid? Weren't we going to look for him today?"

"Not finding him online is nothing but a minor speed bump. I'll figure him out somehow. But not today. I need to rest.

"Now, here's the thing. I'm going to give you my cell phone. We don't want Kaj knowing I let you skip out today …"

"… I don't need to go, Zoe."

"No, no, that's not what I'm concerned about. I'll be fine here, resting. There's food in the fridge, and I've got my pills. But I don't want him unnecessarily tripping out about me being alone. So if he calls or texts, please just respond by letting him know I'm sleeping and everything's fine. Okay? And this way you'll have a phone with you."

"You want me to lie?"

"Did that sound like a lie?"

Lucy ran it back in her head. "No, I guess technically it's not."

"Exactly. I'll be resting, and all's fine. Just let me check my messages one last time before you head out." Zoe opened the phone to find a text from Kaj.

"BIG GALA @ CONNIE'S SATURDAY NITE. HOPE UR WELL ENOUGH 2 MAKE IT."

"But why don't you just keep your phone and answer him yourself?"

"Cuz, I really do want to rest—as in sleep. But mainly, I want you to have a phone with you," she said. "You know—just in case your car breaks down or something. I'll feel better and get more rest knowing you've got it, okay?"

"Sheez, Zoe. You always roll like this?"

"What do you mean?"

"Lying and shit."

"Only if I have to—now. Used to be worse. And that's the truth," she said, one side of her mouth lifted in a mischievous grin.

"Ready?"

"Yep." Zoe nodded toward the cell phone, "But it looks like I have to make a full recovery before Saturday night."

"I thought you had till next Monday off."

"I do. But Kaj just invited me to a soiree Saturday night. One I do not intend to miss."

"Well then, I guess it's good you're staying home after all. Last night your breathing was a little ... I don't know what to call it ... hard, I guess. I could hear it from the other bedroom."

"Labored?"

"Yes! That's it!"

"Medical term." And Zoe knew it to be true. "Don't worry, a day of rest will do the trick—and a day with Phillip will be one you'll never forget," Zoe fought to smile, feeling her cough threaten again. "Now get going."

"On it."

As Zoe watched Lucy pull out of the driveway, she called Ray.

"Anything on the Angie's business?"

"Found Grace—who had nothing to offer. Claims she left that night for a trip to the casino. Also say's she didn't see much because of all the commotion with that phantom 'jumper.' She locked onto that along with everyone else."

"Do you think ransacking the till was connected to the murder?"

"Gotta believe so, but who knows? Could have been an opportunist."

"Yeah."

"What are you thinking?"

"That it might be the other way around and the murder could have been the opportunistic event."

"Murder takes a little more mental preparation, don't you think? Unless it's one of those 'in the heat of passion' deals—which I believe to be a lame excuse, by the way."

Zoe didn't want to examine her own past on that account—after all, she knew how that kind of passion could follow you through a lifetime. "I think that kid is a Traceur—the one who came in shouting about the jumper. Maybe that'll help you track him down. I bet he's your thief. Created a distraction and emptied the till."

"Yeah, I've kind of got him figured for the thief, but how'd you find out he was a runner?"

"On the way home from that artist rendering session yesterday, I think I saw him. He was doing his thing—saw him jump rooftops."

"Thanks, I'll look into it. You still home sick?"

"Yes, sir," Zoe said as she gathered up her bike panniers. "Sucks."

Ray laughed, "I bet it does. You hate being down for the count. Lucy still staying with you?"

"Yep. We're planning on a nice relaxing day at home. At least she can cook."

"Okay, then. I'll let you get to it—and stay in bed."

"Thanks, Ray. I plan to. Bye now."

And for a moment, Zoe had to wonder why she wasn't going to follow her own advice. Instead she dressed for the November chill.

Pam Leonard

BIG PAYOFF—JOSH COUGHED UP A LOT BEFORE HE DIED. And he'd cooperated, actually thought it would save him. The boss handled it personally, after all, he'd missed out on Jeb. It also meant this one had been done right.

That he'd enjoyed it had been a bonus—a perk.

This particular boss had been labeled a sociopath when he was young—and from what he understood, it meant he had no empathy, hence, no conscience.

But that was all wrong—because he could read people. How could you read people if you had no empathy?

And he had power.

It was in the accurate reading of people that he discovered his power. He knew what their motives were. A conversation, to him, was not simply an exchange of information; it was a reading of subtext, an archeological dig for the underlying motives and expectations—fears and weaknesses.

But it required distance. To mine the subtext, you couldn't allow your own emotions to be tapped. Oddly enough, he hadn't found that hard at all. Perhaps it was what made him so good at it. The distance.

As he thought about it, maybe others were good at reading subtext, too, but maybe they let their own emotions get so tangled up in the process they couldn't sort out whose emotions were whose anymore.

He just wasn't sure what that would feel like.

WITH HER PANNIERS SECURED AND AN EMPTY backpack strapped on, Zoe's first stop was the nearest Target store. She locked the bike and made quick work of her shopping.

Zoe stuffed the panniers full and set off for the homeless camp nearest to Angie's. As Angie's was on the way, she slowed the bike to walk past, looking around for anyone familiar to her from that day. No hits.

She mounted the bike again and sped toward the railroad tracks. The wind picked up as she approached the site and a November sky made empty threats of snow. It was unusual, not having snow yet in Minneapolis. Zoe tucked her face against the cold.

Arriving at the bluff, she shouldered the bike and made her way down the steep incline toward the camp. Her goal was to find a familiar face—hopefully one she'd sent away happy from the hospital—but the encampment looked deserted. Zoe made noise as she approached, not wanting to surprise anyone. Even so, no one emerged from the lean-to tarps or the recycled refrigerator box. She leaned her bike against a tree and felt over the ashes of a fire pit. Someone had been there recently.

Wanting to make sure, Zoe called out, "Anybody home? I've got food."

Nothing.

Emboldened, Zoe looked into the variety of shelters.

Within the side-turned refrigerator box were a tangle of blankets, several large plastic bags—which she imagined being used to keep this person's belongings dry during a rain, a hand-carved wooden spoon, and what looked to be a tin bowl fashioned out of an old rectangular gasoline can. The top of the can had been cut off and slits cut at the corners to about halfway down. Then all four sharp-edged sides had been rolled down to create smooth handles—probably rolled over one of the branches that littered the surrounding woods, long-since used as kindling. The knife used to cut the can apart was missing. Zoe backed out of the box and scanned the woods—still no one around.

The vibration and whistle of an approaching train made her pause to watch as it went by—Amtrak, crawling slowly. With the trees bare of leaves, several passengers turned sleepy morning-eyes toward her as they passed. This train had started in Seattle and would be Chicago-bound. A long trip for these travelers, and trackside shelters wouldn't have been an oddity along the route.

Zoe returned to the shelters. Underneath a plastic tarp used as a lean-to was a tattered, down-filled sleeping bag with a nylon shell. Part of the bag's foot-well was melted—its occupant probably too near the campfire on a cold, drunken night. A small cardboard box sat on a tree stump table—a roll of toilet paper, eating utensils, a plastic bowl and a fire-scorched coffee can inside. On the sleeping bag were two paperback novels, their edges curled and dirty.

To most, these things would have represented refuse, but they were precious possessions in this universe. The other shelters, including one actual tent, contained similar items, with the addition of a small mound of pocketed individual servings of jelly and peanut butter. A small lump caused Zoe to lift the edge of the sleeping bag and look underneath. A crowbar and two small uneaten bags of Cheetos, along with empty individual serving bags of a variety of chips and discarded candy wrappers painted the picture of a late-night snack obtained forcibly from a nearby vending machine.

If the occupants of this camp had anything else of actual value, it would have been carried with them. Zoe left the site undisturbed and shouldered her bike back up the slope.

Although it had been fairly calm in the encampment—the tarps snapping only with extreme gusts—the wind accelerated along the street above in a venturi effect between buildings. Zoe leaned into it along her ride to the next homeless camp. This one would be along the Mississippi and was probably the nicer of the two, if one could call a homeless camp nice—and Zoe knew there were many who would. On more than one occasion she'd tried to get shelter for patients who'd refused the offer. Many actually preferred sleeping rough.

Zoe's cough caught her on the way—made her stop her bike to double over with the effort. She reached into her pannier and came out with a plastic bottle of water and used it to wash down another opiate. She fought off a shaking chill as she stood over her bike, along with a simultaneous urge to remove her jacket. Despite the cold, her fever had worsened and sweat was evaporating, making her feel even colder— hot and cold at the same time. She replaced the water bottle and continued.

This time Zoe was able to guide her bike down a well-worn trail in the woods. It led to an encampment along the river. She stopped and dismounted, greeting the only resident who appeared to be home—thankfully, Zoe recognized him. His last haircut looked to have been fashioned around the edges of a cereal bowl tipped over his head, but at least it was trimmed—and his beard was clean of debris. He actually looked pretty good, as she compared him to her recollection of their last encounter.

"Abel. Hello. Remember me?"

"Sure do, doc. What are you doin' down here?"

"Brought you some stuff," she gestured toward her bike. "Where's everyone else?"

Abel smiled. "Around. So what's the catch?"

"You know there's no catch, Abel. But I was sort of hoping we could talk."

He said nothing.

"Just a little information—between you and me. Doctor-patient confidentiality."

"What you got?"

Zoe began pulling things out. She tossed him a packet of tube socks—clean, dry, new.

"What else?"

A long round of salami flew in his direction and he immediately pulled out a jackknife to open it. He cut a piece off the end and offered it to Zoe. She declined.

"Go ahead, Abel. Eat. Can we talk?"

"Sure, why not? Take a seat."

Zoe rested on a tree-stump, while Abel settled into a worn folding chair of the variety that soccer moms carried in their cars at all times.

"The last time I saw you it was hunting season. What happened?"

Abel laughed. "Yeah, that orange jump suit isn't too bad when it's colder than hell out."

"That's what I figured. Bought a night in jail, eh?"

"Yeah. Got me a shower, a place to sleep, and a few meals outa the deal. I told them I didn't need to go to the ER, but I don't guess they liked the way I smelled—wanted me cleaned up. Though I have to admit that a night in the hospital woulda been better."

"Well, like you said, there wasn't anything wrong with you that time. Couldn't really justify keeping you there."

"I know, doc. You'da kept me if you could. So, what's up?"

"I'm looking for a guy named Wolf. Veteran, with a dog—skinny guy, long hair."

"Yeah, I know him. He in trouble?"

"No, just want to talk with him. I promise, this is just between you and me. Just point me in the right direction and we'll leave it at that. He doesn't have to know."

"It's not that . . . but you know how it goes."

"Sure I do. But you'd be doing him a favor. I've got some dog food for him, and a few other things."

Abel kept eating.

"Got more for you, too."

Abel looked toward her bike, and Zoe patted one of the panniers.

"This side's all yours."

"Deal. But don't tell him I said hello."

"I'd never. Here," Zoe began emptying the contents of the pannier. Out of it she pulled a variety of non-perishable food items, some sweatpants and a sweatshirt for layering, more socks—one could never have too many dry socks, a flashlight and two packs of batteries, a dozen chemical hand-warmers for putting inside gloves and boots, and some heavy-duty fleece-lined mittens that came half-way up his forearm.

"What shape are your boots in?"

Abel lifted his legs for her to see the soles.

"Not good. Here," she gave him a fifty dollar bill. "For boots, and boots only, Abel. If when I see you again it's not in new boots, I'll personally wring your neck. And you know I'll be seeing you in the hospital eventually. Winter's coming."

He laughed, but of course promised nothing. She knew this was a crapshoot. He might or might not get new boots. He might or might not buy alcohol with the money. But if he bought food, that'd be a fair trade.

"So, where can I find him?"

ABEL HADN'T EVER ACTUALLY SEEN WOLF'S OTHER CAMP—only heard rumors of it. The gist, according to Abel, was that Wolf came around only during benders—kind of like it was a vacation. He'd hang out with the crew in Abel's camp for a while, but then had the good sense to wean off—or would find himself in detox—and then gather his things and say, "I'm going home now."

Apparently, Wolf was fairly secretive about where "home" was, and it was only while drinking heavily that he gave a few details away. His place was at the end of the bus line that rayed out toward the suburbs from the street above. "Convenient, I suppose," Abel had said and, according to Abel, Wolf had quit taking the bus since he got the dog. Instead he was riding one of those old balloon-tire bikes with a basket on the front. That's where Thor would ride. And that had all started this summer. Abel wasn't sure what Wolf would do once the snow came. He half expected not to see him again until spring.

Zoe had asked several times, trying for details, "The end of the bus line? That's all you can tell me?"

"That's all he told me. What can I say?"

"Think, Abel. There's got to be something else."

And Abel thought, while he continued to work on the salami. Finally he'd offered one small detail, perhaps meaningless, but she'd find out when she got there. Apparently Wolf had said something about his place being for sale. Of course that had gotten everyone around the campfire to laughing—because none of them had anything worth selling. So they'd written it off as drunken bullshit. "But it was kind of funny—him saying that," Abel said. "Like . . . it had to come from somewhere, you know?"

So now, Zoe followed the bus route on her bike. Her head swam with the addition of another pill, but at least her cough had been quieted. The fever had her a little concerned—it wasn't breaking, even with the medication. But it wouldn't be breaking any easier at home, she decided, and forgot about it as she kept track of the bus stops as they passed.

It was a long route, taking her well into what would be considered suburbs; in fact the area was semi-rural. She'd seen from a bank's temperature and time display, that it was nearing noon and only twenty-eight degrees. It felt even colder in the wind.

At the last bus stop she dismounted to survey her surroundings—asking herself where she'd hide a camp if she were forced to. In one direction, was a farm—clearly active. Any farmer would know his land well. There'd be no way to hide out there for long.

In another direction a strip mall spread out on the brow of a hill. Zoe biked to the rear of it and looked down the slope. It looked to be an illegal garbage dump—with old mattresses, plastic bags full of debris, and even old furniture. It had been picked through to a certain degree, with someone having started a small pile of wood next to some old packing crates. It actually looked as though the crates were being disassembled—probably for firewood, she thought, sensing that Wolf must be near.

From there she scanned the other two directions. In one, back toward the city, was a small housing development where quite a few of the homes were for sale. Thinking of Wolf's comment about his place being for sale, she decided to wander through the few streets on her bike. Stranger things were known to happen, she thought. Perhaps Wolf was a guy leading a secret life. Maybe he was a vet who liked the feel of living rough and had come home with a drinking problem. It wouldn't be unheard of.

She scanned the mailboxes as she rode—not expecting one to actually read, "Wolf." What she was looking for wasn't exactly clear. There were no dogs matching Thor's description in any of the yards, even though there were some annoying blue heelers who actually thought they could chase her. She gave special attention to the houses with "for sale" signs—some in tough shape, perhaps foreclosures.

Maybe he was squatting. Now that was an idea. She decided it was within bounds to get off and inspect the properties that were for sale, given the fact that any potential buyer would want to look around. She walked the bike next to her as she circled, peering in the windows. One was completely empty. There was no one living there, and certainly no one squatting. Two others were clearly lived in, and taken care of. In both were children's toys—making neither likely to be Wolf's. In three others, someone—not Wolf—came out to greet her, asking if she cared to see inside. After hearing about the loss of a job and the sadness over an anticipated move to another school district—"because this one was so good"—she declined.

Back near the bus stop, Zoe looked in the final direction. Another farm—appearing not to be active. The structures on the property seemed, from a distance, to be falling apart. There was a small sign next to the long driveway leading toward the rotting buildings. Now, there's a thought, at which she smiled—then coughed, and rode in that direction.

At the entrance to the driveway, next to a deteriorating barbed-wire fence, was a small sign that read, "for sale." Having clearly been there for a long time, the name of the realtor had weathered to unidentifiable. Even the "for sale" was indistinct, with vines having wrapped their way around both legs and over the top. What remained readable was partially covered and protected from the elements.

Zoe looked down the driveway and began walking slowly, scanning the ground on either side as she did. There looked to be a deer trail through an opening in the fence that picked up through a breach on the other side about twenty feet down the drive.

There were prints on the driveway—of the deer, human, and dog variety—and bike tire marks.

She'd found him.

Zoe peered into and searched all the outbuildings surrounding the collapsing farmhouse, discovering no trace of Wolf. Next she crawled into the house proper through an opening in the cellar. The extra flashlight she'd purchased for Wolf came in handy as she navigated the collection of old cans, boxes, and furniture littering the basement. She tried the pull-string of an overhead light with no response and decided the power had probably been disconnected. The basement smelled of mold. On the floor were recent footprints in the dust. Zoe studied the piles of debris. It appeared to have been sorted, and the central pile—consisting primarily of old furniture—had been recently harvested, as there were some surfaces without dust.

She made her way through the rest of the house—the situation being the same. Piles, sorted into furniture, cans, and empty glass jars. But there was no sign of Wolf, or his dog, and clearly no one had been living in the house. Over the fireplace she noted the beginning of a tag—not a gang symbol, but rather some teenage love pledge—which had been interrupted. The can of spray paint remained on its side beneath the misspelled oath. It was in the wall next to the fireplace brick that she noticed a bullet hole.

Zoe felt over the ashes—the fireplace hadn't been used recently. She moved to the kitchen and scoured the cupboards for any sign of life—food, refuse, blankets, anything—but only found that half the cupboards had been emptied. Not ransacked, not vandalized, but literally taken away.

Next she climbed water-damaged steps to the second floor. She had to sidestep rotting wood over gaps in the upstairs flooring. Upon closer examination, the roof seemed to have been pried away in places, leaving no trace of the material. She stepped outside again, and circled the house. There was missing siding. One would expect the material to fall off—remaining where it fell. But it was gone.

Looking back toward the outbuildings she'd previously examined, the same held true—parts of the buildings hadn't just fallen after years of disrepair. They were being picked clean—as efficiently as a rotting corpse.

Zoe circled the outer perimeter around the collection of buildings. There were clearly prints leading to and from the driveway—and if someone were scavenging the buildings, they'd have to cart the materials away in something. But as she walked, periodically crouching low to view the ground, she had to admit that while this had seemed to be a good prospect at first, there was no sign of Wolf or his dog—other than those tracks in the driveway.

She'd been gone a long time, and the sun would set early this time of year—probably around five-thirty. If she were going to bike home, it meant starting soon. But something caught her eye as she was trying to convince herself of the need to go. Stooping low to the ground, she examined bruises on the un-mowed grass. Following the direction of the damage, her eyes fell on woods in the distance—and the suggestion of an opening along a direct path from where she now stood. Feeling the earth underfoot as she walked toward the opening, she discovered a double-track that had been largely reclaimed—not only by time and elements, but also by having been farmed over at some point remote to the present, but sometime after the road had ceased to be maintained. While the old ruts no longer existed in the tilled areas, by keeping on a straight path toward the opening in the trees she hoped to pick them up again by the perimeter of the field at a place the plow had missed. But as she continued to the tree line, there was no sign of them.

Zoe knelt, examining the ground. She cautiously made her way into the woods, a mix of deciduous trees—empty of leaves—as well as pine and cedar. And beneath the pine needles and leaves, was a heel strike. She fanned out from there in several directions. Each time, after finding nothing, she backed to her starting point and tried a different radius. It was in that way that she noticed the broken twigs, and in following them, found the marks that indicated something had been dragged through the woods. From there she eventually picked up the old double-track again. Apparently it hadn't entered the woods where she'd expected—instead it had followed the perimeter of the field for a stretch, obscured by the history of having been plowed, and dove into the woods through a camouflaged opening. In the woods, walking her bike became effortless without the old ruts of the tilled field and the path was easily followed. As wooded darkness gave way to another opening, the setting sun illuminated the unexpected.

"Well...I'll be damned."

HE LOWERED HIS RIFLE—it had been trained dead center "T-zone."

"Ma'am," he tipped his head.

"Wolf," Zoe tried to focus on his face, but the gun was hard to ignore.

He turned to lean it against the wall of the pole barn. "Sorry about that, but a man has to be careful out here."

Zoe lifted her hands, palms up, "Not really a threat here, Wolf."

"That's what I liked about you when you took care of me in the ER. You're funny," he smiled, "and you don't bullshit."

"So you do remember me?"

"Yeah. I thought about it and it came back."

"That's one helluva weapon you've got there. Is that a Leupold scope?"

"Yep."

The scope was of a quality that professional snipers used—and what amazed her was the fact that the weapon hadn't been hocked yet.

As if reading her mind he added, "I never bring it into town with me."

And Zoe remembered that, according to Abel, Wolf's trips into town were when he binged. Right now, he appeared sober. Not cleaner, and still scrawny—but sober.

"What are you doing way out here?"

"And you?"

"Looking for you. No bullshit."

He laughed. "Okay, you found me. What's up?" But then his face darkened. "How'd you know where I was? Did I tell you when you helped me? I don't think I'd do that."

Zoe ignored the question. "How's the dog?"

"Thor? He's around."

At the sound of his name, Zoe heard Thor bark from inside the old pole barn.

"So he's okay? No more problems?"

"Nope." Wolf still looked concerned.

"I brought him some food."

Then Wolf walked toward her, finally interested.

Zoe unloaded the second pannier, pulling out socks, food for Wolf, and a package of dog food for Thor—even a small rawhide bone.

"Should we carry this stuff inside?" Zoe nodded toward the pole barn.

"No. I can do it."

"Wolf?"

"Yes, ma'am."

"Remember when you said that you'd help me if I ever needed anything?"

"Sure do. I was stone cold sober when I said that. I was ready to come home. I never drink out here."

"So this is home?" Zoe figured it for a pretty good place to squat. Funny he hadn't been kicked out though.

"Sure is."

"Is there somewhere we can talk?"

He looked around, seeming to struggle with the question.

Zoe added, "Anything we talk about is private. Doctor-patient confidentiality."

He looked at the pole barn, and then at her, "I suppose we can go inside. But you can't tell anyone?"

"No."

"Okay, because if word gets out, they'll be all over me out here."

The two loaded their arms with Zoe's offerings and moved toward the large sliding door of the pole barn. Wolf transferred his holdings to one arm, and with the other he pulled on the heavy wooden door as he said, "Remember, don't tell anyone."

Zoe's eyes adjusted to the darkness, "Holy shit." And Zoe knew that this was going to be a hard thing not to talk about.

Confidentiality was a bitch.

LUCY PULLED OVER AND PARKED in order to view the text message—then mumbled to herself, "Good grief, I can see why she ditched the phone with me." It was the fourth communication that day.

She took a moment to answer back, "ZOE SED 2 PLZ LET HER SLEEP, SO I DON'T WANT 2 WAKE HER RIGHT NOW."

Lucy waited for the reply. He seemed reliable in that way. She drummed the steering wheel and watched the traffic go by as she waited the minute required.

"NO PROBLEM, LUCY. DON'T WAKE HER. I'LL CHECK BACK 2MORROW. KEEP TAKING GOOD CARE OF HER. APPRECIATE IT."

Shadowland

Lucy hated lying to him, but in the end it was better this way. At least Zoe was getting the rest she needed—and like Zoe had said, technically, it wasn't a lie.

Lucy replaced the phone in her pocket, and steered back into traffic. She planned to take the back roads home, avoiding the freeways at rush hour. It might actually take longer this way, but it seemed safer, and more tranquil. After her day with Phillip, tranquility was her goal. There was a lot to think about.

First there was her plea to embark upon a vision quest. His reply—"Go ahead." She'd pushed him, even though it had become obvious to her that pushing him was an impossible task. But of course all she'd gotten was a cryptic response about visions and dreams coming at any time, at the right time—in their own time. He'd only said to pay attention. And it was, in fact, more than she'd expected from him.

They'd spent time discussing vision quests earlier in the day, too, while walking by the river. It was to Lucy's great relief that although they used to be considered a requirement for boys, they'd always been at least an option for girls. Apparently a female's childbearing abilities justified her existence—no vision quest required—but if desired, it was allowed. Thank God, because if not, she might have chucked the whole idea of exploring her ancestral spirituality.

Secondly, there was his remark about "shadow people"—as if they were all around us, even in us. It was kind of creepy, but he'd approached the topic in such a matter-of-fact way that in the end, it didn't exactly scare her. What it did was to make her intensely curious.

But by far the hardest thing to accept out of all they'd talked about was this notion of Ojibwe heroes—every one being crucially flawed. Lucy had always viewed heroes as, well . . . heroic. But Ojib stories were full of heroes and half-gods who seemed to stumble their way through heroic deeds despite their inadequacies and fears. She'd considered that perhaps that was the whole point, because if you didn't fear anything, or have anything to overcome, then where was the heroism in the deed? Was there even any story to tell? But though that made sense, and was probably true, it still didn't seem to be enough. There was more to it—she could feel it, but just couldn't explain it. "I'm not getting it," she said to herself as she drove, "maybe Zoe can help," because vision quests, shadow people, and bumbling heroes were about all she could absorb in one day.

ZOE'S BREATHING MATCHED THE CADENCE of turning pedals and her cough reacted to the cold air. She raced at her top speed and yet, given the pneumonia, reaching home would take twice as long. She needed to beat Lucy home at any cost—even through the stabbing inhales and the coughing exhales. No way she wanted to compound the lies she'd maneuvered the kid into telling.

As Zoe skidded around the last turn she looked toward the house—no lights on yet—and accelerated into the driveway. She got out to enter the code and scooted under the opening garage door, parked her bike, and then hit the button to close the door behind her.

Within seconds of hearing the garage door close, she heard it open again, and smiled. What were the odds? All in all, it would have to be considered a charmed day. Then she darted into her bedroom and, in the dark, chucked her clothing before diving under the covers.

"A HOMELESS GUY AND A DOCTOR?" The boss was interested.

"Yeah. That's what I hear. They've got some interest in your merchandise. With what Josh said, it makes sense. She's a doctor, and she was grilling him hard—I was in back, I heard the whole thing."

"But it doesn't make sense. Josh said she'd come looking for Christie—that means she doesn't know where Christie is, right?—so it doesn't make sense."

"No, but my other source tells me it's got to do with a homeless guy and a doctor. Who else would it be?"

"I don't know, but we're not going to move on this one too quick. We'll watch her. You got a name? An address?"

"Yeah. And she works at Minneapolis General. We got it all. Everything we need."

"Keep an eye on her. Start now."

"What abut the homeless dude? We're pretty sure who he is. She was seen talking to him. Why would she be doing that if he weren't the guy?—I mean, a doctor and all. It doesn't make sense."

"No, it doesn't. That makes it something to pay close attention to. Homeless guys come and go. This one is going."

"Ojib Heroes?"

"Yes. It's driving me crazy."

"Why?"

"Because our heroes are supposed to be strong—better than us. Half the Ojib heroes and gods seem . . . I don't know . . ."

"Lacking?"

"Yes! Doesn't that bug you? Why put your faith in someone weaker or duller than yourself?"

"So you're not flawed?"

"Well, not that bad."

Zoe said, smiling but not joking, "You're old enough to know better."

Lucy said nothing.

"I guess the way I see it, Lucy, is that it's because of our imperfections that we struggle—and that's how we gain strength, by having to push against something."

"Oh," but Lucy looked hurt.

"In hockey, one of the grand traditions is the post-tournament handshake. You know why it's so grand?"

"I suppose because it shows good sportsmanship."

"In a way, yes. But then what is good sportsmanship?"

"I guess it's dealing with victory and loss graciously."

"Sure, but that just requires behavioral discipline. There's more to it. It goes deeper than that."

"How so?"

"It's a genuine respect for your opponent. After a loss, I'm even more grateful for a good game, a good contest, as when I win—perhaps even more so. Do you know why?"

"No—and you're starting to make me feel stupid again."

"Lucy, that's not my intention. Please get over that—and just pay attention."

"That's the second time I've heard that today."

"Well then, take it to heart. But the reason I'm even more grateful after a loss is that my opponents have pushed me to my limits. I owe them for that, because it strengthens me, and it makes me wiser—teaching me about the world, and about myself."

Lucy's eyes brightened—a smile slowly forming. But then her forehead knotted up in frustration. "But there's still more. I can feel it."

"Good for you, Lucy. You are paying attention. I've never said this to anyone before, because I'm not too comfortable talking about such things, but since you've pushed me to my limits," Zoe smiled, "what you might be sensing is that the Ojibwe 'take' on such things makes the gulf between all that's human and all that's divine not seem so vast. And about faith—why is it necessary?"

"I like that—about the gulf not seeming so vast. But faith—isn't it essential?"

"Why?"

Lucy pressed the heels of her hands into her eyes.

"Too much for one night?" Zoe asked, half-laughing, half-coughing. "Let's eat."

"No kidding. I'll check the oven. Dinner should be about ready by now."

"Thanks, Lucy." Zoe grabbed the television remote and pushed ON. She switched channels to the evening news and lined up the two pills she still needed to take—an antibiotic, and the narcotic that would allow her a night's sleep without coughing.

Lucy called from the kitchen. "Kaj tried you several times on your cell. I can see why you gave it to me. At least this way you got some actual, uninterrupted sleep."

Zoe thought of all she'd experienced that day, and all she wished it would be possible to share with Lucy—or anyone for that matter. As Wolf had pulled open the pole barn door everything in Zoe's arms had dropped and she'd coughed uncontrollably for several minutes after a sharp intake of cold air.

It was just so unexpected—a house within a house.

A small cottage erected within the structure of the pole barn had been Wolf's project for the last two years—or at least the sober parts of those years.

Although assembled from scrap wood and other found supplies, it was finely crafted. The reason, perhaps, that he was careful to leave this place and go into the city for his binges. Remarkable, was how careful he'd been to wean himself off booze each time before returning to his "home."

He'd been gradually disassembling the farmhouse and scavenging the dump she'd seen, only to return everything to a useful purpose in his cottage.

Shadowland

After seeing the astonishment on her face he'd said, "Some day I'm going to unwrap it as a great big present to myself!"

When she'd asked him why he chose to build inside a pole barn he'd mumbled something about not being able to afford a building permit, and about how it allowed him to build it slowly—the rain couldn't get at it. She didn't dare ask him what would happen when the property owner found out about it.

Lucy returned with their dinner and drinks on a tray. Both sat on the couch, facing the television, and Zoe downed the pills before eating.

"So what's this, Lucy?"

"An oven risotto."

"No shit? I thought you had to slave over a stove to make that."

"Sara doesn't have time for nonsense like that. She's taught me all kinds of shortcuts."

"Well, this works. It's good."

"Thanks."

Zoe quit talking and ate—it was the first thing she'd eaten since breakfast—and so did Lucy. Out of fatigue and hunger, both allowed the evening news to take over their conversation.

Zoe's eyes fixed on the television as an image of the second homeless camp she'd visited that morning played across the screen. And at the sight of a body bag being removed, her spoon dropped to the floor.

"You okay, Zoe?" Lucy moved to pick up the spoon.

"It's okay. I got it," Zoe waved her off and grabbed the spoon, but kept her eyes on the screen. "Shit."

Lucy looked toward the television. "That's the place, isn't it? The place we were going to go?"

"Yep."

"You knew the guy?"

"I might have." Zoe reached for her cell phone and hit the well-used number. "Ray? Just saw the news. What do you know about the dead homeless guy?"

Lucy watched Zoe's face break out in a reluctant grin as she listened to one side of the conversation.

"Well, hello to you, too."

Zoe laughed.

"Yes, it's good to hear your voice, too."

Then through several minutes of Zoe's silence, her expression sobered.

"Okay. Thanks. Talk to you later." Zoe put down the phone, looked at Lucy, and teared. "I knew him. It was Abel."

The door opened, as Kaj let himself in. "Surprise!"

"Kaj! What are you doing here?"

"Giving Lucy the night off." He swept Zoe up in an embrace and looked over Zoe's shoulder at Lucy. "Pack up your stuff, kiddo. I'll drive you back to Sara's and then pick you up again in the morning."

"SHE'S GOT A VISITOR. Still want us to keep watch?"

"No. Go back in the morning. See what she does."

"Probably just going to work."

The boss was getting irritated. "Yeah, probably. But we won't know until you verify it. Now I'm letting you go home and fuck your girlfriend and come back in the morning. How about a little enthusiasm? Think about what your night was going to be like!"

"Window peeping on that chick? Not so bad."

The boss actually laughed. "That's why I keep you around, wiseass. You crack me up."

"That's good, boss. Thanks for the night off."

"Just make sure to get your ass back over there bright and early. Before she makes a move. I've got to think about this."

"SO, WHAT WAS WITH THE TEARS? I couldn't help but notice when I came in."

"You remember Abel? Homeless guy. He's in the ER occasionally. Has a tat that reads 'momma warned me.' Hard to miss—it's written across his chest. You see it every time you listen to his heart."

"Sure, I remember. What about him?"

"He took the westbound today—traveling light."

"Huh?"

"Hobo speak—he died."

"Did you know him well?"

"No—but it's still sad as hell. He didn't have much," she said, knowing that he'd died with what to him had seemed like riches, and wishing she'd taken the time to give more generously long before needing the favor from him.

"He didn't come through the ER. How'd he die?"

"Ray said it was probably an accidental drowning."

"If Ray's involved, it's not an accident."

"It's referred to as ambiguous circumstances, so homicide gets called in."

"What's his opinion?"

"He says it's one of those cases where we'll probably never know."

"They got nothing?"

"Only that it wasn't a robbery, because the guy had food and McDonalds gift certificates in his lean-to. And there was no evidence of a struggle, even though Ray said the camp was a chaotic mess—so it was hard to tell."

"You have skin in this game? Something personal?"

Zoe looked away, "No. Let's just go to bed. I have to get myself right before this big shindig Saturday night."

He grinned, "I'm counting on it. I want to show you off." His eyes sparkled with mischief.

Zoe chuckled. "Seriously? Look at me. I'm a mess. I just want to be able to make an appearance, but I won't exactly be in 'show' form, pal—that's up to you. I'll be showing you off—while I'm trying not to honk and cob."

"You're still coughing?"

"Like you wouldn't believe. Thank God for the meds or I wouldn't be getting any sleep at all."

"Okay, to bed it is. Let's go," and he picked her up.

Zoe let go of her doubts as she buried her face in his shoulder. He gently placed her on the bed and began with her socks, undressing her, kissing her—massaging her after removing each article of clothing.

But the doubts crept back. She imagined him with Dr. Pink. Imagined them standing close, conferring over a patient. Operating as one efficient unit. Admiring each other's skill and dedication. Growing close. Touching each other—casually at first, and then with anticipation. And just where had she seen this play out before?

She worked to rid herself of the intrusive images, even as Kaj worked his magic on her. He brought about the sheen on her skin—had her breathless and coiled in anticipation. His pace quickened, before releasing them both to the winded rush of their fall back to earth.

And as she slipped toward sleep, her final conscious thought was, "If you ever fucking do this with Dr. Pink . . . I'll sure-as-shit kill you."

Abel cried out to her. "I was warned—now look at me." And she did look at him—rattling chains and all.

Warned? Was his death her fault? An enormous weight came over her. She couldn't move.

Then he said, "Wolf doesn't know. He hasn't been warned."

Warned?—by who? His dog?

"You have to warn him."

But still she couldn't move. She could visualize Wolf—in his cottage. And she could see people approaching him out of many directions within the woods. Some carried guns, others knives. But Wolf's dog didn't bark—didn't warn him. And though she struggled to speak, to shout at him, her voice didn't work either. Instead she started coughing, and among the many faces in the woods, she saw him—the Canadian. The man who'd terrorized her and murdered her family. He was laughing at her—even as he crept closer to Wolf's shelter, keeping his eyes on her as he made his way skillfully through the woods—and still she couldn't move, couldn't talk.

As the armed intruders swarmed the pole barn, she finally found her voice and screamed herself awake.

"Zoe! Are you all right? You were dreaming again, hon."

Zoe looked up into his eyes—hers still terrified. And in those few moments before she moved and lost the dream, she identified it. The overwhelming weight she'd felt—it was guilt.

"I'm okay. Did I actually scream? I dreamed that I did."

"Yes. You did. Quite loudly."

"Sorry."

"Was it the usual? The Canadian?"

"No. He's dead."

Kaj said nothing, simply looked at her with a question in his eyes. She knew what it was.

They'd never found his body, even after Lucy's accurate gunshot. The evidence—a considerable blood trail—had later proved that Lucy had indeed hit her mark before pushing him off the cliff and into deep water. It was the same water Zoe had rescued Lucy from after the kid's running tackle of the man had sent them both over the cliff.

But they'd never found his body.

"He's dead—I know it."

Still nothing from Kaj.

So she shouted at him. "I know it because he haunts me! Okay? He haunts me!" Then quietly, "He's dead."

"Of course he is," Kaj pulled her into his arms.

The dream was disturbing—nothing new there. Zoe had learned to anticipate that. But what in the hell did it mean? Why did she feel so guilty? And what was with this "warning" shit? Warn him about what? Maybe it was just the guilt she'd felt after manipulating Abel—creeping itself into her dream, about why she hadn't helped him sooner.

"Listen, Kaj, there's no need to get Lucy back over here today. I'll be fine."

"Well then, I'm coming back after work tonight. Okay with you?"

"Yeah," she smiled, "last night was . . . therapeutic."

"I'll let Lucy know she's off the hook," he grinned.

CHAPTER FIVE

HRISTIE FELT FOR HER SON IN THE DARK. She could hear him breathing and was amazed by how late he'd slept. Normally he was an early riser, jumping up and down by her bed and asking for breakfast—almost always after a night of work followed by a mere two hours of sleep. It would be her habit to wake, make him food, and then see to his preparedness for kindergarten. The arrival of the school bus would be her snooze alarm.

She leaned in closer, feeling his breath on her cheek. It was the absolute darkness of this place, she guessed, that was why he slept so long—the darkness, and the silence.

As for her, it was getting a full night's sleep that allowed for such an easy awakening. Without the bedside clock, she'd have had no idea of the time.

She felt over his forehead and gently pushed damp curls aside, fighting her memory of the blood she'd had to wash from him—right now his bangs were damp with sweat, not blood. His bangs were always sweaty and stuck to his forehead—hard-play sweat, she smiled in recalling, his body a mini-furnace and constant motion his fuel. She curled around her "little man," feeling his warmth, and wished for only one thing—that from now on, she could protect him.

***

FINALLY ALONE IN THE HOUSE, Zoe lingered in a steamy shower. Expectorated sputum circled the drain in red. Each attempt at a deep breath was accompanied by stabbing chest pain and an uncontrollable coughing fit. She had to compensate by breathing shallowly, trying not to test her lungs.

Soap ran down her legs and the red washed clear. When she massaged shampoo through her hair Zoe's eyes tracked high along the wall, landing on a red stain. In looking closer, she saw red sputum clinging to the tiles in several places. She reached toward each and scrubbed them free with a soapy hand until red trails converged on the drain again. And then she began to cough some more.

This time she redirected the spray by covering her mouth, and spit directly at the drain.

Zoe wrapped up in a towel and made her way toward the kitchen, acknowledging to herself that she'd been enjoying Lucy's cooking and was already missing it. A long stare into the fridge didn't result in anything. Neither did her peek into the pantry.

Finally she started the water heating and opened the freezer to scoop Peet's coffee into a filter. She lined up her pills and debated whether or not to take the narcotic. If she did, she was limited to her bike. When the coffee was ready, she poured it through the filter and watched it drip into the cup below. Then she palmed the antibiotic and tossed it into her mouth. The narcotics she left on the table. Instead she threw on her clothes and grabbed the car keys.

"Zoe?"

"Yep. What's up Lucy?"

"Is this an okay time to call? I figured you'd be up and eating by now."

"You're right, kiddo."

"Oh, good. I didn't want to wake you."

"It's okay." Zoe pulled to a stop at the red light. "I'm not doing anything, just lying around, resting."

"Good."

"Well?"

"Ah, well, I'm headed back over to Phillip's place. He said we could hang out again today. Pushpa let me use her car."

"That's great. And?"

"Sara kind of likes the idea. She said it'd be good for me to connect with him. But she wants your assurance that he's okay—you know, safe."

"He's fine, Lucy, or I never would have sent you over there. No need to worry. But I get Sara's point. She's right to question things. Have her call me if she's still concerned. I'm glad you two talked about it. Okay, then?"

"Yeah, but…"

"What?"

"Well, it's just that something's been bugging me."

"Go ahead, shoot. What is it?"

"Well, it's what you said about faith."

"Ah—so that's it."

"Yeah, it bugs me. And I wanted to talk to you about it before I go to Phillip's place."

"Okay." Zoe pulled into the intersection. "I'll share my take on it. But you still have to wrestle with this stuff on your own—and I can tell you right now, Phillip won't spoon-feed you. He'll expect you to work for it."

Lucy laughed. "I know. That's why I'm talking to you first."

Zoe grinned as she pushed her car to get through a changing light on the yellow. "Ask yourself, do you have to have complete faith in a religion to practice it?"

"I suppose not, but doesn't that just make it a hollow gesture?"

"Why should it? Religion is about action—it's a behavior, a discipline, believing isn't a necessary component at all. Sure it gives us a lot. It gives us a sense of place and purpose. It connects us with others who wrestle with the same questions we do—and connecting people is damn important—but faith isn't necessarily required to live within a religion practice."

"But doesn't God see that?"

"Perhaps. But if so, can't God absorb the truth? In our hearts, we all have doubt. Why deny it? Truth isn't about being perfect—it's as messy as our lives are."

"But…"

"Listen, why would we accept that human beings, flawed as we are, actually have the last word on interpreting such things?" Zoe pulled up in front of Angie's and parked the car. She turned off the ignition and continued her conversation. "The Ojibwe's narrowed gulf gives me both a sense of reassurance and caution."

"Oh, man. Now I'm even more confused. But I think I sort of get what you're saying. It's just that we're human, and God is more than what we can imagine."

"Oh, you're good, kiddo. Did Phillip tell you what many translate Kitchi Manitou as?"

"Kitchi Manitou is the great spirit, the creator, right?"

"The Great Mystery." Zoe scanned the people coming and going from Angie's. Among the patrons was one she recognized. "I come from a scientific background, Lucy. I look at things differently. To me, mystery is the reason we're here. Without it, why bother? I'm not threatened by what I don't know or understand. It's okay. In fact I view it as a gift—from God, if you will. It gives us purpose. We have to be curious in order to make progress and survive. In fact, if everything were perfect, why bother?"

"I remember Pushpa saying something like that to me once. About mystery being the reason she gets up every morning."

Zoe laughed. "Exactly. It allows us to experience the joy of creativity and imaginative leaps. So to me a mature belief is faith in a spiritual essence even though our understanding of it is undoubtedly imperfect."

"Imagination? But I thought you were a scientist."

"Oh, my, I think you may have an inaccurate idea of what scientists are. It's science that brought me back to God—not religion."

"What?"

"Lucy, I did the practice thing. I did the praying—and I'll bet you did, too. I prayed obsessively once, wanting a certain outcome." Four daily prayers, Zoe recalled—and it had to be four—done exactly the same way each time. They were meant to protect her father and brother from her mother's fate. The prayers were meant to keep them safe. Zoe had been convinced that if she didn't do the ritual something awful would happen to them. But it happened anyway.

"Well anyway, it didn't work. It was only magical thinking. So for a long while, I turned my back on anything religious—even spiritual—until two things happened. One was that I met Kaj and rediscovered something." Zoe cleared her throat and was glad this conversation was happening through the phone. "The other was prompted by Kaj, but it was still science that directed me back toward God."

"Wow. How?"

Zoe kept watching the man through the window. She had to get in there quickly, or she'd miss him. "How about we talk about that another time? I think I've dumped enough on you for one day. And Phillip will be challenging you as well. Okay by you?"

"Sure, okay. But thanks ... for everything. For talking to me about this stuff, and for introducing me to Phillip."

"No problem—and, Lucy? Try thinking about prayer differently, too. Let go of any preconceived notions about it, okay? Just see what happens."

"Okay, Zoe. I'll try. Get some rest."

"Will do, kiddo. I'm putting my feet up as we speak."

ZOE APPROACHED THE BAR AND PLACED an order for scrambled eggs, hash browns, and sausage. Without Lucy, it would have to do. The bartender—not Josh this time—left to put the order in and then came back with coffee.

She asked him, "Who's the guy in the corner? The one with the laptop?"

"You don't know?"

Zoe rolled her eyes. "I guess not, or I wouldn't have asked."

"He's a writer. Mystery novels. Writes in here almost every day. They're actually pretty good—I have a couple."

So this bartender can read, she realized. "What's his name?"

The bartender squeezed his eyes shut, trying to think. "I can't remember."

And she wondered why that didn't surprise her. "Thanks." A writer, eh? She called to the bartender, "Send my food over there." Zoe pointed to the corner table with the writer and his laptop.

Before grabbing her coffee mug, she pointed at Kelly's picture above the bar, "Were you here the day that happened?"

"Yep."

"What went down?"

"It had to do with a frozen pizza."

Zoe smiled, and turned toward the mystery author.

WHEN ZOE APPROACHED HIS TABLE he looked up, "Hello."

Zoe pointed to a chair, "You mind?"

"Well," he looked down at his work, but then back at Zoe—working the smile—and said, "I suppose it's okay. What's up? You an aspiring writer?"

Zoe's smile transitioned into something cautionary, "No, I'm the story."

"Huh?"

"Never mind. Lame joke. Actually, I was wondering how much you remembered from last Monday. I recognize you from that day. You didn't leave with the others, did you?"

"No, I stuck around. Told them everything I'd seen."

"Which was?"

"The kid running in here on the heels of that homeless guy, then looking up toward what we all thought was going to be a jumper only to see his shadow instead."

"His shadow?"

"Sure. He jumped the buildings. But I only noticed his shadow do it—on the street. I didn't actually see him."

"Okay, that's good." She'd seen a shadow, but hadn't realized it might be a Traceur. Instead she'd expected a body on the pavement. "What else did you see?"

"Listen, it's not that I mind telling you but, what's your interest?"

Zoe puffed air into her cheeks and let it out slowly—wondering what lie to choose. Then she decided on the truth. "The lead investigator is a good friend of mine. Used to be my partner when I worked the force. Just helping him out."

"Okay. I'm cool with that."

"I assume you didn't see who rifled the till?"

"Nope. I was looking out at the street, same as everyone else."

"Almost everyone. You noticed me that day?"

"Of course, I'm a writer. I notice all sorts of stuff. Things others don't see."

"What did you notice about me?" she grinned, testing him.

"That you were watching that woman at the bar, and the guy you were sitting with had his picture on the wall. He wasn't supposed to be in here."

"Do you know why?"

"Yep. I was here that night. It had to do with a frozen pizza—and it's too good a story not to be in my next novel."

Zoe laughed and had to stifle the cough. She quickly drank some coffee. "I'll make sure to read that one. But back to Monday—mind sharing what else you noticed?"

"I gave your friend the facts. But he didn't seem too interested in anything else."

"Well I am. Let's start with Grace. What did you notice about her?"

"Grace?"

"That hard-drinking woman at the bar."

"Oh." He smiled. "Probably the same thing you did."

"That she was drinking hard? And that people were staring at her?"

"Yeah. I know what you mean. But I also saw it in her eyes—that she recognized the homeless guy."

"How do you know?"

"Just saw it—like I said, in her eyes."

"Weren't you looking at the kid?"

"Eventually, when her eyes finally went to him."

"Help me out here. What exactly did you see in her eyes?"

"Fear."

"Come on, a lot of people fear the homeless."

"Not like that. It was an intimate fear—a fear of something she knew, not something she didn't know."

Zoe thought about it while shoveling more food onto her fork. She raised it, poised before a wide-open mouth, and said, "Who was she looking at before the homeless guy walked in?"

He smiled.

"Well, you said you'd been watching her. And you noticed her eyes," Zoe persisted.

"She was watching the little dancing kid, with the woman—and the back of the guy making his way toward them."

Zoe's smile grew lopsided over a mouthful of hash browns. She forced a rapid swallow, "And just what did you make of that?"

"Kid's been doing that his whole life."

"Exactly!"

"He was getting in between his mom . . . and trouble."

"Right! That's what I thought, too. Or dreamed, maybe," her voice fell off and she refilled the fork as she considered the possibility that Grace might know Wolf. Then she asked, before stuffing in the next bite—an activity that seemed to amuse her new author friend, "You must know most of the regulars here. You know those folks?—the little kid with the woman . . . and the guy?"

"Sorry."

"How about Grace?"

"Nope. I see her here a lot, but don't know her. This is the first I've heard her name. She's kind of like wallpaper, you know?"

"What about the kid who came running in? Recognize him?"

"Don't believe I've ever seen him in here before either. But remember, it's not as though I live here—even though my girlfriend might claim otherwise."

Zoe kept eating, with one eye on her new friend, and she was pretty sure she might also rate a few lines in his next novel. He seemed to be paying very close attention to the rhythm of her filling the fork, then her mouth, and then the swallowing of half-chewed food. Comic relief, she thought, maybe some dubious character in a bar who ate fast and sloppy—a bad guy. Maybe even something to do with a frozen pizza.

They finally exchanged names and he gave her his card. "Charles Morgan," it read, along with all his contact information.

"Glad to meet you, Charles." She pushed away from the table, an empty plate left at her place, and threw a five and ten down. "Hope to see you again. I'll look up your books."

"Appreciate it."

ZOE PUNCHED THROUGH THE GEARS, making her way to the head shop above which Grace was known to live.

Grace's apartment was on the second floor, accessed via a narrow, windowless stairway that she found only after going through the head shop and being redirected through the back door. Her apartment was one of four at the second floor landing, one of only two overlooking the street. Zoe was greeted cautiously.

"I remember you."

Zoe smiled.

"From last Monday."

"Yes. That's what I'm here to speak with you about."

"Why? And who the hell are you? I already told the cops everything I know."

"I'm a colleague of Detective Perry's," she lied—but only sort of, Zoe reasoned, as she still occasionally did consulting work for the MPD—"and I'm helping him track down a few things."

Grace didn't ask for any ID, and Zoe figured being female was what really got her through the door.

"Well, come in then," Grace said, clearly impatient, "what is it now?"

"Can we sit?"

Grace looked around and then grabbed a pile of newspapers off one of the chairs. "There, sit. But make it quick." Grace sat across from the chair on a well-worn couch and dropped the papers next to her. As she did, Zoe scanned the room.

Everything was old, stuck in the '80s, she guessed. Grace's morning's coffee was still on the table along with a half-eaten bagel, a knitted throw tossed casually over the back of the couch, a take-out menu from the malt-shop down the street, a photo album, and a stack of books—one of which had a bookmark located half-way through the pages. But if it weren't for the plants, Zoe would have been hard-pressed to believe someone actually lived there. The whole place just felt dead.

"You didn't stay. Why?"

"Why should I?"

"To help the police."

"I repeat, why should I? I didn't realize anything had happened until they came to question me later. It was simply time to leave. So I tossed my money on the bar and left after I walked out to see the jumper."

Zoe's recollection jibed—she hadn't noticed Grace after coming back into the bar. In fact, several people had taken the opportunity to leave—not all of them paying their tab. But this made sense. Grace was apparently a regular and wouldn't have skipped out. So maybe she truly had nothing to offer about the theft and murder, which is exactly what Ray had told her—but what about Wolf?

"You know the homeless guy."

"I do?"

"You recognized him, when he came in."

"And just how do you figure that?"

Zoe debated . . . and then said, "That mystery author, in the corner, he could see it in your eyes." Feeling immediately foolish, Zoe added, "Says he has a way with observation."

Grace laughed, "And he must have an active imagination. He's a writer, for cripes sake. Fiction, apparently!"

"Well?"

"Well what? I don't know him from Adam."

"Would it be so bad to admit to knowing a homeless guy like Wolf?"

There was no apparent surprise in hearing the name Wolf, but Zoe could almost see the hairs on the back of Grace's neck stand on edge and decided that the writer had a point. You could see a lot in her eyes. Grace Prescott was angry—and this conversation was definitely going places.

"I don't have anything against the homeless! And being a war hero doesn't make any difference either, I mean to tell you that!"

Oh, no, Grace, Zoe thought, *you most definitely did not mean to tell me that.* But Zoe was careful not to point that out. "Really? He's a war hero? I didn't realize that. What did he do?"

Grace stopped. She stared at Zoe for what seemed like a full minute, blinking maybe once. "I just figured, what with the army outfit and all."

In returning the stare, Zoe asked, "So if he's a war hero, why is he homeless?"

"Do you actually think there's an easy answer to that question?"

"No. Did I say that? I just asked why."

"Because he blames himself, because he blames the world, because he can't hold down a job, because he drinks, because he doesn't much care for people, and maybe because he was . . ." and that's where Grace stopped again.

"Was what?"

"How should I know? Just hypothesizing. Aren't there always a lot of things contributing in that situation?"

"I suppose there are." Zoe searched for a way to resume the conversation. Get her angry again? It might be worth a try.

"So you've helped him then?"

"I do a lot to help people. You have no idea."

"You're right. I have no idea. I don't know you at all. So tell me, what do you do?"

"And just how does that have anything to do with what happened at Angie's?"

She'd lost her. Grace had shaken free. No point in continuing. "It doesn't. I was just curious."

"Well, I have things to get done. Can we wrap this up." It wasn't a question.

"Of course. Thanks for your time. One more thing, do you know where I can find Wolf?"

And in that moment, Zoe was pretty sure she saw what the writer had—a flash of fear.

"Of course not—I don't even know the young man." She seemed to think for a moment, "I just hypothesize."

"Sorry, I forgot. It's a reflex to ask."

As Zoe got up to leave, Grace finally asked, "Can I see some ID?"

Zoe made a show of searching her pocket. "Sorry, I guess I forgot to bring it with—technically, I'm off-duty."

Grace hurried to position herself between Zoe and the door, "Well then, how about some contact information—you know, in case I remember anything. How about an address, a phone number . . ." and she appeared to think for a moment, "a name, for cripe's sake! You never even told me your name!" Grace picked up a pen and ripped off the edge of the newspaper, shoving it at Zoe.

"Name's Zoe Lawrence, and here's where you can contact me," she wrote down her cellphone number, handing the pen and paper back, and noting that the hand reaching out for it was shaking. "Thanks again for your time."

ZOE'S OLD CONTACTS FROM HER YEARS on the Minneapolis Police Department were still useful. Next stop was the local café known to be a morning-after hangout for the area's prostitutes—one or two notches down from Angie's, and not pretending to be anything else. Zoe knew the owner and namesake, Betty.

"Zoe. It's been a long time."

"Hi, Betty. Yes, it has." Zoe took a stool at the counter and glanced at the tables. The woman she was looking for wasn't here.

When she turned her head, Betty was grinning, "Looking for someone?"

Zoe chuckled, and nodded.

"I thought you were a doctor now."

"I am," she grinned, "and it would be in the interest of this person's health if I could find her."

"Coffee?"

"That'd be nice," she looked at the pastries on display, "and one of those." Zoe pointed at a cream cheese Danish.

When Betty returned with Zoe's order she leaned in close. "Who you looking for?"

"Woman with a kid of about five or six years old. The lady has bottled blond hair, wears it long, with brown eyes and eyebrows that don't match the hair. Last time I saw her she was wearing a sexy red number under a drab brown woolen coat. High heels in a different shade of red—which even I know to be a fashion faux-pas."

Betty laughed, and looked at her own shoes. "Oh, I'm not so sure about that. So, does this woman have a name?"

"Christie." Zoe took a chance, "And she comes out of a stable that's now missing its stallion."

"Ah, Christie—and Jeb. Yeah, terrible thing about Jeb." Betty's amusement was thinly disguised.

"Apparently no one reported him missing?"

"Don't know. But I'd certainly never bother."

"Where's Christie now?"

"Haven't seen her since Jeb passed. I'm hoping that's a good sign. If she has family to go home to, now would be the time."

"What can you tell me about her?"

"Not much, hon, but you could try the other gals. The ones at the far table—they know her."

"Thanks. By the way, do you know Jeb's last name? I'd like to give Ray something to go on."

"No clue."

"Any idea where he lived?"

"Again—no clue. Sorry." She pointed at the women. "Try them."

THE OTHER LADIES HAD NOTHING TO SAY, and they were on their game—used to the long con. It was rare that they weren't. Zoe couldn't get any toehold with them. Their talents were clearly being wasted, Zoe realized, and wondered what a resume intended for the CIA might look like. How could you positively spin a tits-up career?

NEXT STOP, WOLF'S—and she decided to bring him some lunch. Zoe stood in line at Surdyk's deli, waiting for the Reubens, chips, cheesecake, and sodas. Best Reubens in town. Her cellphone sounded. Caller ID had it as Lucy's place.

"Hi, Lucy."

"Hi. Sorry to bother you, but I figured it was around lunchtime and you'd be up getting something to eat. Was I right?"

"Yes, I am getting something to eat," Zoe answered, marveling at how easily that question had been dodged. "What's up?"

"How are you feeling?"

"Much better." That answer was a definite lie.

"Well then, do you have a minute?"

"Sure, what is it?" Zoe handed her payment to the server and grabbed the parcel of food.

"I spent the morning with Phillip. He kicked me loose to go home and help Sara."

Out on the street, Zoe unlocked her car and slid in.

"What's that noise, Zoe?"

"TV."

"Oh, okay. Well anyway, I've been thinking about what you said. And it bothers me."

"That's not surprising," Zoe chuckled. "I say a lot of bothersome stuff. What exactly are you referring to?"

"About mystery. About how that's the reason, you know, that we go on."

"And? Teach me something then, kid—what exactly bothers you about it?"

"Well, it's not true. I mean, it is, but it's not all of it. I love finding things out, just like you do, but I get up every day for other people, just like you do."

Zoe coughed when she started the car, and it turned into the real thing. She couldn't stop for a minute or two and grabbed one of the sodas, gulping until her throat quieted. As she pulled out of the parking lot, heading north, she listened.

"You love taking care of your patients. You solve the mysteries of their ailments because you want more than anything to make them better. And when you were a cop, you worked so hard because you were serving people. It's even on the side of cop cars—'to protect and serve'—the mysteries you solved were on account of someone needing you to do it."

Zoe felt a wide smile work it's way across her face. "Did Phillip put you up to that?"

"Nope. But we talked about how everyone casts a shadow, and about how everyone is tugged-on—you know, by other people, by their community."

"I'm not sure I like the idea of getting tugged on."

"It's that we all have free will, but we're not really free—both at the same time."

"And I don't much like the sound of that, either, Lucy."

"Come on, Zoe, you know it's true."

"How?" Zoe navigated the lunchtime traffic, kept moving—and kept challenging Lucy, as Phillip had undoubtedly done.

"Well, the real heroes aren't good guys who just sit around and don't do anything—you know, the guys who just address their adoring crowds and leave it up to everyone else to protect their sorry asses—right?"

"Mmm-hmm," Zoe fought a smile.

"They get to say and do all the right things while others have to do the rough stuff on their behalf. I mean, what are cops, anyway? And they do it out of duty—they're tugged on something fierce.

"And take what you did in the Boundary Waters. You wanted to kill that guy, didn't you? I saw you looking out at the water. You wanted in the worst way to go out after him and make sure he was dead. But you didn't. You looked at me, at how much I was bleeding, and changed your mind. Instead, you chose to help me."

"Got me there."

Lucy laughed. "You know, you're a lot nicer than you think you are."

"Aw, shucks," Zoe said, grinning into the phone. "And what about you? You went out on a limb for me, too. You could have been killed. So I guess it was the least I could do—getting you some medical attention."

"Don't sell yourself short, Zoe."

Zoe was quiet. So was Lucy. There was only the wind outside her window, the odor of the food, this young girl—talking sense—and the realization that helping Lucy had become just as important to her as it was to Kaj. But it always seemed to be the other way around—Lucy helping her, holding her accountable, tugging at her, in admittedly good ways.

"You're right, kid. But you'd better do the same. Trust yourself."

"Should I come by after I help Sara?"

"No. I'm fine. You take the night off. Are you seeing Phillip again tomorrow?"

"Yep. And guess what?" Lucy asked with enthusiasm.

"What?"

"He's thinking about a naming ceremony for me."

Zoe realized that Phillip was doing all that he could to release Lucy from her troubled past while at the same time helping her to make some sense of it. Release her from it, but not forget it. It was still important—still what formed her. Lucy needed to incorporate it somehow, welcome it as a teacher—just as Zoe was only beginning to do with her own past. Phillip had been a good call. Thank goodness he'd been willing. "That's great, Lucy. Does he have a name picked out yet?"

"No. Not yet. He says he needs more time with me. And Sara's fine with that. She said that I can meet up with him as often as I need to."

"Yeah, well, Sara's a good egg. How's Walt, by the way?"

"Sick. He had a fever last night. But he was better this morning. Last night was fun, though. He cuddled with Sara and we all talked. Walt didn't seem nervous about it either. He even shared some stuff with us. I love times like that, because it's always so hard to know what in the hell is going on in that boy's head."

"That's right—the fever thing. Almost forgot. I need to look into that. It has me wondering."

"Maybe fevers aren't totally bad after all."

Zoe felt her forehead and said, "Let's hope not."

ZOE'S APPROACH HAD HER WONDERING where to park. Wolf had seemed dead-set on secrecy and a car might be noticed at the abandoned farm. She opted to park in the strip-mall lot across the highway and walk in. Zoe took off at a jog, hoping to make it before the warmed sandwiches lost all heat.

As she passed the abandoned house and outbuildings she accelerated to an all-out run, breaking into the field and hopping tilled ruts in Parkour fashion. Wormholes, she thought. Parkours were like the wormholes in string theory, traversing cosmic distances by way of the most efficient route, reducing the time required in traveling between two points.

Zoe had to laugh, even out of breath. Why did she have thoughts like this when she was running? Or maybe it was the fever.

The idea of entering another universe through a wormhole was what she moved on to as she dodged brush and branches and emerged into the clearing where the pole barn stood. This time the dog barked.

Zoe stopped, and Wolf once again lowered his gun.

"Ma'am..."

"Call me Zoe," she smiled.

"Zoe, you really shouldn't be here."

She lifted the bag. "Just wanted to bring you lunch. Can we eat?"

He scanned the woods, and then looked back toward the structure. "All right." He stepped aside to let her pass through the door.

"Can we go all the way in? You know, into your cottage?"

He nodded and opened the door. Zoe walked in, amazed as before. She set the package of food down on his handcrafted dining table. It was a combination of found timber and cement—as were the kitchen counters.

She pulled out a chair and waited, "You joining me?"

He seemed reluctant, but sat down anyway.

The dining table was located next to a large window—one that was fashioned out of a utile, functioning double-hung window, probably scavenged from the farmhouse, and a large pane of fixed glass in a shape that looked to have been formed out of something broken. When combined they created a trapezoid of appealing proportions. It was unfortunate that all they looked out on was the inside of the pole barn.

"Here you go. You like Reubens?"

Wolf looked at the bag. "From Surdyks? Yes, ma'am." His arms rested on the table, surrounding the food. He grabbed his sandwich with both hands and ripped off a large bite. Zoe opened both bags of chips, unwrapped the desserts, and offered him a soda, which he used immediately to wash down the food.

"This place is absolutely amazing. Can I get a tour after lunch?"

He nodded as he chewed another quarter of the sandwich. Zoe set her sandwich in front of him, "I just ate a huge breakfast."

"You sure?"

"Yep. Couldn't eat another bite."

He accepted it and kept eating. As she studied his arms, she wondered how in the world he could have been a war hero—if Grace was more than hypothesizing. He was sinewy strong, but had no real bulk at all.

"So, you were in the military before?"

"How'd you know?" He stopped chewing.

She raised her eyebrows and pointed to his clothes.

"Oh, yeah," he smiled. "I was."

"And you said the name 'Wolf' came from your guys in Iraq." She pointed to her head, "Another clue," and smiled.

"I guess I was a little worked up that day, what with Thor almost dying and all. It's not something I talk about much."

Zoe knew she was being asked to drop it, but she didn't. "So, where did they get 'Wolf' from? What happened?"

He stopped eating—and as on the day they'd first met, he stared at her without any apparent concern for her discomfort. As before, Zoe didn't look away.

Finally he said, "I'm not much for talking."

"I heard a rumor that you were some kind of a war hero. That true?"

"Listen, I told you I owed you, but please don't push it."

"It's just normal conversation. And it's just between you and me. It must get lonely out here. Don't you crave someone to talk to once in a while?"

"Not really."

She laughed. He smiled.

"Well then, someone to laugh with?"

"Maybe," his smile remained.

"Must have been hard, running through enemy fire," Zoe took a chance— a wild guess.

"Not really. But that's where the name came from. Apparently I was howling as I ran. They said I sounded like a wolf."

"It wasn't hard? Somehow I can't believe that."

"I guess I didn't have much time to think about it."

"Why did you have to run through crossfire?"

"Hank was shot already—in the back. Shattered his spine up high. He couldn't move anything. All he could do was breath and talk. Told me he wished he could die a hero, but that I should just…"

"What?"

"Nothing."

"So then what?"

"I made a hero out of him." He set his sandwich down. "Ma'am, this is really hard to think about."

"I thought you were the hero."

"Damn it! Stop!"

Zoe held up her hands. "Sorry. Just trying to get to know you." And though she debated saying it, "I'd like to help you if I can."

"Help me? Why would I need help?"

"Because that war is still going on inside your head. I can see it—and I can get you help with that. It'd be confidential, just like this conversation. Remember?—I promised."

"I don't need any help."

"Well then, how about a friend? Still confidential."

"Okay, listen. You asked, I'll tell you. Apparently someone out there thinks they know me, so I'll set the record straight—just between the two of us."

"Fair enough."

"Hank wanted me to put a bullet in his head," he paused, put down his food, and closed his eyes for a moment. Finally he took a deep breath and said, "I wasn't friend enough to do it. But running with him sure fucking did the trick anyway. By the time I got him into the chopper, he'd been hit enough to kill him ten times over—and I didn't have a damn scratch on me! There. Now can we leave it be?"

Zoe now understood the aura of guilt surrounding this guy. "Yep, we can leave it. Except to say . . . what else could you have done? There's no fault in what you did."

"Did I say there was?"

"You didn't have to."

"Drop it, please."

"Sure. But if you do want help, please let me know. I have some pretty good connections with a woman who can give you just what you need. I swear."

"No offense, ma'am, but you have absolutely no idea what I need."

"If you said that to most anyone else, I might say touché. But with me— you're wrong. Don't underestimate me, Wolf—in any respect. And don't think for one minute that I don't know what you're going through. But I promised to respect your privacy, and I will. What we talk about is between us—and wanting help is up to you."

Wolf's eyes tracked from Zoe's face down to her clenched hands, and he broke the tension. "Underestimate you? You don't seem all that big and strong."

She laughed. "Neither do you."

Wolf smiled. "I used to be."

"How about that tour?"

HE SHOWED HER THE CENTRAL PLUMBING AND UTILITY CORE—it ran off an old well on site. His meager electrical needs for light and hot water were, for the time being, met by "scavenged"—although Zoe figured stolen—solar panels on the roof of the pole barn. Heating the space was accomplished with a massive stone fireplace—its chimney carrying up through the pole barn roof. Of course, the fact that the whole structure was located inside a pole barn contributed to an easy retention of heat. And for emergencies, there was a generator—this time, admittedly stolen.

Zoe took notice of her surroundings. He had very little, but had made a home of it nonetheless.

She asked, "So you know Grace Prescott, then?"

He stopped. If his war history was a touchy subject, this seemed worse. "Why in the hell would you ask me that?"

Out of the three reasons she could have given him, she chose the easiest, and pointed to a tiny picture above the fireplace mantel, "There she is."

He grabbed it and turned it facedown. "That's none of your business."

Zoe held up her hands, once again. "Sorry. I didn't realize it was off-limits. I've met her. Seems nice enough."

"What were you doing talking to her?"

"My business."

He eyed her, apparently debating, then said, "It's time for you to go."

"SHE WAS IN THE HEAD SHOP for a long time, then she went to Betty's. I saw her talking to Betty, and to some of the girls. I lost her after that. Had to go in and deal with Betty, first—like you told me to. It took time."

"What did you find out?"

"Betty told us she's looking for Christie."

"So, nothing new, then?"

"Nope. But I made sure Betty'll think twice before talking to her again."

"Betty knows the score. She shouldn't have to be dealt with."

"One would figure."

"What the fuck is she doing? Keep an eye on her, too."

"There's only one of me."

"Make it happen!"

"Sure thing, boss."

ZOE THREW HER COAT IN THE CLOSET and went straight for her medications. The cough had been getting worse all day so she downed two of the powerful pills and then jumped into bed, expecting Kaj to arrive at any time. After lying down, the change in position had her coughing again. She amused herself with a game of basketball, wadding up tissues full of bloody sputum and aiming for the wastebasket. At least she didn't have to get up. Then she grabbed the remote and flipped on the television. Friday nights were reserved for college hockey whenever she could work it into a busy schedule—her beloved Gophers. Problem was, she was pretty sure she'd be asleep before the game started.

KAJ MADE HIS WAY IN QUIETLY. All the lights were off except for a television glow from Zoe's bedroom. As he'd expected, she was asleep—a hockey game playing in the background. He imagined another day of rest had done her some good, and left her to sleep a little longer.

After unloading the groceries he started work on their dinner. The familiar odors of one of Zoe's favorite dishes, Italian sausage and peppers, should be expected to wake her. But as the food was prepared, there was no sign of life from Zoe's room. He loaded a tray with their meal and brought it to her. She was still sound asleep.

Even after gently touching her, she failed to waken. He moved his hand to her wrist and checked the pulse—rapid. Her breathing was clearly labored, and the tissues that had missed their target littered the floor—bloody. Finally he shook her awake.

"Zoe, you okay?"

"What time is it?"

"Just after eight. Have you been sleeping this soundly all day?"

"No. I tried not to take anything for the cough today, and that was a big mistake. I finally gave up and took two of them so I could get some sleep."

"What about that bloody sputum? I wonder if we shouldn't get you back in for a second look."

"Don't be crazy. The air is so dry—those are from a bloody nose."

"Well then, let's get you fed so you can go back to sleep."

She sat up in bed, her head swimming from the medication—feeling a little nauseated even—and did her best to eat.

Kaj watched her pick at her favorite dish.

"Look at me," he said. Her pupils betrayed the large dose of narcotic. "You sure you're okay?"

"Having pneumonia sucks . . . but I'm okay. How was your day?"

"Distracting me?" he smiled, and ran his finger down her nose and over her lips.

"Yep."

"My day was pretty interesting. Connie and I were on the receiving end of a building fire. A little café called Betty's. Someone torched it."

Zoe sat up straighter. "What?"

"Firefighters think it was arson."

"Anyone hurt?"

"Well, of course. That's how I got involved. You sure you're okay?"

"I mean . . . did anyone die? How bad was it?"

"Why? You know someone there?"

"Sort of, I guess. When I was a cop I used to check the place out once in a while. I'm familiar with the owner."

"Betty? She's okay. Fortunately no one was seriously hurt. A couple of ladies sustained a few second-degree burns, but not extensively, and Betty suffered some mild smoke inhalation trying to get everyone out. Apparently the damage wasn't even all that bad—Betty had a fire extinguisher."

"When did this happen?"

"Late morning."

Shadowland

ZOE DID THE MATH. MUST HAVE BEEN RIGHT after she'd left. What the fuck?

Zoe rose unsteadily and looked out the window—hoping to see what exactly? She didn't know. Despite the attempts to hide her activities from everyone who wanted her to rest, was it paranoid thinking—or the drugs—to imagine that someone hadn't been fooled? And then she began worrying about Wolf.

No, she reasoned, if someone had been busy torching Betty's, they couldn't have followed her out to Wolf's. And that was how she would force herself to think if she expected to get any sleep at all.

Chapter Six

ZOE WOKE TO A HAND ON HER FOREHEAD.

"God, Zoe, you're burning up."

Zoe turned in bed, sticking to damp sheets. She joked, "You'd think I'd remember a night that sweaty and wild. But sorry, stud, I don't."

"Zoe, I'm not kidding here, you must have one hell of a fever." Kaj went out to his car and came back in with his stethoscope. The cold metal felt good on her skin.

"Give me some deep breaths, hon."

"Deep breathing? Sorry, babe, you have to earn that."

"Zoe, I'm not kidding around."

Zoe tried, but with each deep breath she broke out in a coughing paroxysm.

"Keep breathing," Kaj said as he kept listening. "Lord—it's noisy as hell."

Zoe reached for a tissue in which to deposit her wad of bloody sputum. He grabbed it from her, took one look, and said, "You're going in, now. Get up. Get dressed."

She turned toward him, an argument ready, and then began coughing so hard that she doubled over with a sharp, stabbing pain in her side and seriously thought she might have broken a rib. All she could do was to reach out for his hand, stand unsteadily, and then shuffle to her closet—trying to breath shallowly, not testing her cough or the painful rib. She threw on jeans and a sweatshirt, and then grabbed his arm as he led her out to his car.

"SHE DOESN'T LOOK SO GOOD, BOSS."

"And that's a bad thing how, exactly?"

"Figured it for good news. Anyway, I got here in time to see her leaving with that same guy who came by last night. But he was kind of helping her, like she was hurt—or sick."

"You still with her?"

"Yeah. Looks like they're heading for the hospital."

"Okay. You know what to do."

THE WATERS WERE PARTED—ER personnel knew Zoe well from her days as a trauma surgery resident. She'd worked long, hard hours with these people, formed life-long bonds, and when she walked in on Kaj's arm there was genuine concern and a hasty response. Zoe found herself gowned and seated comfortably in a cube—an IV running into one arm and a phlebotomist on the other, drawing arterial blood gasses from her wrist. The inside of her elbow was already bruised by the venous blood draw, and the oxygen saturation monitor's beeping had been silenced.

A nurse at her side fussed with the oxygen tubing. "Dr. Parker is calling your attending right now—from Pulmonary. He'll be by shortly. I listened to your lungs—they sound gawd-awful, Zoe."

Zoe started to talk but was once again overcome by a coughing fit. The nurse handed her water, and Zoe gave up trying to do anything except breath shallowly and sip from the plastic cup. She eased back against the raised head of the gurney, and looked around, thinking—wondering if all she'd done in the last few days had contributed to this or if the antibiotics had been the wrong choice from the beginning. An answer to that question would remain her mystery, because she sure-as-hell wasn't going to let on what she'd been up to. She had absolutely no energy for an argument with anyone, and had been promising confidentiality at every turn.

The narcotics had worn off from the night before and with each inspiration she felt the urge to cough violently. She sat, almost unmoving, trying not to bring on another fit—breathing fast, but shallow. The walls were some awful peach color—not blue, like the stabilization rooms. The room smelled of disinfectant, and one corner of the ceiling had been water-damaged. When she finally began counting the tiles, Zoe forced her eyes shut.

Her brain was in iPod-shuffle mode—swinging from one topic to another. There was this fucking pneumonia, the killing at Angie's, Lucy's quest to learn more about her heritage—along with all the damn questions she'd been asking, and, oh, yes, Dr. Pink, and tonight's soiree. It was Saturday, wasn't it? How did Abel die? Why was Betty's place torched? Was she thinking straight? Was it the drugs?

Her eyes shot open. Better to count the tiles, she thought. Then her attending walked in, alongside Kaj.

He said, "You'll do just about any damn thing to get more time off, won't you?"

And when she laughed, she coughed.

He drew close and placed his stethoscope first over her heart, and then along her back. "Deep breaths."

And she began coughing again. He listened, undeterred, moving the stethoscope over every region of her lungs. Kaj stood watching.

"X-rays. Sputum samples. I'll meet you upstairs, Zoe." He turned to the nurse. "Got a room number yet?"

"Yes, doctor." And the two walked out of the cube, leaving Zoe and Kaj alone.

He leaned a hip on the side of the gurney and pulled her close. The movement made her start coughing again, and it was a full minute before she calmed down. Her head rested, exhausted, on his shoulder.

Zoe risked speaking, softly and slowly, hoping not to precipitate any more coughing. "I don't want to stay."

"We'll wait and see what the x-ray shows. They'll be coming for you soon."

And then Dr. Pink walked in.

KAJ STOOD AS SHE WALKED IN—and leaned into a fucking kiss on the cheek.

"I thought it was your day off," Connie said in a soft, sexy voice—purposely so, Zoe decided. It certainly wasn't the voice she reserved for the ER patients—or for her interns.

"It is, for both of us, but Zoe's pneumonia has other ideas."

Connie finally looked at Zoe. "Oh, you poor dear. Poor lamb." Then she turned to Kaj, "It's a shame she won't be able to make it tonight . . . especially since you're the guest of honor."

"You're the guest of honor? This whole shindig is for you?" Zoe asked, in her softest voice, in her case, not wanting to cough—and yet wanting to shout at Dr. Pink to take her fucking hand off Kaj's arm.

But Connie wasn't letting go. Instead, Zoe saw her squeeze as if to emphasize the point. "He'll be in his element, an adoring crowd gathered to witness the unveiling of his painting."

"Painting? What painting?" Zoe's anger was starting to include Kaj.

"He didn't tell you? His latest painting was chosen as an Arts District winner. Well now, Kaj, why wouldn't you share that with the girl?"

The girl? We're about the same age, *Cosmo* cover. Difference is, I don't need a magazine, or shrink-wrapped jeans, or bottled-blond hair, or even that ridiculously luscious shade of pink lipstick to feel sexy.

Zoe's breathing started to deepen, and the cough surfaced again. So did the question . . . if that were true, why confide in Dr. Pink and not in her?

Zoe looked at Connie; seeing that "doubt" was exactly what she was selling. Problem was—Zoe was in no mood to fight her off. She shouldn't have to. Kaj, in his infinite fucking wisdom, should recognize what was going on here and make it unnecessary.

"Well, I didn't think it was such a big deal, really. Besides, I don't think I should even go now. Zoe may have to stay here overnight. I'd like to be with her."

"Well, isn't that a lovely thing. How unselfish," and she looked pointedly at Zoe.

Fucking bitch is trying to make me look bad, or make me behave. Either way, I don't like it—is what she thought. But what she said was, "Kaj, you should definitely go. Everyone will be there on your account. I'll be fine here. I mean really, what better place for me to be?"

And instead of declining, he said, "I suppose so." He stroked Zoe's hair and added, "I won't stay long."

Didn't even put up the tiniest fucking fight. Did she know this man anymore? Since her transfer to Internal Medicine she no longer worked side-by-side with him. Did he have secrets? New interests? New women? Zoe wasn't the *Cosmo* cover kind of girl—never had been. And she certainly wouldn't change to satisfy him. But it was that kind of woman he'd been used to.

And now "doubt" was exactly what she felt.

The curtains parted as an assistant peeked in. "Dr. Lawrence?"

"Yes."

"I'm here to transfer you to radiology. After the x-ray, I'll take you to your room."

She only nodded. Speaking had become too hard. He undid the locks on the gurney wheels and then guided it out of the room. Zoe looked back to see Connie lean into Kaj and whisper something in his ear. He chuckled and said to Zoe, "I'll meet you in your room."

Yeah, well, fuck you, too—she wished she had the wind to say. She did think about saying, "Don't bother," but in her head, that sounded too passive-aggressive. Instead she said nothing.

ZOE, PRETENDING TO BE CHARITABLE, finally encouraged Kaj to go home, change, and to be on time for his big night. She didn't ask him to explain why he'd neglected to tell her about the painting. She didn't ask why he'd never bothered to show her any of his paintings—or his art studio, for that matter. Apparently it was somewhere in his freaking mansion on Lake Minnetonka, where his mother—who she'd also never met—had her guest quarters. She didn't continue that line of questioning to ask how he'd managed to accumulate so much money that he could afford a lakefront mansion, a downtown penthouse, and a North Shore cabin. She didn't even ask him what Dr. Pink had whispered in his ear, or why he'd laughed, or if he had any clue that he was being played. And she failed to mention her suspicions that he liked it.

So he'd left, but not before kissing her passionately—which she tried and failed to reciprocate—and checking in with her physician. After being convinced that she would be all right, he left. He walked away. He got in the damn elevator and rode it down—perhaps with another stop at the ER to see Dr. Pink, Zoe imagined. Then he got in his damn SUV to go home and select his most appealing and finely crafted outfit for the evening—but probably not before a brief workout, no, not before maintaining his taut, muscular physique. He would be center stage tonight, and he'd always been damn good at that.

Zoe swung her legs over the side of the bed and let them dangle for a moment. She waited, taking note of the dirty off-white wall color while her blood redistributed and she no longer felt light-headed. Then she tied the gown securely and threaded the IV bag and tubing through the arm of her hospital-issue robe. With the robe on, Zoe stood cautiously and wheeled the IV post out into the hallway.

A nurse looked up from her charting. "Can I get you something, Zoe?" They were on familiar terms, as this was the very floor where Zoe spent countless hours taking care of medical patients—and Zoe knew she was busy, would rather not be bothered, and wouldn't argue the point much, if at all.

"No. Just a little bored. I'm going to check and see if one of my patients is still in the hospital. Just curious about his status."

"I can do that for you."

"No. I don't want to bother you. I'll do it. It'll give me something to do other than to stare at the walls."

"Suit yourself."

Zoe sat at a computer terminal and parked the IV post securely next to her. She logged in and scanned patient names. Betty … Betty … Betty … what in the hell was her last name? Cooper! Betty Cooper! Zoe saw that she had been admitted through the ER and discharged the same day.

Problem. Betty had never been a patient of Zoe's. And that was a problem because electronic records and patient data privacy laws would detect that Zoe had no reason to look at Betty's medical chart. All she was entitled to see was some basic identifying information and that she'd been admitted and discharged on the same day. If she opened Betty's medical record for a more detailed look, there were tripwires—alarms that would sound somewhere in some tech-tyrant's office. Bottom line—she could get in serious trouble.

Zoe drummed her fingers on the desk, memorizing the numbers, and caught the eye of the nurse. Zoe smiled and logged off.

"Was he still in the hospital?"

"Nope. Think I'll go for a walk down the hall. Move my legs a little."

"Okay." The nurse glanced at Zoe's chart. "You're next dose is coming due shortly, don't wander far."

"I know." She'd prescribed the very same medicine countless times. Could do it in her sleep. She'd be back in time, anyway—what she had to do required only a moment.

"SHE'S STAYING, BOSS. THE GUY LEFT ALREADY."

"Okay, then take the night off. You'll be busy tomorrow."

The boss had it figured out. Or at least he thought he did. What still didn't make sense to him was that the doc had been looking for Christie. It was the only thing that prevented him from making a move on her. If he could figure that out to his satisfaction, he wouldn't hesitate. But he couldn't make it work in his mind. And until he did, maybe the doc was worth more to him alive—just in case.

He glanced through the French doors leading from his den out to where the kids played. He'd never been good at playing. His playground days had been spent cutting other kids' achievements off at the knees. Play was where kids figured out what they were good at—and then got better at it. But the boss had learned at a much younger age what his skills were. He'd been perfecting them through countless encounters with other kids, but also with adults. In fact, adults were even easier to con. They'd forgotten how much kids know, how much they understand—and how easy they are to underestimate. But despite that strategic advantage, most kids were too weak for the long con. They'd give up under pressure—it was always guilt that got them in the end.

The boss never understood guilt—and he was glad he didn't. He maintained his status through insight and intimidation. There could be no other hero—no one else who could impress, or call the shots. He'd been born a bully, and he was damn good at it.

So he decided—that after the doc's usefulness was exhausted he'd have to find a way to get rid of her. After all, docs came and went, too—just like homeless people.

"MINNEAPOLIS GENERAL, EMERGENCY DEPARTMENT. How can I help you?"

"My name is Betty Cooper and I'd like to speak with Dr. Zoe Lawrence. It's important."

"I can check. Just a moment."

Zoe waited on the line, knowing the outcome.

"I'm afraid she's not scheduled to be here today, can I leave her a message or would you like to speak with another physician?"

"No. It has to be Dr. Lawrence. Can you note that I want her to call me as soon as she sees the message?"

"Certainly. But if this is an emergency I can connect you with another physician, or you can simply come in to the Emergency Department."

"No. I'll wait. But you'll leave her a message—and she'll see it?"

"Yes, ma'am. The messages are electronic. She'll be required to follow up on it. Can I verify your birthday, and a number where she can reach you?"

Zoe gave her the memorized numbers, "Thank you. Goodbye," then got up from the public telephone, made her way back to the room with dirty, off-white walls, and fell onto the bed. It was hard to imagine that only a couple of days ago she'd been chasing a kid through the streets but was now shuffling next to an IV pole. Even without the damn pole, she wouldn't make it half a block.

Her nurse came in with a new IV bag and another dose of antibiotics. "How's the cough?"

"Better, but it's starting to break through again. Can I get something for it?" Zoe decided that what she intended to do later that evening would require silencing the cough.

The nurse checked her watch. "Sure thing. I'll go get you another dose after I hang these."

WHEN THE NURSE RETURNED WITH HER PILL, Zoe palmed it—saving it for later. A large dose might be required. Then she made another trip to the computer terminal.

At the nurse's glance, Zoe said, "Got a message about another patient. Might as well take care of it now."

"Suit yourself. It's not as if you ever do any work around here anyway," she said, sarcasm in her voice. "But if I were you, I'd just take the day off. Seems to me you've earned it—I saw your chest x-ray."

"Yeah, it looked like a snowstorm, didn't it?"

"Good thing you're pretty healthy overall, or you'd be in the ICU with this."

"Lucky me."

"Can I help you with anything?"

"Nope. Am I good on this terminal?"

"Yep. Knock yourself out."

Zoe logged on again and was met this time by the message from her virtual Betty Cooper. Zoe opened Betty's chart—a chart she now had license to look at—and began reading.

Betty's visit had been a brief one, according to the note. She'd been advised to remain in the hospital but had checked out against medical advice. It was a judgment call. Her condition seemed stable enough, but her admitting physician had wanted to keep her overnight for observation. From what Zoe could discern, Betty could be expected to do just fine but her doctor had been covering his own ass—pretty hard to blame him.

Betty had also been adamant—despite the firefighters' suspicions—that it had not been arson, but rather a grease-fire. "Her mistake," she'd been quoted as saying.

Zoe looked back at Betty's older records from previous visits. Betty didn't appear to have a regular physician—a good thing for Zoe. This way her little foray into Betty's electronic chart wouldn't raise any other kind of suspicion.

Betty had been seen for a variety of complaints, most notably a remote history of being victimized in several violent attacks, and some visits for sexually transmitted diseases. The docs who'd seen her hadn't shied away from naming her occupation.

So, Betty had an intimate knowledge after all—the lives of the working girls that populated her café were all too familiar.

Zoe scanned the rest of her chart, memorizing what was important—this time, without having taken the narcotic yet, her mind was clear and sharp. It was interesting to note that Betty lived on the edge of town rather than the community in which she worked. Her home address wasn't far from Wolf's hideout. Not far at all—in fact if Zoe had to guess, it was within a stone's throw.

Before logging off she charted that a return phone call had been made and the question answered. Then she returned to her room and watched the clock—timing her escape.

HER CELL PHONE WOKE HER out of a light sleep.

"Lucy. What's up?" Zoe worked to clear the sleep from her voice.

"How are you today? I didn't wake you did I?"

"Nope. Just resting my eyes."

"Oh, crap. I did wake you, didn't I?"

"No. Seriously, you didn't. Now what's up?"

"I had another morning session with Phillip. Well, 'session' isn't exactly the right word, but I don't know what to call our meetings. Well, 'meetings' I guess."

"Good Lord, Lucy, you need a boyfriend—or some other hobby."

"I don't have time for that right now."

"I was joking."

"Oh. Well, sorry."

"Lucy, get over it. Quit apologizing all the time. Guess what? You did wake me. And you know what else? It's not the end of the world. We'll all be just fine, even though you woke me. Not really a big deal at all."

"Okay, now you're making me feel stupid again."

"Gawd, Lucy. Get over it! Just spit it out, will you?"

"It's about the science thing. About how you said it brought you back to God."

"Did I say that?"

"Quit it, Zoe."

Zoe laughed. "Yeah, maybe I do remember saying that. What in the hell was I thinking?"

"You'd better remember, or I'm personally coming over there to wring your neck—pneumonia or not."

"There we go! That's the Lucy I'm willing to wake up for." Zoe glanced at the clock and repositioned herself in bed. Once comfortable, she said, "It's about quantum mechanics and string theory."

"What? We only talked a tiny bit about that in physics—not in much depth. How did those things bring you closer to God?"

"It's all about possibilities, Lucy—and probabilities. Not to mention miracles—or at least perceived ones."

"Keep going."

"Okay, the science of string theory requires multiple universes where each and every possibility can be played out."

"Still not seeing God in any of this."

"That comes later. Stick with me. Particles aren't at the heart of everything, but rather strings of energy. They can either be closed loop and independent, or open, and connected to their surroundings—at least that's how I understand it. Anyway, they vibrate, wiggle, and jump around––they're unpredictable in where they are at any given moment. This diversity of possibilities is exactly what is required of multiple universes. If there're an infinite number of possibilities, eventually our number will come up again and there'll be a duplicate of our universe, and even a duplicate of you and me—but perhaps with different outcomes. Eventually everything lines up like it did for us."

"Whoa."

"Yeah. Crazy, isn't it? And remember about Parkour? About taking the most direct route between two points?"

"Yeah."

"Well, imagine closed-loop strings traveling through space and forming tubes that link cosmic distances as if there were no space in between them at all. But I'm getting a little off-track. Back to the vibrating strings. And here's the miraculous thing. If you were to shoot a bullet through someone and you had an infinite number of attempts, within all the possible outcomes exists at least one in which every string—every bit of energy—would line up so that the bullet could pass directly through and not damage anything. In fact there'd be no evidence that it had even passed through at all. In effect, a miracle."

"But that doesn't qualify as a miracle. It's science."

"Oh, Lucy, but that's exactly why I was able to come back to God. There should be no conflict between the two. It's not a matter of one or the other— that is, if science truly exists within the mind of God."

"Hmm."

"Yeah, hmm. But I can already tell you don't like that."

"Well, maybe I'm just confused."

"It's in the possibilities that I see God. To me, God absorbs all the possibilities, but with a desired outcome. And there are an infinite number of chances for us to get it right. In essence, a very generous God."

"But why does God have to wait for us to get it right?"

"Because we're involved. God set this in motion with us as involved. So, we do have free will, but as you and Phillip talked about, we're tugged on—by God."

"And by each other!"

"Of course, and we're all tugged on by God. I view the Great Mystery as always whispering to us when decisions are made—whenever there's a fork in the road leading us down one possibility or another.

"And still, as you've noticed, without connections in our own universe, without links to those around us, we lose our sense of place and dimension—of home, even. We become like closed-loop strings—there're called gravitons, by the way—escaping this universe and slipping into another, perhaps to loosely vibrate there, not knowing if they'll remain. I mean we're no less involved than the laws of physics, are we? We can no more easily escape the physical laws—say gravity, for instance—than the spiritual pull. We're a part of it all. We matter."

"Whew."

"...And connectedness is what creativity is about in science. Scientists link what we know—what we've discovered—with boundaries and limitations, and through those connections, they invent. Science is all about those kinds of imaginative leaps—often making unlikely connections.

"But we also invent in the spiritual realm. I sometimes think we're the creative link between facts and meaning. As humans, we've evolved to reflect our environment, changing as an adaptation. In much that same way, the facts change, too—or more accurately, the meaning behind the facts changes. So, connections are important—very important. My guess is that in order to progress as a society, we have to make unlikely personal connections, as well."

"Phillip spent a lot of time trying to get me to see the importance of accountability...and responsibility—that what I do affects everyone else. Which I get, of course, but I couldn't see why he had to keep at it. I mean I get it. But this kind of puts a different spin on it. It's being accountable to yourself, first, maybe even to your shadow, and then to the person right next to you—no matter who they are."

"It's a thought," Zoe smiled, and thought of the huge gulf between her own Karma and Dharma. "I wonder sometimes if that isn't one of the biggest limitations of religion . . . and politics for that matter—in both we tend to rub elbows only with like-minded people. If that's all we're doing, how can we truly advance?"

"Maybe if we all align our energy in the way God wants, we get miracles—and the fast track to a better understanding. You know, like wormholes, or Traceurs!"

Zoe's eyebrows arched. This kid was something else—taking Zoe's crude explanation, indeed her incomplete understanding, and creating with it. What

Zoe decided not to say was that in all of this she also saw the possibility that at death we slip into the next universe, awaiting those with whom we have latent connections—perhaps even seeking them out again. For most that might feel comforting, but for Zoe and Lucy, the idea that either of them could be tugged on by the murderous people who had populated their lives up until then would sound more like a version of hell.

Zoe looked at the clock. "Gotta go, kiddo. Getting tired."

"Okay, Zoe. But, hey, thanks! I love this stuff. It gives me a lot to think about."

"Sounds like you and Phillip have really hit it off. He's got you questioning things—and that's good."

"Yeah. He said the very same thing. That it's more important to know the right questions than to have all the answers. Something about how the answers keep changing anyway."

"I suspect the answers keep changing right along with our decisions. See you later, Lucy. Thanks for the call."

ZOE CALLED FOR A TAXI AND ASKED the driver to wait for her outside the hospital. Then she did a dance with the nurse in charge—said she had something she needed to do, but that she'd be back in time for lights-out. The nurse was about to argue until Zoe stated the obvious—"Not much you can do about it"—and that convinced her to unplug the IV and heparin-lock the access. The two wrapped a bandage around the site and then Zoe changed into her jeans and sweatshirt, threw on her jacket, and was out the door.

The taxi driver had arms like a blacksmith, and he played that whiny country music that made Zoe want to put a dagger through her heart. Zoe wondered if it wasn't against the rules to play music in a taxi—she rarely took one—especially music like this. She gave him her address and, once there, asked him to keep the meter running and wait outside.

"No problem," he said, then turned up the volume and smirked, "I can be paid to turn it off."

"And I can be paid not to complain about it."

He tilted his head, seemed to think about it, and then turned the volume down—very low this time.

Zoe laughed. "Yeah, that's what I thought. I'll be back out in a few. See if you can find something funky on that radio. I'm in a dancing mood."

He grinned.

SURVEYING HER WEAPONS, SHE WAS ACUTELY AWARE of the superiority of her opponent's armament. The closet held jeans, sweatshirts, tees, bike clothing, flannel shirts, and some corduroy pants for winter. Her dresses were stuck in the back corner, a layer of dust over the shoulders. Zoe visualized her sortie, and the enemy territory she'd be entering. Deployment—all at once, or should she carry out her campaign in waves? Zoe held two options at arms length. One was a sexy red spaghetti-strapped dress, requiring something over it in this weather. It highlighted her broad, toned shoulders and a cleavage that would attract any man's eye. The other was black and less revealing, but dramatic—its fabric draped in Grecian folds. The black dress would catch air in movement—perfect for dancing. But the red dress loved her shape—revealing every curve, every muscle, every shadow, the silk moving seamlessly over her skin.

"Waves." She selected the red dress, along with a wrap that would hide her biggest assets at the outset. Mindful of the meter running outside, she took a fast shower, changed into her outfit, threw the palmed pill into the back of her throat and swallowed it dry, then grabbed two more pills out of her stash to bring along. The medicine cabinet held only a small assortment of rarely used, outdated make-up—nothing to compare with the killer shade of pink that Connie wore. Zoe did the minimum—lipstick in a pale pink, and a touch of rouge to hide the pallor of her illness. Her hair she simply brushed. The last thing she did was to climb onto her shoes—adding a good three inches to her height—and hope she wouldn't break an ankle.

BACK IN THE TAXI, HER DRIVER HAD MANAGED to find some funk. She nodded with satisfaction and kept nodding to the beat with eyes closed as he headed in the direction of Lake Minnetonka. Apparently Dr. Pink lived close to Kaj's other home—one Zoe had spent exactly zero time in. And that pissed her off, too. Why was that? Was it only that he spent most of his time at his downtown condo—busy as hell? Was it that they were both busy as hell? That was what she'd always thought, and what she would have believed—until Dr. Fucking Pink.

———

ZOE GAVE THE TAXI DRIVER A GENEROUS TIP, and then promised another if he'd agree to come back at 10:00 P.M. and wait for her. He looked at the clock on his dash and nodded. It was a long drive, but an easy one—in fact, a pleasant one. He'd be there.

"Wait for me, even if I'm late. I'm good for it."

"Besides, I know where you live," he joked.

"You can change the channel back now. But do not—I repeat, do not—make me listen to that country western garbage on the way home. I might have to kill myself in your taxi," she teased.

An attendant opened the car door and offered a hand in helping her out. She stood a moment, acclimating herself to the high heels, and scanned her surroundings. The lakefront mansion was a fake. It was made to look like an Italian villa—in Minnesota of all the incongruent places. Its size, and the degree to which it had been adorned, spelled money—lots of it. Affording the lakeside property alone made this woman rich. Zoe's eyes traveled from an ornate entry decked out in early Christmas display, to the side garden—lit artificially in the premature darkness of late November. Even devoid of leaves and the autumn colors having faded to await winter snows, Dr. Pink's garden was a cascade of shapes and textures, clearly designed by a pro—undoubtedly an expensive one.

The house was lit from within, seemingly every room awash in gold tones. A large Christmas tree was visible through the windows framing a two-story foyer and, gauging by the number of cars parked by valets in an adjacent field and the movement behind every pane of glass, the house was at capacity. That suited Zoe's purposes—she'd timed her arrival perfectly. As Zoe approached the front door white noise emanating from within the house clarified itself—a mixture of laughter, chatter, and music. The impression of gold took on highlights of color in the many dresses worn by laughing, drinking women, as well as from artwork on the walls. As Zoe entered, she was greeted by some sort of house servant—an entirely alien creature in Zoe's experience—and asked if she'd like to check her wrap. Zoe declined, and made her way in to join the crowd as inauspiciously as possible, her wrap serving as camouflage.

Shadowland

The party was divided into several rooms, all somewhat open to each other and visible from most vantage points. In one room a band played an appealing funked up jazz and bodies responded in intriguing ways. Some were content to simply stand and let a subtle movement of their heads keep time with the beat, while others were making love to the music—and their partners, shimmying front to back, front to front, in each others arms, seemingly reenacting every position in *The Joy of Sex*—albeit fully clothed.

Zoe's throat itched with an impending cough and she signaled a server who immediately brought her a drink—something with alcohol. She tossed it back, coating her throat, and reached for one of the two additional pills she'd brought along. After washing it down with the rest of her drink, she signaled for another. The server quickly refreshed her drink and held out some canapés—a welcome offering. Zoe indelicately grabbed a handful and made her way toward a corner of the large central room.

The room she stood in was largely cleared for use as a dance floor with a variety of seats and tables around the perimeter. The other rooms adjoining this central room must have been where the too-fascinating people were—they'd attracted attentive clusters around them, rapt in whatever was being spewed, all laughing on cue.

Zoe scanned the artwork, an eclectic mix—perhaps selected by someone who didn't know her own taste, yet clearly original and expensive—not particularly to Zoe's liking, even though Dr. Connie Sayre had the good taste to choose that killer shade of pink. For the most part, they were realistic landscapes, a few nudes in provocative poses, and some portraiture. Out of the few abstracts—Zoe's preference—were some composed of particularly attractive colors. She wondered if one of them was Kaj's—his award winner. And then she looked into the far room where, in front of a wall of lakeside windows, there stood an enormous easel—black fabric draped over the painting underneath. Apparently some sort of unveiling was in the works.

Zoe settled into her corner of the room to observe. She hadn't seen Kaj yet, or Connie, but they had to be somewhere in the mix. She shrank back for a moment, a doubt emerging. What in the hell was she doing? There was still time to leave and abandon this stupid, stupid plan. And she was seriously ready to give in to the voice inside her head, calling her out as stupid, until she heard, "You clean up nicely."

The writer. "Charles. Nice to see you again."

"You here for the big unveiling?"

"Yes. You?"

"Couldn't resist. Heard some rumblings about this being a particularly erotic painting."

"Erotic?"

"Yes, but no one's actually seen it yet—other than the Arts District Committee members. The artist wouldn't allow it. They sort of forced his hand into making it public by selecting it as the winner ... and then of course by tying it to this fundraiser. It would have been pretty callous to decline."

"What fundraiser?"

"You didn't get the invitation?"

"No, I was asked to accompany someone. I don't see him here yet. We had to arrive separately."

"Well, it's a fundraiser tied to an organization that shelters abused women and victims of violent attack."

So that was it, Zoe realized. It wasn't just a simple matter of having been awarded for the painting. He'd been given the opportunity to contribute toward a cause near and dear to his heart—and to Zoe's. She'd been such a victim herself. She wanted to find him, to hold him, to apologize for having ever doubted him.

"That's admirable."

"Yeah—and this is a great place to people-watch, don't you think?" he smiled.

"I suppose for a writer ... it's the bomb." Zoe looked out into the room full of laughing, dancing couples, and the singles—some smooth and effortless in their socializing, others awkward and obvious.

"Take that guy, for example," he pointed to a rather homely man chatting with an exotic-looking and alluring woman. "Bit of a mismatch, wouldn't you say?"

Zoe took measure of the exchange. "Oh, I don't know. He might be one of those intensely smart, highly entertaining and humorous geeks who can be expected to run the world some day. And she might be a lot smarter than she looks—hitching up with him."

"You're good. You'd make a good storyteller. That would be one spin on it—and a fertile one if writing a murder mystery."

"How about those two?" He pointed to an elderly couple, the man bending down to pick up a napkin dropped by his partner, the woman almost reflexively reaching a hand out to hover an inch away from the balding spot on his head.

"I get nothing from that," Zoe said.

He shook his head and smiled sadly. "Undoubtedly, you haven't gotten to that point with anyone yet."

"What point?"

"She's thinking about his lifetime of giving, sacrifice, and generosity."

"You get all that from the way she's looking at his bald spot?"

"Yes, I do."

"Wow." Zoe looked around. "What about her?" Zoe pointed to a woman dressed in casual clothes—jeans and a leather jacket.

"Her? She's confident—wouldn't show up here dressed like that if she wasn't. And she's here for the art—I mean, look at her. She's not trolling for a guy—she's waiting impatiently. Has a 'let's get this show on the road' look about her."

"What's her back story?" Zoe tested, grinning.

"Okay. Let's see—she's here to steal it. Casing the place."

"I like that. Yeah, that works."

"Now those two—they're an item." He pointed as Kaj entered the room—confidently, all class, handsomely dressed—with Connie on his arm.

Zoe felt herself shrink back behind the author, out of sight. Her throat went dry and her goddamned cough threatened again. She reached for a second pill and pulled a fresh drink off a passing server. The pill went down as she coated her throat by drinking it all in one pull and, at least temporarily, quelling the urge to cough.

She stared. Watched them. The chemistry. The intimacy. Then quietly asked, "What makes you say that?"

"Well, she's all over him. Look at her pawing his arm, leaning in, brushing her cheek against his, whispering in his ear—she's not shy about it."

Zoe watched as one of Connie's hands grasped his, the other continued to hold his upper arm—guiding him through the room. Her breasts, barely covered, brushed up against his arm as she allowed for no space between them. Zoe saw the same thing the author did. Felt the same way. But she said, "He's not really doing anything."

"Well, that's the whole point—he's not exactly resisting."

"But that would be rude," she said quietly. Zoe looked closely. There was nothing but a smile on his face—no apparent discomfort. He certainly wasn't trying to pull away. As if she expected him too, she thought. As if she should have any goddamned expectations at all.

"And there, see? She's led him to the dance floor. A little public display of affection."

Connie pulled him into a dance. Those who recognized the two even clapped as a small circle opened up around them. Kaj pulled Connie into his arms, circled her, and moved her over the dance floor—but Zoe felt it in her body, as if she were with him, next to him, in his arms. As if he were making love to her, not Connie—and yet there was this betrayal.

"Let's dance," she said to the author, removing her wrap and tossing it over a chair. "Charles, right?"

He looked surprised—and stared at her oh-so-barely covered skin. "Yes, it's Charles. You want to dance with me?"

"Yes, in the worst possible way."

"Sure," he grinned. "I didn't exactly see this coming."

Zoe fell into his arms and whispered, "Well then you're not quite as good a writer as you'd like to believe. Real life, pal—this is real life." The two moved smoothly onto the dance floor—Zoe working a sensuous encounter for all it was worth. She felt Charles come alive in her arms.

"What's our back story, Charles?" she asked, one eye on Kaj and Connie. "Make it good." Charles was surprising her—not a bad dancer.

"You and I share a secret—one neither of us realizes. And yet, the truth always finds a way—it always comes out. Tonight, we discover each other."

Zoe pulled her head from his shoulder and looked directly into his eyes—she couldn't help but smile. "Thank you, Charles."

He pulled her close and, as the narcotic flooded her brain, they seemed to float across the dance floor. She felt his rapid heartbeat through the sheer red fabric of her dress—merged with him, and forgot about Kaj and Connie because, after all, this felt so much better than anything they could possibly be feeling.

They moved, turned, entangled—she didn't pull away as his mouth went to the soft side of her neck. Instead she leaned into it, closed her eyes, and trusted him to lead as they swept an effortless path across the room. They never slowed their pace, though she felt a vague sense of other bodies and the occasional brush of fabric against her bare arms as he guided her between couples, darting through openings in the crowded room—finally claiming their space at its center with the music's ending.

She opened her eyes to see Kaj next to her—and Connie, with an amused smile, her eyes alight with mischief. Kaj's eyes spoke of something else entirely. Anger? Pain? Good, she thought—and it had to be after 10:00 P.M.

She kissed Charles—with far more passion than she felt—and darted away. Without Charles to hold her up, it was an awkward exit, a slightly stumbling one—navigating high heels while awash in the dizzying narcotic. But instead of embarrassment, all she felt was a red, hot anger. She didn't look back.

Zoe slipped as she jogged down the walkway to her waiting taxi and felt Kaj's hand around her arm. He pulled her out of the impending fall, and spun her to face him.

"I didn't expect to see you here tonight," he said—with far more composure than she was entitled to, she knew.

"Clearly."

"Stay."

"And watch you with Dr. Pink? I don't think so. I don't really need that."

He looked at her quizzically. "Dr. Pink?"

"Connie."

"You can't be serious."

She turned to leave.

He wouldn't let go. "Please stay. I can't exactly leave."

She twisted her arm out of his grasp. "And another thing. Why haven't I met your mother?"

Kaj paused for a deep breath. "Are you okay?"

"No."

"Really? You actually want me to answer that?"

"Yes—why?"

"She's been out of the country for the past two years."

"Well, that doesn't change what I saw in there."

"Nor does anything change what I saw." He looked at her pupils. Have you been taking that narcotic—for your cough?

"Fucking doctors." Zoe ran for the taxi just as Connie called Kaj's name from the doorway of her over-the-top home.

ZOE ASKED THE TAXI DRIVER TO INDULGE HER in one more stop. She ran into the hospital and instructed the nurse to give her the next dose of IV medication—Zoe wouldn't be staying the night. The nurse put up a small fight, phoned the doctor on call, and was told not to bother signing her out AMA. It would be fine for her to follow up in the urgent care clinic tomorrow—which Zoe agreed to.

Back in the taxi, she let her head fall back on the seat and caught the eyes of the driver in his rearview. He reached down and changed the channel. Zoe's tired smile lasted only a few seconds. When her eyes closed she heard Dr. Pink calling to Kaj. Saw them dancing, embracing one another, Kaj dressed for another way of life, another place—next to Connie, not of Zoe's kind. She heard his smooth, sexy voice say, "I can't exactly leave."

No, but she fucking could. It brought her back to the struggle she'd had with her trust in Kaj, and with their intimacy. At one time she'd worked to drive him away, to make him say no—as she'd not had the strength to resist. But he'd stayed—and earned her trust.

Or so she'd thought. Did she trust him?—maybe not, apparently not, decidedly not ... because she'd run out on him. Left him with Dr. Pink. Left him to another life, another woman, and other tastes—running back toward her own anger, her mistrust, the familiar comfort of solitude. She started coughing and the driver eyed her in the mirror again.

After tipping the cabbie generously she fumbled with her key and stumbled into the door of her beloved home on Mississippi River Boulevard.

The fridge was—thankfully, blessedly—fully stocked with beer. She drank one completely and reached for another, opening it as she made her way to the pantry. She tipped the bottle back again, one eye on the shelves. Candy—red Swedish Fish and Atomic Fireballs, pink jellybeans, malted milk balls, even pink cotton candy—pink. She drew her arm across the shelf, spilling it all on the floor, and retreated to the bathroom.

Even her own image, adorned in lipstick and rouge, drew her ire. Zoe turned on the water and splashed it over her face, scrubbing until her skin was sore. She looked back into the mirror, and then toward the empty beer bottle—at least she might sleep.

Standing in her bedroom, the red dress remained—she hadn't removed it yet. It felt sexy—she felt sexy. She felt drunk, drugged, ecstatic, but not enough—because she was also lonely and despairing. Would that ever go away?—would there ever be enough alcohol, drugs, and sex?

For a moment, she actually thought about calling Ray. "And then what?" she asked herself. Use him, as she'd used Charles? Make love to him?—angry love, selfish love, childish love?

A quiet knocking on the back door interrupted her thoughts. Zoe made no move to answer, and the knocking grew only slightly louder.

"Shit. Can't even fucking be lonely by myself." Zoe hurried to the back door, angry, and turned on the overhead light as she looked out the window. The figure shrank from the light, looking around as if caught in a prison break. The woman's eyes pleaded with Zoe to open the door and, as soon as she did, the shadowy figure bolted through it and out of the light.

Zoe locked the door behind her and said, "From Betty's, right?"

IT WAS A BRIEF CONVERSATION—shared over coffee at her kitchen table. As the woman spoke, pleaded, begged and relayed the message from Betty, Zoe listened and said very little. She fought nodding off, and noticed the tapping of a leafless branch on the windowpane, the refrigerator turning on and off, the knocking of hot water pipes, and a vague sense of the wind outside. She was aware of her ridiculous red dress next to this woman in fishnet stockings with a low-cut sheer blouse and a barely-there mini skirt. The woman's coat, however, was more utilitarian—trimmed with fake fur, the hood covered her identity in shadow.

Zoe waited until the woman had warmed herself over coffee and delivered the message for which she'd been dispatched. In response, Zoe promised nothing, although she did admit to a genuine sorrow over the trouble she'd caused and agreed to think about it—all of it. Which should have made the woman nervous—because it was clear to Zoe that she hadn't been told all of it—but instead the woman seemed not to care, or to notice, that Zoe had stressed the words "all of it." She simply pulled the hood over her head and, through the rear door, hurried back into the night.

Pam Leonard

WHEN ZOE HEARD A KEY IN THE FRONT DOOR LOCK, she ran a hand down over the sheer fabric of her red dress, rose from her place at the kitchen table, felt again over the fabric as it draped over her breasts, then ran toward the door—and jumped into Kaj's arms as he entered.

He only said, "I tried the hospital first, they said you'd left," then lifted her and carried her to the bed—smooth, like dancing, like Zoe had seen him doing with Connie. Zoe rolled him over on the bed and straddled him, nearly attacking—and they made angry love.

CHAPTER SEVEN

S HE WOKE COUGHING, AND PUSHED KAJ'S hand away as he felt her forehead again.

"Goddamn it, Zoe, you're still burning up."

"I'm going in today for more IV antibiotics. I'm on a Q8 schedule. I'll swing by the hospital three times today. Then on Monday, when I'm back at work, it'll be easy to get dosed. Besides, I'm much better than before. Believe me."

"You didn't cough much during the night. But then again, you were zoned—I could see it in your eyes, at the party. Might explain a lot of things."

He looked a question at her, but she said nothing. Taking three of the pills in rapid succession had indeed stopped the coughing—and a lot of other things, like rational thought, maybe.

"I was supposed to work today, but I can try to cancel—find a replacement." His hand went again to her forehead.

"Of course not. You can't exactly leave."

There was no recognition on his face—of the phrase he'd used the night before. There was no apparent detection of Zoe's pissed-off state of mind either. It was a phrase that was, in fact, simply true. And they'd made love—angrily, intensely, as if to purge all that was wrong.

"What happened after I left?"

"I stayed long enough for the unveiling."

"And?"

"We raised a lot of money. That was the whole point."

"Did you sell the painting? Auction it?"

"No. That one's not for sale. We sold others. But in the agreement, I had to unveil that particular painting during the event. People apparently paid a handsome sum to come and see it. Imagine that?"

"I'd rather not feed your ego at the moment."

He took her into his arms and laughed. "You already did—last night. Or don't you recall?"

Zoe looked around at her wrecked bed and toppled nightstand. "Oh, yeah?" She looked a challenge at him. "What, exactly, did I say?"

"Other than 'again'—and my name—over and over?"

Zoe felt her anger ease, and an involuntary smile work its way across her face. She pinned him against the sheets. "Again."

IF HE'D BEEN ANGRY OVER HER DISPLAY with the author, he hadn't shown it—and it made her wonder if that was because he felt guilty himself. She shook her head violently to rid her brain of the image—of her doubts, of the persistent mistrust—and watched his car back out of the driveway. Zoe opened her kitchen window to the cold while runners padded along the running trail under a low gunmetal sky that threatened snow. It lied, too. Steam rose from the cup of coffee in her hand.

Zoe let shit out, she always had, couldn't help it, and it drove people away—which was often her subconscious goal. It's not that she let the facts out—instead, for a long while, she'd kept her history carefully hidden from anyone. But she did let loose with her anger—her mistrust of people, of happiness, of herself. And still, everyone needed an escape valve. Maybe because she so secretly guarded the miserable facts of her life Zoe's outlets had been drinking, sex, risky biking, all-out hockey, and any number of other self-destructive and sabotaging behaviors.

But this habit of letting it out without thinking, without reflection, impulsively—she'd often lived to regret. She needed to take a damn breath before jumping to conclusions. Hadn't she learned that by now? It always screwed things up to assume shit. To assume everyone else thought like she did—behaved like she did.

Kaj, on the other hand, was the kind of guy where it was all happening on the inside—relentless work on an ulcer, bothered by things he had yet to share. And while his Nordic roots demanded stoicism, it had eventually become his way. For Kaj to explode in frustration, in pain, took a lot of provocation—and Zoe had brought him to that point on more than one occasion. Each and every episode she'd regretted, while each and every one, he'd forgiven. Where was he now?—at what point along the trajectory? Was it even necessary for her to ask if she was in the right? On those rare occasions when she was, she never handled it well—screwed everything up, leaving it for him to fix. That, she knew, was wrong.

And where was she?—at what point along her well-worn path, the rut that distanced her from commitments? Could she change course? Did she even want to? Was it better for him if she just kept going—a wreck waiting to happen. Then he'd be free—for a different world, another life, a better relationship. And she'd be free—to what? To what end?—to ruin someone else's life?

This line of thinking—if one could even call it thinking—she'd been down before, during several bouts of untreated depression. She'd toughed each one out—and again, she shook her head, shivering in the cold, "Stop it," she said aloud, and closed the window. She reached for one pill, and one pill only, swallowing it with the last of her coffee, and then decided to opt for a free breakfast at the hospital—one she didn't have to prepare. After lingering in a warm shower she dressed for the cold and mounted her bike.

ZOE FIELDED ANOTHER CALL FROM LUCY while getting her dose of IV antibiotics and finishing a second cup of bitter hospital coffee.

"Zoe, I'm afraid. I had a dream last night, and I think I should tell Phillip about it. It was different from anything I've ever dreamed before—and it has me worried."

"Where the hell is she? Have you seen her? Her name is Lucy. You know—sixteen years old, about five-foot nothing, raven-black hair?"

"Come on, Zoe."

"No, I'm serious. This girl I know—Lucy—drove an SUV to the Boundary Waters before she even had a license, then took on a homicidal maniac because it was the right fucking thing to do, and then she took on everybody over making sure the old folks, Sara, and Walt, all still had a place to live. Brave as hell. So where is she now?"

"Okay. I get it. What's there to be afraid of? But you don't know what I dreamed, and trust me, you don't want to. It's just that I have to tell someone. And I think this dream was a different kind of dream. As in, like, maybe a vision quest one. But it found me, instead of me going after it. Maybe that's what he meant by 'go ahead' when I asked him about a vision quest. Like it didn't have to be all ceremonial and shit."

Zoe straightened in her chair. "Sorry, Lucy. I didn't mean to make light. I just want you confident—trusting yourself. I can't stand the idea of you hesitant, not after what you've been through—you've earned your stripes, kid. Sure you don't want to share this dream with me? I'm happy to meet you today and we can talk it over."

"No, you're the last one I can tell."

"Okay, not me, then. Would you rather talk with someone other than Phillip? Like maybe Camilla? You're aware that she's a psychiatrist—expert on all the shit that goes on in our heads and in our dreams. I talked through a dream with her once and actually found it kind of helpful. If you want, I can hook you two up."

"No, maybe later—but not now. I don't even know why I called you. I guess it's just that I'm feeling afraid, and I probably needed to hear exactly what you told me. So thanks, Zoe. I'll talk to you later."

"Bye, kiddo."

Zoe hung up—uneasy. It was just a damn dream, she told herself. She'd never done the vision quest thing herself. It had never occurred to her. After all, she'd identified her strengths and found a place through her own culture—the white man's way, the tradition in which she was raised. While her understanding of vision quests was pretty superficial, she viewed them as a way to find one's calling. So why bother? But then again, in thinking about her serpentine course through law enforcement, trauma surgery, and then internal medicine, perhaps it would have been more efficient to embark on a damn vision quest at the outset. She chuckled as she closed her phone. It was just a damn dream.

The nurse came back in to disconnect the IV. They decided to simply heparin-lock the IV access and bandage over it so it could be reused with each dose over the next several days. Better than getting stuck over and over.

Zoe stopped in the ER on her way out, saw that Dr. Pink wasn't working, kissed Kaj in what was a passionate and teasing preview of their upcoming evening, and then bundled up for the cold.

Back on her bike, she made for Angie's.

"YOU SHOULD HAVE SEEN HER FACE when they unveiled that painting." The author seemed very amused.

"Who?"

"Don't even mess. You know who—the chick he was with, remember? The guy who chased you out of the ballroom? Dancing?"

"Oh, her."

"Yeah, her." Charles eyed Zoe closely, while she worked to look disinterested. "I might have missed something in my reading of that little scenario," he smirked.

And Zoe had no idea as to why. "Something you want to say?"

He just smiled, and shook his head. "Probably for the best that you left, even though I'd have liked for you to stay."

"Why? Why for the best?"

"It might have been embarrassing."

"I'd say I embarrassed myself sufficiently—long before I left. That's kind of what I was hoping to talk to you about."

He laughed, and waved her off. "No need. I get it. You and the artist are an item. That's clear enough," and his smile widened.

"Good, so we're okay? No hard feelings? We had some fun, anyway, didn't we?"

"Yeah, fun—plenty of fun. Wish there'd been more, but I get it. And yes, we're fine."

"Great. Then I'm off. See you again, I imagine."

"Oh, yes. At least I'll be seeing you—in my dreams, every night," he teased.

Odd thing to say, she thought. But then again, being odd generally enhanced a writer's career.

BACK ON THE BIKE, SHE THOUGHT ABOUT how to accomplish her next task. It might require finesse.

Betty was waiting for her at the alley entrance to her restaurant. She ushered Zoe into the back office and turned on her angrily, "What are you doing here? I asked you to back off."

"No, you didn't. You sent one of your minions—some streetwalker who's been doing only what she's been told to do for far too long. Fucking got no mind of her own left."

"Don't you get it? That's the whole point!"

"Get what? All she said was to back off or someone was going to get hurt. Sure, she hinted that it might be me next time, but what she said made no sense—none whatsoever. You're the one who insisted it was a grease fire. So why should I be concerned? I have to say that I'm not. But if you want to convince me, go ahead."

"It was a message, all right?"

"From who?"

"I don't know," she looked past Zoe's shoulder toward the door.

Zoe turned to look, but no one was there.

"Who, Betty? Who's been hassling you? And why?"

"I told you, I don't know. I really don't."

"Then how can you be so sure?"

"Someone came in here, after you left, and asked what you were after. When I told him, he freaked on me. Grabbed a pitcher of water and threw it from across the room at the hot grease. It was a grease fire, just like I said. We were all damn lucky not to be hurt worse."

"What did you tell him—about why I was here?"

"That you were looking for Christie—and her kid."

"Why'd you do that?"

"The guy had a bandana over his face. It was obvious I had trouble from the moment he walked in—and I wasn't going to make it worse by lying. Besides, I'm not very good at that."

"So, you really don't know who this guy was? Didn't see his face?"

"No, end of story. Not knowing stuff is how I stay in business. Now, I've told you everything I can. Leave us alone. Besides, you're not a cop anymore, you're a doctor, why do you have to get involved in all this?"

"Old habits, Betty."

"Yeah, well, just leave it as justice. Jeb deserved what he got. Doesn't matter who did it."

"Thought you didn't know any more than what you already told me."

"Come on, one look at him with Christie and the kid, you'd know. The guy was a bully. And now, just maybe, it's possible for quite a few women to get out of the life. Their time is now. Don't screw it up for 'em. Don't make someone hunt them down."

"Someone?"

"Whoever has Jeb's back—doesn't matter who. There's always someone. You know that."

"All right. I won't be coming around anymore . . . as long as you take my damn phone calls. Don't put me off, Betty. I haven't dropped anything on this, but I'm not forgetting it either."

Betty looked again toward the door and said, "Okay. Now get out of here and don't come back. I'll take your fucking calls."

"One last thing—still no idea where Christie and the kid are?"

"None."

ZOE GUIDED HER BIKE TOWARD ABEL'S OLD FLOP and paused at the street above. There was activity below—laughter, louder than necessary, drunk voices, and wood smoke.

Zoe took out her cell phone to check the time. She calculated, then decided to go home and prepare. She would hit the hospital again for her second dose of IV antibiotics on her way back to this place. She also wondered if they'd consider switching her to an equivalent antibiotic requiring only once-a-day dosing. She would ask.

AND THE ANSWER WAS YES, STARTING TOMORROW, but only if her temperature was consistently down at the third dosing later that night. At this visit, it had finally returned to normal. After the medication was run in, Zoe made her way to the bathroom and opened her backpack. It was time for a few alterations. She locked the door behind her.

The first thing was to discolor her hands with carbon paper. Then she put both hands to her face, up her arms, and around her neck—touching any exposed skin that would be expected to get dirty. She followed that with a purposefully half-assed job of cleaning it off, making sure to leave convincing smudges here and there—around her nose, in the creases formed by wrinkles or by bending and twisting body parts. Special attention was paid to her hands and around her nails—nails were always dirty. She even went back to the carbon paper one more time when she deemed her cleaning job to have been done too well.

Zoe withdrew a brush and teased her hair into a matted, untamed mess. She hid most of it under a black watch cap, the messy ends falling away from around her face.

She stripped, and replaced her clothing with layers—multiple layers, more than would be required even in the cold. It needed to appear that she was wearing her closet, and each layer had to be convincingly threadbare. She'd raided her outdoor clothing—the items used for years to garden, mow the lawn, and shovel snow from her driveway. She wore almost nothing that had even started out as expensive, and used the carbon paper to smudge each layer with a convincing degree of filth. She was careful to select items that would appear to be slightly oversized—although Zoe was naturally lean, she was also fit, but now had to appear to be slightly emaciated.

Finally, the boots—her old pair of insulated Herman Survivors, the one thing that had started out as expensive. But in years of use as her winter mountain biking boots the leather had been scuffed and worn so as to be barely recognizable. In fact, they were even bloodstained from a time when her pager went off during a weekend outing while on call. She'd responded to the emergency department in her mountain bike clothing and despite the gown and gloves, her boots had been in the way of some serious blood splatter. But she loved those boots too much to discard them, and had kept them in use.

"SHE WAS IN ANGIE'S TODAY, BOSS. Someone saw her. But by the time I got there she was already gone."

"Where are you now?"

"Camped outside the hospital. I have eyes here that place her coming in a little while ago."

"Okay, good. Keep watching."

THE WOMAN WHO UNLOCKED THE DOOR and walked out of the bathroom bore no resemblance to the doctor who'd first walked in. Zoe noticed the glances—and that's all they were—followed almost immediately by a turning away. It was easy to escape without being recognized. Back on her bike, she rode in the direction of Abel's old camp.

Her bike had to be stashed before she walked into the camp. It would be incongruent—a dead giveaway. Zoe locked it to a tree some distance from the path toward the river, and hoped it would still be there when she returned. She kept her small backpack, an expected item—torn in two places, and stained. It had cushioned her back during two epic bike crashes on hard pavement. Zoe viewed it as lucky.

Finally, she silenced her phone.

Her approach was tentative, meek—she said nothing, only stood at the periphery of their circle of fire, waiting. Finally, one of the men pointed to a log. Zoe sat, but kept her head down, still offering nothing. She shivered in the cold and stretched dirty hands toward the fire, sensing their questions—their curiosity. But in this place, they wouldn't pry.

They continued their conversation. Although the laughter had been temporarily muted after Zoe's arrival, there were still things to talk about—such as the guy named Gimpy, and how his knee was predicting a harsh winter. They all looked toward the sky and shook their heads as a few snowflakes began to fall—then they laughed heartily. There would be no whining in a place like this—no time for dissatisfaction or unhappiness. Not because of their freedom, although many did regard that as a perk of this lifestyle, but because they were too busy trying to survive. There was no room in their minds for dwelling on that shit. Another perk?—Zoe wondered.

The bottle was passed, finally making its way around to Zoe. Without talking, she looked a question at them, holding it in her hand. The guy next to her—she thought they were calling him Tex—said in a southern accent, "Go ahead—have a drink."

She tipped the half-full bottle and took a long pull—letting a small amount dribble from her mouth as if frantic for it. After a long look at the bottle—a look of longing—she wiped her mouth with a sleeve and passed the bottle on.

The man on the other side of her accepted it, drank, and then reversed the direction of the bottle, giving it back to her. "Looks like you need it bad, girl. What's your name?"

Zoe didn't answer, but took another drink. Then she carefully placed it back in his hands and gestured for him to pass it on, saying, "Thank you."

He grinned over gaps between his few remaining teeth. Zoe smiled tentatively at him then looked back down at her boots.

A man across from her asked, cautiously, "You found a place for the night?"

"Park bench up near the Stone Arch Bridge," she answered. "Been staying there the past two nights—it's off the ground, and there's a nice curve to it."

The man named Tex offered, "I'm heading south soon. Want to come along?"

The others laughed.

"Hey, just being a nice guy!" Tex defended himself.

Zoe took it up from there, "I'm looking for someone."

The men all looked toward Tex, who asked, "Who would that be, darlin'?"

"Abel."

"You know Abel?"

"Yep. I thought he was here."

The men all shifted nervously, one even got up, turned a circle in place, then sat back down. No one spoke.

"So where is he?" Zoe pressed.

"Why you need him, darlin'?"

"It's personal."

"You related?"

"Something like that."

"Aw, man," one of the men said.

Another said, "He's not here any more. Don't suppose you ever see the news?"

"Nope."

"Well…"

"Go on, tell the girl," Tex said.

"Abel's dead."

Zoe worked to look dispassionate, hardened. She nodded, and then said, "How'd he die?"

They all got quiet.

"How?"

Finally the guy named Tex, said, "Someone killed him."

"Who? Who killed him? You're sure he was killed?" So at least now she knew that it was murder—no kind of accidental drowning.

"Know he was killed. Don't know who did it."

"How do you know?"

"Word gets around. Never can trace where stuff like that comes from. But it's generally accurate."

"Then a guy named Jeb. You know where he is? Supposed to take care of me. He promised he'd take good care of me."

"Where'd you come from?" This time it was the man across from her.

"Little town up north. You probably never heard of it—place called Hallock."

They all laughed and he said, "Oh, we've heard of it."

"Spent a cold winter up there once," another man said.

Zoe leaned in, "Really?"

"Yep. You miss it?"

"Right now I do. It's getting colder. But generally … no, I don't."

They all grew silent—getting the gist. She'd probably only travelled the distance from a greater to a lesser hell. But no one asked.

Finally, one of the previously silent men said, "You wouldn't have wanted to get mixed up with Jeb. How about we steer you to a shelter?"

"Wouldn't have?"

"Yeah, as in past tense. Honey, he's dead, too. You're not battin' too well."

"But he promised."

"He was killed. Like I said, you don't want to get mixed up with his kind."

Zoe looked down, acting ashamed.

The man said, "You're already mixed up, aren't you?"

Zoe barely nodded.

"How long?"

"I came to town last May."

There was a whistle from one of the men. Zoe didn't look up to see which one.

Then Tex said, "I bet you and I can work out a deal."

There was a rustling sound from within one of the shelters. Zoe nodded in resignation. She had to sell it that she was desperate—and that she was used to exchanging this kind of currency.

"My tent's right over there," he pointed to the finest one of the bunch—an old REI two-person, its duct-taped tear indicating it had probably been discarded by someone who could afford to replace it. "Got me a nice futon mattress, too." He reached out his hand.

She grabbed it and stood, ready to follow. There was a nervous scuffling of feet around her, and someone said, "Wait."

Tex turned angrily toward the voice, "This ain't none of your business, Preacher. You got no right."

The man named Preacher dropped his eyes. Apparently Tex had him there.

As they approached the tent, Zoe took his hand up toward her mouth as if to kiss it. He smiled, looking back toward the circle of men. Again she felt the nervous energy behind her. Then she bit him.

He howled and jumped back, but quickly recovered and stood ready to strike.

The first thing she heard from behind her was the Preacher, "Tex, we don't need that kind of trouble here. You'll just bring 'em down on us again."

"No shit I don't need this kind of trouble. She's a fuckin' animal!"

Zoe wanted to ask who the real animal was? But she didn't.

Instead she shouted, "Well then I need to find Christie!"

"Christie?"

The man who'd sat across from her said to the others, "Jeb's girl."

"Where can I find her? I'll scream if you don't tell me! So help me God, I'll scream bloody murder!"

The men laughed nervously and one of them said, "Gal can handle herself. I'd advise you not to mess, gentlemen."

"No shit, Professor," Tex squeezed his hand in pain and kicked at the dirt.

"Where is she? If you know Jeb, you must know her! She'll help me!" Zoe raised her voice, disrupting the sanctity of their little enclave. She had one shot with these guys and so far she'd sold it—that she was damaged, feral, unpredictable, maybe even a little crazy, definitely more trouble than she was worth. They had it good down here—as far as homeless camps went, this one wasn't bad. And they would simply want to get rid of her. How far would they go?

Most of them were okay. Zoe knew that. Not that she knew these men, but she'd met others. The composition of any homeless camp was always a mixed bag—no different from any other group of men. Only a few were truly dangerous. Most were decent. But almost all of them were afraid of something, and wouldn't want trouble.

Finally one said, "She's with a guy named Wolf."

"Fuck, Stu, what the hell!"

"Well, she's not gonna leave lest we tell her."

"You think she's trouble? You just wait!"

"I won't say where I heard it. I promise."

"You best not, girl. If you do, you'll have a whole new kind of trouble. And what you got now?—Honey, it won't even compare."

Zoe had to stick with it. "Where can I find this Wolf guy?"

"Don't know. None of us know. And that's the truth. Nothing you can do to change it."

Another reinforced, "Come back in a month and you might find him here. He comes and goes."

"I'll find him."

As she walked away, she overheard one of them say, "It'd be good if she did."

ZOE KNEW WHERE HE WAS. She rode through a bitter wind to the outer edge of the bus line—her layers of clothing welcomed in the cold, and made one stop at an electronics store along the way. At the abandoned farmstead she used the approaching darkness to her advantage—traversing the long driveway, around the abandoned buildings, and across the field wasn't risky. Twilight had decreased visibility, lessening her concern over being seen. The real worry was over Wolf. Had she allowed herself to be conned?

Despite the cold, having navigated her bike over the tilled field and through the woods had frost collecting on the outer layer of Zoe's clothing—she was damp and overheated underneath. Zoe paused at the periphery of the clearing and caught her breath, calming herself and studying the pole barn's structure.

Wolf had done an excellent job of camouflaging the place. One would never know from looking at the outside that it was fortress to a house within—another layer between Wolf and the outside world. In fact, the entire farmstead was added protection. It had obviously been abandoned for quite some time and anyone interested in poking around it he'd managed to scare away with a few well-aimed gunshots. As trespassers, they'd been breaking the law anyway, so he'd have no concern over being ratted out. They'd just leave—probably never to come back.

There was the tilled field, the woods, and a lack of any obvious road into the woods. The land was posted with no trespassing signs, so that would keep the snowmobilers, hunters, and ATV riders away. Then there was the pole barn itself, and finally the locked door of the cottage within. Even if someone did wander by and see the pole barn, they'd have no concept of what was inside.

Being inside a house that was located within another structure made it hard to get any bearing in space when looking out the windows. The view through each was identical—the same pole barn wall. And still, as Zoe recalled her previous visit, the interior had seemed so small compared to the volume of the pole barn. There was the main living and dining area, a small kitchen, and a short hallway that she supposed led to a bathroom and bedroom.

Curious, she leaned her bike against a tree and silently approached the pole barn. "Thank you," she mouthed, as she found the pole barn door give way just enough to squeeze through.

Zoe walked to the front door—it was opened before she had a chance to knock. "How'd you know I was here?"

He didn't answer. "How'd you get in?"

"Look at me—skinny," she shrugged.

He did—then said, "What's with the get-up?"

"Long story. Wanna hear it?"

Wolf looked over his shoulder, at the interior of his cottage, and then nodded. "Okay."

Zoe walked past him as he held the door—then pointed toward a chair. "Okay?"

"Yep. Have a seat."

He sat opposite her on the sofa.

The story she made up was too implausible not to believe. Zoe felt the influence of her new author friend in every word. It had to account for her clothing, and offer a reason to have shown up at Wolf's doorstep. She made it sufficiently detailed and confusing, too—hard to follow, hard to question. It had to do with a trail-biking contest not far from there—a really weird deal, some sort of a charitable fundraiser. A good cause though, after which she thought she'd stop by and say hello to her new friend.

She pointed to her appearance, "I crashed a few times. Mind if I use your bathroom to freshen up?" Before he could respond, Zoe pulled an offering out of her backpack, "Thought you might like this for your place." She held it out—a small radio. "I didn't notice one here before. Got you some batteries too."

He accepted it, "Thanks," and pointed down the hallway toward the bathroom as he inspected the radio.

Zoe moved slowly down the hall, lingering at the entrance to his bedroom along the way—it was empty. When she glanced back toward Wolf. He was watching her. Zoe smiled, and continued toward the bathroom.

With the water running she looked in the medicine cabinet—it was an old one, probably scavenged from the farmhouse—and inside the small handcrafted linen closet. There was nothing to suggest that anyone other than Wolf occupied the house—very few items, the bare essentials, and not much in the way of duplicates.

She probably should have brought him toilet paper, she realized.

Zoe came back out and asked, "Mind if I get a glass of water?"

"I'll get it. Have a seat."

He came back out from the kitchen with water and two cookies. "Here you go."

"Thanks. So, do you ever have anyone out here? Friends?"

"Nope. And I want to keep it that way. You still understand that, right?"

"Certainly. I won't say anything. I promised. But it just seems like it'd be lonely."

He pointed at Thor. "Not really."

Zoe raised the cookie before taking a bite. "Thanks, I owe you."

"Let's get something straight, you don't owe me anything. I owed you. I still do—you saved Thor's life. I'll always owe you—end of story. But don't go and make it any more complicated than that."

She paused. "By the way, what's your given name?"

"Why?"

"Small bet with myself. I pegged you for Scandinavian—am I right?"

He laughed. "Nope. Mark Murray. Scottish. How about you?"

"French Canadian—and a little Ojibwe."

"Yeah, I guess I see that in you."

Zoe smiled. "I need to level with you about something, Wolf, and I don't have any time to tiptoe around it. I get pretty riled about assholes who abuse women. So you see, I got this thorn in my side about a gal named Christie—she was in the bar that day, with her kid, and the guy who died was her pimp."

Wolf showed no emotion. Only asked, "What's that got to do with me?"

"Well, I've been trying to find her, make sure she's okay—but she disappeared, and your name came up."

"Who? Who gave you my name?"

"Not saying. Another promise. But the theory is . . . she's with you."

"She's not. I mean, look around. You see anyone else here? And why would she want to be here? Who knows I'm here? Tell me!"

"My source didn't know where you were. Just that she might be with you, wherever you were. So why would your name come up?"

"That's what I'd like to know. Must be someone trying to get me killed."

"How so?"

"You mess with someone's stable, well . . . let's just say you can run, but you can't hide."

Zoe looked around her and raised her eyebrows—not exactly buying the not being able to hide part. "But he's dead, anyway. Why worry about him?"

"They're like rats. Where there's one, there's more. And a dead man's empty space gets filled—fast. My guess is she's already working another street, for another piece-of-shit. Keep looking—and although I wish you luck, you can leave me the hell out of it. I don't even know the chick."

IT MIGHT BE POSSIBLE TO SCARE THE DOC. She was slight, and presumably sick—that is if what he'd been told was correct—and she lived alone. She had a male friend, but he didn't live with her. She had a good job, one she would want to protect. And she undoubtedly valued her life. So maybe, just maybe, he could avoid another death. Only because too many, all at once, well . . . even in a city this large, it drew unwanted attention from the wrong crowd.

Cops had a way of noticing the death of a WASP woman.

But this particular WASP woman was presumably bright. Smart enough to know when to let go and think about her future. Disciplined enough to stick with it. After all, weren't those the qualities required to become a doctor?—and in the end, she had things, things she'd want to hang on to. She had a good job, a boyfriend, a house—even if she didn't value her own life, she'd value her things. She'd want to protect them if threatened.

The boss had always recognized the importance of adjusting his plans to fit the situations—never get too attached to Plan A. But…if she didn't react in the way he expected, his Plan A could still be made to work. Maybe just a disappearance, without a trace, no body would mean no murder to prosecute—just a disappearance. After all, docs come and go—just like the homeless.

OUT ON THE STREET, ZOE TURNED HER CELLPHONE back on and checked messages before mounting her bike.

One from Kaj, "HOME SOON."

She texted back, "HOME AFTER LAST DOSE @ HOSPITAL."

And one from Lucy, "Y ARNT U ANSWERING PHONE?"

Zoe called her.

"Lucy, is this an emergency?"

"No, just checking on you—to make sure you're okay."

"I'm fine. Just on my way to the hospital for today's last dose of IV antibiotics, then I'll be going home. Okay with you?" she teased.

"Why are you on IV medication?"

"The pills weren't working, but it's okay now, kiddo. I'm fine. Why are you so worried?"

"No reason. Just that I'd sort of gotten used to looking after you, I guess."

"Well, mission accomplished. Now you've got more important things to worry about than me. How's it going with Phillip? Been able to spend a lot of time with him over the weekend?"

"Yes." Lucy paused.

"And? How's it going? Have you worn him down with your questions yet?"

"No." Lucy laughed. "He's got stamina."

"You still sound bothered."

"I don't know, I guess I am."

"Here's something fun to think about, and it has to do with this connectedness stuff you and Phillip have been tossing around. There's this scientific theory called 'entanglement,' and it holds that each thing—for instance an electron—has a shadow, a mirror-image duplicate, that it's linked to. Even at great distance, they're linked in such a way that they still communicate with each other. If something happens to one, it impacts the other instantaneously, no matter how far away they are—as if the space between them doesn't even exist."

"I guess that's pretty cool. But right now, it only makes me more nervous."

"Why's that?"

"I don't know." There was a pause. "No, you're right. It's cool. I'll think about it some more."

"Good. Maybe it'll keep your mind off whatever's bothering you. Gotta go, kiddo. I'm on my bike and it's getting cold standing here talking."

"Oh, sorry. Talk to you later. And, Zoe?"

"Yeah?"

"Be careful."

ZOE'S THOUGHTS RAN FROM ONE EXTREME to the other as she biked. Why indeed? Why would Christie be at Wolf's? Did he have some sort of a copper kettle going?—a meth lab, maybe, hidden on the farmland? People like Christie would put out for that—probably had been for a long time.

But what if Wolf was telling the truth? Hard to keep a meth lab quiet in certain circles—and anyway, she'd have noticed the odor. Could Zoe have read the homeless men wrong?—been thrown on Wolf's trail purely as a way to get rid of her, or as revenge against Wolf? Mark Murray. She stopped, dug out her phone, and called in a favor.

THE NURSE TOOK ONE LOOK AT ZOE and shook her head.

"Long story," Zoe said, and added, "You don't want to know."

"Well then, be quiet," the nurse stuck a thermometer under Zoe's tongue.

Zoe grinned and asked, after the nurse pulled it out, "Normal?"

"Yep."

"Good, then tomorrow I'm on a once a day regimen."

After the medication had been run in, Zoe was disconnected from the IV and her access bandaged over. As Zoe took the stairs down to unlock her bike, her cellphone chirped.

"Hi, what have you got?"

"That name you gave me?—birth certificate indicates he was born to a single mother but he took his dad's last name. Mom's name was Grace Prescott. Dad's was Colin Murray. I looked them both up. It appears they eventually married—after the kid was born. Dad is currently presumed dead. Disappeared. Mom waited and eventually had him declared."

"Thanks, I owe you."

"You sure as hell do. I was having a quiet Sunday till you called."

"Too quiet, probably."

The man on the other end laughed. "Yeah. Bored out of my mind. Talk to you later."

ZOE CAME HOME TO SOMETHING HOT—hard and muscular. A Kaj she recognized—but didn't. He wouldn't lose control, but on this night he didn't wait for the normal sequence of events. There would be no casual dinner, only time enough to strip and shower. He wouldn't bother her with the mundane activity of putting one foot in front of the other—instead he lifted her out of the shower, still dripping, and set her, supine, on the bed. The change in position, thankfully, no longer made her cough.

His hands kneaded her muscles, almost to the point of pain—but not quite, he would know the limit. His mouth teased her at every responsive place—a landscape he knew well. Her lips, neck, hips,—he synchronized to bring about the shock wave that followed. Only then did he acknowledge his own needs. Still under control, Zoe thought in her foggy aftermath, still under control—even as Zoe wondered what truly being under control would feel like. Maybe she was even glad she didn't know.

LUCY WOKE IN A PANIC. SHE JUMPED OUT OF BED TO PACE, shaking her head to loosen the dream—but this one wouldn't disappear with waking and movement like most dreams did. It chased her around the room, held her gaze as she focused on the tree fort outside her window, even behind her closed eyes.

It dogged her until she didn't feel like herself, even questioning her own history—maybe a meaningless history. Lucy ran a hand over her arms, checking for actual mass and structure. Checking for something with which to mount a muscular defense. She was real, she was here—her body existed. She was strong. Wasn't she?

Zoe's words echoed. Where was Lucy? Where was the girl who was unafraid? But in Lucy's dream, it was Zoe who had disappeared into an expanding universe, her heart ripped apart by dark energy—and the dark energy was evil, something of our own creation.

ZOE LIFTED KAJ'S ARM FROM ACROSS HER BELLY as she twisted in bed to answer her phone.

She saw the caller's I.D. and in a hoarse, sleepy voice, answered, "Lucy, what is it this time?" by now assuming that, with Lucy, it wouldn't be an actual emergency.

"You okay?"

"Of course I'm okay." She felt Kaj shift in bed, his arm reaching around her waist again and squeezing her rear. Zoe worked not to laugh. "Are you okay?"

Lucy hesitated, "Yes. I guess so."

"What is it, kiddo? Just save us the time and tell me."

"Well, I had a dream about the universe expanding and people breaking apart."

Zoe couldn't help it—she chuckled. "Sorry, Lucy, but you've been watching too many Woody Allen movies."

"No—I haven't."

"Well, then, apparently you're starting to think like him."

"What do you mean?"

"A young character in one of his movies argued against doing his homework, because, after all, the universe was expanding . . . so why bother?"

Lucy chuckled a little. "I hadn't thought of that."

"Yeah, but John Wayne movies are good antidotes."

"How so?"

"He's quoted as saying, "Life is tough . . . but it's tougher when you're stupid." Zoe paused. "So do your homework!"

She could hear Lucy exhale into the phone, and only hoped it was an exhalation of pent up stress and anxiety—a release.

"Lucy? You still there?"

"Yeah, but I still feel like there's no hope. Like something awful is going to happen. Maybe it's not the expanding universe, maybe that was just a symbol . . . or whatever."

"So, what … are you ready to tap out over a damn dream?"

Kaj stirred, waking up. Listening now.

"No, it's just that …"

"I messed your head up with all that physics talk, didn't I?"

"No! I like that stuff. Don't stop it."

"Well, then, what is it? Is it Phillip? Did he say something that bothered you?"

"No! Quit thinking it's someone else. It's me."

"Well, I guess that's a start at least. Apparently you've finally found Lucy."

To Zoe's great relief, Lucy chuckled into the phone.

"You gonna be okay, kiddo?"

"Yep. Sorry I woke you."

"Don't be. I always want you to call me if there's a problem, okay?"

"Yep."

"You want to meet tomorrow night? We can talk."

"Maybe. Maybe—I don't know. I'll call you if I do. Okay?"

"Sure. I'll be back at work. Just text me if you need to talk. Remember what I said about Camilla … or maybe Phillip. And Lucy?"

"Yeah?"

"Pay special attention to your math homework—it's the only multi-universal language. That way, if the universe does break apart and we're hurled into another—at least you'll be able to communicate."

"Very funny."

"You think I'm being funny? I'm totally serious."

But Lucy laughed anyway, and said, "I'm okay now. Go back to sleep."

Kaj asked after Zoe hung up, "She okay?"

"Yeah, but she won't get back to sleep tonight."

"Why?"

"Because I've sent her on an impossible task."

"What's that?"

"Understanding the unpredictable—people will never conform to mathematical formulas. I should have told her to study poetry, instead." Zoe laughed and shook her head. "She just had a bad dream—a nightmare." Zoe turned to look at the clock. "We won't get back to sleep either."

He grinned and grabbed her, "Then let's not waste the time."

CHAPTER EIGHT

ER ANTIBIOTICS HAD BEEN ADMINISTERED, the IV access bandaged over, and now Zoe was on the run—meeting every new patient admitted on the service during her absence. It was twice—no ten times—as hard to get to know someone through reading their chart, as opposed to admitting them in the first place. She had to familiarize herself with all of them, and then formulate a plan for each one before attending rounds. In addition to that, she was already getting called by the ER to come down and pick up a new admission—and it wasn't even 9:00 A.M. yet. This didn't bode well for her on-call night ahead.

She decided to rely—albeit uneasily—on her interns to present the patients they were familiar with, and she would focus on the new admit. Attending rounds started at ten. There was no other way to divide the work.

Taking stairs down to the ER and avoiding the crowded elevators was faster. When pushing through the double doors, she expected the usual chaos, but not this. It was out of control. There was shouting, running—which rarely happened, even under extreme circumstances, as it would invite an accident—and she immediately noticed the glut of attending physicians. The staff from the night before must not have gone home yet—out of need. They'd overlapped for a couple of hours already—an oddity, as everyone in the ER prided themselves on being able to handle just about anything.

Zoe noticed the blood trails on the linoleum, still waiting to be cleaned. So that's why she hadn't sensed the pandemonium down here from her place on the medical wards. They were dealing with surgical emergencies—probably trauma of the motor vehicle accident or gunshot varieties, maybe both.

But this would eventually translate into a busy day for her anyway. Whenever things became too chaotic, ER personal wouldn't have time to scrutinize the nuances of each patient. Instead, whenever there was even a question about whether or not a patient required admission, under these circumstances they would be turfed to the medicine services without bothering to explore social service options that might keep them out.

For Zoe, it would probably mean a day of admitting only marginally ill people who would be discharged the next day after social service consults. She looked at the board for her patient's name, picked up the paperwork, and went looking for the actual patient. On her way past one of the stabilization rooms she glanced in to see Kaj and Dr. Pink working side-by-side over a bloodied body— one that from another glance at the cardiac monitor and the blood volume at their feet, appeared to be barely alive. The rapidly emptying red IV bags were trying to keep up and the two surgeons were fully focused on the open chest as Connie performed open cardiac massage. But this guy wasn't going to make it. She continued on to a small cube at the end of the hall.

The small, almost emaciated woman on a gurney woke as Zoe entered. Her awakening was more of a startle, and Zoe wondered just how tired someone had to be to sleep amidst all that noise and chaos on the other side of the curtain.

Zoe reached out, "Dr. Lawrence," and took the patients hand in hers. She noted the weak grip, dry skin, and a slight tremor. The woman's eyes were dark and sunken. "Sally? Sally Taylor?"

"Yes, ma'am."

"I'll be your doctor while you're here. They called me from the internal medicine department. I understand you've been having difficulty urinating? And pain?"

"Yes." The woman's eyes darted away from Zoe's every time Zoe looked directly at her.

"How long has this been gong on?"

"About a week."

"Fever?"

"I think so, but I haven't checked. I don't have a thermometer."

Zoe looked at the chart. "According to this, your temperature is one hundred and one degrees. So you think you may have had this fever all week?"

"Maybe just a few days. But the burning—when I pee—that's been at least a week."

"Foul odor?"

"Yes. It's getting in the way of my job." Sally looked at Zoe expectantly, and Zoe looked closer at the chart.

"Your job?"

"Mmm Hmm. The odor, not the pain," Sally added, somewhat defiantly.

"Ah. I see." Zoe quickly scanned the multiple ER visits to find sexually transmitted diseases and several childbirth admissions. The story was told there. A streetwalker. All her kids had been given up.

"I'm ready."

"Good. Let me take a closer look. Abdominal pain?"

"No. I mean I'm ready."

"Ready for what?"

"To go."

"I'm afraid we need to keep you here for a while." Zoe started her exam. "Could you open your mouth please?" Sally's mucous membranes were dry. Zoe rechecked her blood pressure, finding it to be normal, and her pulse high. Zoe listened to her heart and lungs and then laid a hand over one of Sally's kidneys, pounding the other hand into it. Sally jumped.

"Please lie back." Zoe listened to Sally's abdomen with her stethoscope, and then proceeded with a manual exam. Sally's bladder was tender.

"When was the last time you had anything to drink?" The tremor was concerning.

Sally didn't answer.

"As in alcohol. Ever had the DTs before?" Zoe knew from the chart that she had.

"Yes."

"We're going to have to order a few tests, get some fluids in you, and some antibiotics. Looks like a bladder infection, at a minimum—a kidney infection, most likely."

"Okay."

"Don't worry. I imagine we'll get you out of here soon. I'll be doing a pelvic examination before I bring you upstairs. Any chance you could be pregnant?"

Sally looked away. "I don't know."

"Don't worry, I'll be checking for that anyway."

"But, I thought . . ."

"What?"

Sally eyed Zoe with suspicion—Zoe felt it.

"Never mind."

"We'll talk some more when I get you upstairs, after my rounds with the attending doc. I'll come back and we can figure things out, okay?"

"I guess so. But I've been sitting here for hours."

"That explains your ability to sleep even with all the noise," Zoe smiled.

"Yes, but it was supposed to be Dr. Sayre taking care of me. She saw me first."

"Yes, that's true. But she's an ER doctor. You've probably got a kidney infection, and that requires that you be admitted to a medical service. You're too sick to be treated in the ER and let go."

"Can I still talk to her?"

"Dr. Sayre?"

"Sure, I can let her know that you'd like to see her. I'm sure she'll stop by. But I have an idea that it might be a while—maybe even tomorrow. They were hit pretty hard in the ER. It's going to take them awhile to dig out from under everything. And Dr. Sayre's been up all night. She'll need some sleep."

Sally's eyes brightened. "Okay. Tomorrow is okay. But you will tell her?"

"Absolutely."

"What did he have for breakfast?"

The intern looked helplessly toward Zoe—and then back toward the man who'd asked him the question. Zoe hid her smile.

"Ah, I can check."

"You mean you don't know?" the attending physician asked, exasperation in his voice.

"No, sir. I don't."

"Aw, for cripes sake, make something up!" Zoe inserted, nearly shouting.

Then both she and the attending laughed.

"Oh. Oh, I see. Okay, you guys think that's funny? Well, what if it mattered? What if it was important what he ate?"

Zoe smiled, "Then you'd have known what it was."

His face brightened just a little. "Yeah, I suppose so," and he laughed, too.

The attending left, with an admonition that the intern should try lightening up a little bit.

"Okay, you guys get going on your patients, I have to go finish up with my new admit. Renal infection. Let's meet over lunch. From the way the ER looked, I'm predicting we'll get our next patient any time. Which one of you is up next?"

The embarrassed intern, Joel, spoke up. "I am."

"Okay, I'll page you if we get one before then."

ZOE HEADED TOWARD THE FAR END OF THE HALLWAY—one that literally spanned two city blocks. Sally's test results should have begun trickling in. Long strides guided her past door upon door of the sick and dying. A few, disoriented and tethered to their beds, called out to her. From some, an odor of bodily fluids overpowered the disinfectant. Pings of cardiac monitors and ventilated breaths followed her down the hall—familiar background music. But her mind was on her patient.

Long strides gave way to a jog when she noticed the commotion up ahead. She slid to a stop at the nurse's station. "What was that all about? What happened?"

"She signed out AMA."

"Who did?"

"Your patient."

Zoe looked into Sally's room. It was empty.

"What the hell? Why didn't anyone call me?"

"No time. He swooped in here and had her up and ready to leave before we knew it was anything more than a routine visit. We made her sign out against medical advice, but she almost left without doing it."

"She wanted to leave?"

"As far as I could tell. She sure wasn't resisting—and she signed the AMA form."

"Aw, shit. Was there any argument in there? Did you hear anything?"

"No. The woman was quiet as a mouse the whole time she was here."

"Test results?"

"Here, let me check." The nurse pulled the records up on screen.

Zoe looked over her shoulder, "Fuck, she was pregnant after all," and ran toward the stairs. She pounded through the door to level one, only to catch sight of Sally being led into a parked car. The man slammed the door shut and then ran to the driver's side while Zoe ran toward the car—calling Sally's name. The car almost hit Zoe as it swung backward out of the parking spot, and then accelerated toward the street. Zoe had to let go of Sally's eyes, scared, almost pleading, as she redirected her gaze toward the license plate.

No time to waste on facts—this doc had to be discouraged.

Sally argued that she really was sick—but wasn't this how some of the others had disappeared? Too many had disappeared lately. So the boss would give them both one chance—both Sally and Zoe. But they'd each have only one chance to get it right. His man was already in position at the hospital—on task. Meanwhile, he would handle Sally himself—and that would be the fun part.

"What do you know about the girl you saw earlier—Sally Taylor?"

"Why?" Dr. Sayre, busy at the computer, didn't even look up from the screen as two interns hung on each arm waiting for some decision or another before they could proceed.

"She was asking for you."

"I'll stop up and see her." Connie handed an EKG printout to one of the interns. "Atrial fib. You really ought to know that by now." And with that, she rid herself of one intern. The other still rocked from foot to foot, impatient at her side.

"That's going to be hard, since she was practically kidnapped out of her hospital room."

"Kidnapped?"

"She signed out AMA, but it was coerced—I'm sure of it."

"Why didn't you stop her?"

"I wasn't there. It was too late."

Connie's face darkened with worry. She looked at the remaining intern. "Get lost."

"So what do you know about her?"

"Nothing. It was so damn busy here last night that all I did was take her as a patient before being called away for the critical cases. Never got back to her. Someone else must have turfed her to you. Could have been one of the interns."

"Nothing was done when I got here—just vitals and presenting complaint. No labs were drawn, not even a urine specimen."

"Like I said—busy as hell."

"Yeah, couldn't help but notice that. I came down around nine. Did that guy make it?"

"No. Gunshot to the heart."

"Figured."

SALLY TAYLOR. WHILE SHE'D GOTTEN NOTHING from Dr. Sayre, Zoe did have his license plate number. Eventually, Sally was going to need medical attention, whether she'd truly signed out against medical advice or not. Time to call in more favors, Zoe decided. Unfortunately, she couldn't leave the hospital until her call shift ended the following evening.

So Zoe made another call.

HIS PHONE CALL BEGAN AT A WALL PHONE within the hospital. From there it was routed to the operator. The operator took the information and paged Zoe. Zoe saw the number and called the operator. From there, the operator gave Zoe her instructions—she was needed for an emergency consult in the next building. It was a surgery patient, requiring an internal medicine consult before being taken to the operating room.

Zoe jogged toward the skyway connecting the two buildings. She'd been given a room number she wasn't familiar with. It took her down to the basement level and, while it seemed odd, she simply tried to find it quickly.

At the bottom of the stairs, Zoe looked down the long hallway, expecting to see some activity. But all was quiet, almost deserted. She checked her pager again and called the operator back while she walked. "You sure? That's what they said?"

The operator reread the instructions.

"Was there a call-back number?"

When she was told that the call had originated from a wall phone in that area, Zoe simply forged ahead. "All right. I'll keep looking. Try the phone back for me, will you? See if you can find someone still at it."

The operator agreed, and in the distance, Zoe heard a phone ring.

She jogged toward it, realizing that she must at least be close. What many didn't realize were the number of city blocks taken up by the hospital and its many attached buildings. It was easy to get lost in some parts.

The man grabbed her from behind as she passed the entrance to an empty room—his arm wrapped tightly around her throat, pulling her back and into the darkened space. Her first instinct was to pull at his arm and struggle away from him, but her training stopped her. Instead she allowed him to guide her backward.

"What do you want?"

He laughed. "I would say that's a stupid question, but in this case, you happen to be lucky."

"Lucky how? I don't exactly feel too lucky right now," she managed.

"Lucky because I've been told to go easy on you."

"Meaning?—you piece of shit," and this time she did struggle against him.

He laughed again. "And to think the boss thought he had the fun part."

"This is fun? For who, exactly?" She felt him turn hard against her hip.

"This goes on much longer, I may not be responsible for my actions."

She quit struggling. "Then I'll ask you again—what in the hell do you want?"

"What I want, and what I've been sent to do, are two separate things."

"Okay, Einstein, what have you been sent to do?"

"Tell you to mind your own business."

"My business? This job is my business. I am minding my business. What in the hell do you expect me to do? What is this? Who sent you?"

"You don't have to know who, only why. And the why is that you have a job you like, a boyfriend you love, and a fucking house. You want all that to go away? Maybe you even go away. Maybe it all goes to hell in a house fire. I mean, who's to say? Anything can happen."

"Does this have to do with Sally?"

She felt him squeeze tighter. A message.

"I'm going to let you sit down on that chair in the corner, facing the wall…"

She still hadn't seen his face—he'd kept her back toward him in the darkened room.

"… Then I'll leave. You sit there for five minutes, and we're good as gold. You do what I say—you never have to see me again."

She was readying herself to take him out—starting to struggle again by pulling forward against him. Then she would use his pulling backward to her advantage and go into his movement—use it against him.

Until he said, "…And your boyfriend won't ever have to see us either."

"Okay. Okay. I'll do it. Let me sit down, and you go. You won't have any trouble from me."

He let his hand drop from her neck to squeeze her left breast. That's when she whipped her head back and into his nose.

"Damn it, bitch!"

"…And I say, if you go, we'll never have to see each other again. No trouble from you, no trouble from me."

He guided her to the seat in the corner, and sat her down facing away from him. "Stay there for five minutes."

"I said I would. Now go!"

She waited only one minute—after hearing that he was gone, then felt along the back of her head. It was wet, and sticky. Zoe tried not to smile about that, as she started worrying about Kaj.

AFTER TAKING CARE OF THE BREAKFAST CHORES Lucy finished her online homework. It left her free for the day by 11:00 A.M. With permission, she grabbed the keys to Pushpa's car and made for Phillip's place. In her pocket was a generous amount of gas money—Pushpa always thought of such details.

Lucy made a stop at the gas station—one carefully selected to allow for the drive-off without paying. There was a lone and lethargic attendant, no security cameras, and quick freeway access. It felt awful, like a backslide into her old way of life, but it had to be done. From there she crossed to the other side of the city, one of her old haunts, and pulled up along side the man—a man she, at one time, had worked hard to avoid, but who, now, she'd worked hard to relocate. Lucy combined what money she'd saved with Pushpa's and, in exchange, the man put a brown paper bag into Lucy's hands. The two separated immediately. Lucy wouldn't take time to look in the bag until she was clear of the neighborhood, trusting in its contents.

She kept driving until turning a lonely corner onto Phillip's street. It dead-ended near the river, and there, she paused the car. Phillip's house would more appropriately be described as a shack covered in tarpaper, but Lucy liked his home—surrounded by urban woods, his yard was a garden of log sculptures guarding a fire pit. She heard the sound of his chainsaw at work on a carving.

Out of Phillip's eyeshot, she looked into the bag. It was old, and probably dirty, undoubtedly linked to other crimes—if it were clean she'd have had to pay far more. And as expected, he'd shorted her on ammo, but there was still enough. All in all, an okay deal, she decided. And that was good, because it made for one less thing she'd have to correct.

Lucy felt the weight of the gun in her hands—cradling it in a shooting grip and keeping it low, below the dash. She turned it over and loaded the clip. It was just like the one she'd fired in the Boundary Waters—the one she'd stolen from a dead man, a man who'd intended to kill her. She'd requested such a gun, one she would feel confident in handling, and her source had delivered.

Lucy looked up as the sound of the chainsaw died—he must have sensed her presence. She put the gun below her seat then put the car in gear and covered the distance to Phillip's driveway. As she pulled in, he walked out to meet her.

"You've had another dream?"

"Yes."

"Did you tell Zoe this time?"

"I can't."

"But Lucy, you need to understand that I'm not really your teacher—she is. I just translate. It's Zoe you need to speak with about this."

Lucy remained silent.

"Perhaps you don't need me to see her properly anymore?"

Lucy looked into his eyes—they were dark, like hers, pulling at her, and she felt hers close involuntarily. "I see her fine—and I know what I have to do."

"Lucy, it's clear from hearing about your past that you have the gift of prophetic dreams, but bear in mind that having a glimpse of what's to come doesn't necessarily mean you can change it."

"I don't see why not."

"Perhaps your dreams are nothing more than time-travel," he teased.

But Lucy could tell he wasn't entirely joking.

"That would mean we aren't free at all, not even a little bit, because then everything would have already happened—I don't buy that."

"Lucy, life is messy, and so is this string theory that Zoe's been talking to you about. It's only one of many theories, and it's so messy that of the scientists who ascribe to it, many don't even like it themselves. It makes them damn uncomfortable."

"So what?"

"There are many people acting in the direction of a certain outcome, Lucy—not just you—and there are many paths to getting there." He smiled. "Like I said, it's all messy."

"That I buy—but not only in this universe, it's happening in all the others, too. I just choose to believe that in this universe, I still matter. Don't you want this one to be the one that comes out right?"

"Of course I do. But in that case, Zoe's perfectly capable of taking care of herself."

"But Zoe's heart ..."

"Her heart?"

"It needs protecting."

Phillip chuckled, "Zoe would argue that she's anything but pure at heart."

"She started out that way! But this isn't only about Zoe," she shot back, marveling at his ability to correspond with her thoughts. "It's just that in order to protect the good, some people always have to turn bad." She exhaled forcefully. "It's exhausting to think about."

Phillip smiled, and added, "Let's just hope Zoe's purity of heart won't have to be tested."

Lucy allowed herself to smile too. "Okay, so maybe I'm being overly dramatic. But I can't ignore what I've seen."

Lucy heard her own words, but they sounded foreign. Where in the hell were they coming from?—who in the hell were they coming from? The Lucy she believed herself to be, or the one that Zoe was convinced resided in her?

Phillip put his arm around her slender shoulder, momentarily mirroring her confused expression, and then invited her in. "It's cold. There's a fire going." He steered her toward his door.

Once inside the drafty structure, Lucy shed her coat and pulled in close before the warm fire. She sat and wordlessly watched Phillip prepare coffee. Her eyes followed his movements until an outstretched hand offered her the cup. Lucy cradled it in her hands and sipped. He'd put milk in it.

"Thanks."

He nodded and sat beside her as they both looked into the fire. Finally he said, "I'd ask if I can stop you, but I already know the answer. So can I help you, instead?"

Lucy did a rare thing, leaning into his shoulder and wrapping an arm around his back. "Thank you."

"How? How can I help?"

"No. It's not that. I don't want you involved. But thank you for offering. It's that you won't try to stop me—that's what I appreciate." Lucy took her arm back and returned to upright. "I've watched people try to tell Zoe not to do this or that—things she feels she needs to do. She always has to hide stuff. It drives me crazy, seeing that. Even though I know it's because people love her. And of course that's good and all—but their love is too confining. She laughs, and makes jokes about it, but I can tell it bothers her. And if they aren't careful, they'll drive her away."

"People love you, too, Lucy—and be honest, Zoe isn't the only one who hides things."

Lucy sensed something—something you notice peripherally, an inconvenient flaw in her logic—and she stiffened.

Phillip smiled at her response. "My dear, when you get angry—no matter who you're angry with—you're nothing like Zoe."

Lucy turned her stare toward him, saying nothing.

He nodded. "See? You're like one of those constricting snakes. You squeeze all the air out of a room. You make everyone uncomfortable, unable to breathe, even without saying a word. Yours is an anger that cannot be ignored. And still you sit quietly, unmoving." He got up to pace and then went to the door. "There, see? You make me move away from you and open the door for air, without saying a word," he laughed, "with just one look. Zoe?—she would have let me have it. But not you—no, yours is a patient anger, and very effective. Hers is not."

Lucy rolled her eyes. "Zoe told me the Ojibwe could laugh about very serious things. I guess she was right," and she smiled.

Phillip closed the door and returned to her. "You've been on your own most of your life, Lucy. Sometimes you forget about the feelings of others. You can't ignore the fact that we're all connected."

Lucy was aware of her breathing, how it had grown deeper and more rapid. Connections, that was the peripheral thing—and her anger?—it was directed inside. How stupid could a sixteen-year-old girl be?

"Listen, I don't know where this will end, but I have to try. If I don't, I'm absolutely certain that something very bad will happen. It's come to me more than once in my dreams—and it's more than a dream. It stays with me when I wake. It even haunts me during the day—as if expecting something. I ask Zoe questions, like you tell me to, and she answers in her own way. You help me to understand the answers. That's all fine. But this is between me, and something bigger. I can't say no—even if it seems irrational. I mean, don't you think I see that?"

"Yes, of course. And I told you I wouldn't try to interfere."

"Good. Because if I was a boy you wouldn't."

Phillip paused before answering. "Okay, you've got me there. And I would love you both equally. That's why I'm offering my help and support, if you'll accept it."

"I'll think about it."

"That's good enough . . . for now."

Lucy turned an angry expression toward him.

"I won't interfere, I promise," he said.

Lucy nodded and got up to leave. She paused at the door, "That's good, because I'm taking no chances. I'll give you nothing to know. Nothing to tell."

ZOE SAT BACK DOWN IN THE CHAIR. The darkened room was quiet. The hallway was quiet. Finally two people walked by, joking with each other, laughing—but Zoe remained silent, still thinking. They passed by unaware of the woman in the shadows as she listened to their voices grow distant, eventually disappearing into a stairwell.

She thought about calling the cops—maybe calling Ray. But she had no idea about the people she was dealing with except that it was more than this one guy. He had someone telling him what to do. All she knew, or thought she did, was that it had something to do with Sally. But they'd threatened Kaj—and that put a different spin on things, a very personal one. They knew where she was, and how to get at her. They'd know the same things about Kaj.

No, this was personal—and she'd handle it herself. If not, she and Kaj would always be looking over their shoulders. But just in case, she opened a pair of sterile gloves along with a scalpel and cut off a small chunk of hair where the man's blood had stuck to it. Then she put it in a plastic bag and stuffed it in her pocket—still considering her options.

"BETTY. A GIRL NAMED SALLY TAYLOR. You know her?"

"Goddamn it, Zoe. I'm not your pipeline."

"You know her, or not? And don't even think about lying to me."

Betty let out an exasperated breath. "Yes. I know her. So what?"

"Can you find her? Know where she lives, or with whom?"

"What is this?"

"She's sick. That's all I can say. I need to find her."

There was silence on the phone. Zoe waited it out.

"I don't know where she is, but I'll keep an eye out for her. If I see her, I'll let you know."

"Fair enough. Any idea of someone else I can ask?"

Silence again—and deep breathing. Finally, "Fuck! Okay, try my competition—Angie's. That's all I know. We run different sides of the trade. Try there. And do not tell them I sent you!"

Zoe hung up and looked at her notepad. She was well into the double digits on patients, with more coming in. She'd see to the critical patients first and then break for a moment to make another call.

"I GOT TO HER, BOSS. Message delivered. She agreed."

"That right? She agreed?"

"Yeah. No questions asked. She's really got the shakes over it."

"That right? Really? She's got the shakes over it?"

"Yeah, boss. It was easy."

The boss waited, just long enough for his man's pulse and blood pressure to rise, just long enough for it to cause his nose to start bleeding again.

"Then how'd you get that?" The boss pointed at the man's swollen nose—dripping blood.

"Ah, she didn't see the wisdom in my advice right at the get-go."

"So what are you saying? Does she have a broken nose, too?"

"No."

"Then why'd she do that? Or should I ask how'd she do that?"

"It was an accident. Her head bumped into my nose."

"Really? An accident? You got bumped into?"

He nodded while pinching his nose shut.

"You asshole! What did you do?"

"Nothing!"

The boss walked up close, and without warning threw a punch at the damaged nose.

"Ah! That hurts like hell!" the man said, but he made absolutely no move to defend himself.

"I'm going to ask you once more. What did you do to her?"

"Copped a feel, that's all! Innocent enough. I don't see why she'd complain. I was nice as hell otherwise."

The boss chuckled and turned away, thinking. Finally he said, "Okay, I suppose it might help to sell the point."

"How's Sally?" It was said with a nasal twang, still holding his nose.

"She tells me we have another problem."

"Like what?"

"As in there's more than one doctor we might have to worry about."

"How'd you get that out of her?"

"Let's put it this way, she's at the warehouse—recuperating. And she won't be able to work for a while. In fact, she won't be able to sit for a while."

The man with the broken nose chuckled. "Guess you did have the fun part."

The boss closed his eyes and smiled, "Exquisite." Then he turned back to face the man with the broken nose. "You know how to get around in that hospital? Ways to get in the ER without going through the front door?"

"Yeah, easy."

"Then get cleaned up. You've got another job to do, and this one's even more important." He closed in on the man's space, "Do not fuck it up."

BACK IN THE CAR, Lucy separated the gun from its clip and then hid both in her coat's lining—one on each side to balance things out. She drove to the place her dreams kept returning her to—Angie's—with an insight, and a vague plan, emboldened by her previous visit there with Zoe.

Lucy scanned the crowd as she walked in. She didn't recognize any faces—although she'd been half hoping to see the Traceur kid. She walked up to the bartender and pointed toward the "help wanted" sign. He reached under the bar and handed her an application form and a pen, then directed her to take a seat.

Lucy selected a spot against the back wall, but near the bar. She could see everyone who walked in, and hear everything that went on at the bar. When the server came over, Lucy asked for water.

"That all?"

"Yep. Just filling this out." Lucy pointed to her job application.

The server chuckled and leaned down toward her. "Where're you from?"

"Up north. The rez."

"Didn't I see you in here the other day? Talking to Josh with some lady?"

"Yeah. That's how I knew about the job—saw the sign. I was panhandling and she offered me a hot meal. The lady seemed nice enough, so I came along with her."

The server waited.

"Can I have that water now?"

"Be right back." The server hurried to the bar and whispered something to the bartender. He motioned toward the back where the server disappeared behind greasy curtains.

When the server reappeared with her water, Lucy said, "Maybe I would like a hamburger after all."

"Cheese?"

"Nope. Plain."

"Okay," she answered—but with a smile this time.

And Lucy thought, but didn't say, "Well, just look at you perk up."

Lucy was no longer the object of attention, just another customer—a paying one. She settled back into her seat with the confidence that having a gun in one's pocket afforded, and started filling out the form.

She noticed two women at the bar. One was an older woman—kind of rough around the edges and drinking something out of a shot glass. The other was young, two seats away, drinking coffee. They weren't talking to each other, but both looked distressed.

At another table a couple sat in silence, interrupting their lunch occasionally to tap into their cellphones. Neither spoke to each other. She wondered if that was really any better than her own parents' shouting matches followed by tearful apologies and drunken clinginess. She liked what Zoe and Kaj had. It wasn't perfect—Zoe was still tiptoeing around, but it was what she imagined real love to be, passionately connected without being consuming . . . alert, attentive, involved.

A lone man in the corner was watching her. Lucy swept her gaze across him as she surveyed the entire room—didn't stop on his face, didn't smile. She could feel his eyes stay with her, but she didn't want to feel self-conscious.

She continued writing, and finally looked directly at him in hopes of driving his gaze from her. It didn't work—he only smiled. Lucy felt her mouth involuntarily respond—it would be bad form not to. But she went immediately back to her writing and thought, but did not write, "Creepy."

There were three teenaged boys in colors at another table, loud and obnoxious—needing attention, and willing to do anything necessary to get it. They were purposefully crass, harassing of the server, and intending for every word they said to be heard by all the diners. They also wanted everyone in the diner to be just a little bit afraid of them. Lucy noticed the zone of avoidance— there was a ring of empty tables around the punks. She marveled at their idiocy— they really didn't get it, how stupid they looked.

At least they were a good distraction from Lucy, who had to make her water, hamburger, and scribbling last as long as possible—long enough to make certain observations. The bartender was not the one she'd talked to with Zoe and, for now, that was probably a good thing—but just in case, she'd offered a good explanation to the server that distanced herself from Zoe, who was a former cop. She watched him take care of the two women at the bar. Once when he was in the back, the server answered the phone up front and called to him. Apparently, his name was Mike.

The man in the corner was staring at her again—quizzically. He seemed to want to get her attention, raising a hand in a slight wave along with another smile. Lucy's lack of response, other than her raised eyebrows, seemed to discourage him. Should she know him? If so, she couldn't remember.

The two women at the bar rose to leave at exactly the same time, but only the older woman actually left. The other sat back down. It was at the same time the punks stopped their verbal jousting in obvious deference to the man who walked in. Lucy watched everyone's eyes turn toward the door.

There were a few things Lucy knew for certain, things you learn for yourself—or discover yourself, like you're part of the experiment. One was that a reputation for being a successful hothead was like an insurance policy—people tend not to want to test it. If you could make a solid case, you were good as gold.

Another was that some of these hotheads loved confrontation too much to pass up a chance—it didn't matter whether or not you wanted to test them, they'd find a way to maneuver you there anyway. While the young punks may have thought of themselves as occupying the center of the universe, this man knew that he did.

Lucy glanced around quickly. The man in the corner was paying attention. The young wannabe posers were silent, watching the man's every move—afraid, it was clear—and Lucy sort of got a kick out of that. The woman at the bar sat again—in silence.

The new arrival walked over to the bartender and whispered a question that Lucy couldn't hear. Mike, the bartender, raised both hands, palms up, as if to say, "I don't know."

Apparently that was the wrong answer. The man grabbed one of Mike's hands, turned it palm down, and pinned it to the counter. He squeezed it, and Mike just took it—just fucking took it. Lucy saw his face cringe in pain, but he didn't try to pull away. He simply endured it until the man released him. Then Mike pointed to Lucy.

ZOE HAD NO TIME FOR A LUNCH BREAK, but made the call anyway—while sitting on a toilet. Her source said he'd get back to her that afternoon. Zoe closed her phone and, with elbows on thighs, she leaned her head into her hands. Something didn't add up.

Zoe ran through the players—and the deaths, none of which might connect at all. A guy named Jeb, presumably a pimp—and Abel, who she really knew nothing about whatsoever. Then there was Christie, presumably a streetwalker, and Sally—likewise employed? The new guy, whose identity had yet to be determined—apparently linked to Sally, and then Wolf—linked to Christie?—or not? Finally there was Grace—linked to Wolf, as his mother, but neither wanting to acknowledge it, and then Betty—obviously in contact with streetwalkers, and somehow threatened—because of her connection to the streetwalkers?—or not?

Zoe heard the code blue alarm and darted out of the bathroom. The disembodied voice routed all responding personnel to the ER administrative offices. As the internal medicine resident on call, she was expected to be present at, and run if necessary, any codes. All she could think of on her way down the steps was Kaj—this was unusual, in fact she'd never once been called to a code in the ER. The ER was a world unto itself, handling anything and everything—competently. It had to be one of the staff, because ER personnel would handle a patient coding there more than ably, and certainly without help. But why would they move on Kaj? She'd promised to cooperate.

KAJ WAS COVERED IN BLOOD, a look of panic on his face unlike any she'd seen before. She almost didn't recognize the calm, controlled man she knew. In fact she'd only seen anything remotely resembling this expression on him when she, herself, had been covered in blood after tackling, subduing, and saving the life of a panicked stabbing victim. She ran toward him, ignoring the gathered crowd. It was only after she touched him, felt his face in her hands and realized that he was walking, alive, breathing—unhurt—that she allowed herself to look anywhere else. She followed the direction of his gaze—the reason for his look of panic. It was Connie, on the floor next to her desk—throat slit almost to the point of decapitation. No code blue would have saved her.

Zoe pulled closer as she heard the sirens scream to a stop outside the ER doors. Connie had been killed by a capable Someone—both carotid arteries severed. It was also a strong Someone—as she'd been fit and strong herself, despite the *Cosmo* cover illusion. He'd come at her from behind, that was obvious—the blood spray probably hadn't hit him. Zoe fingered the plastic bag in her pocket. She'd been surprised, like Connie, and this could easily have been her.

Zoe returned to Kaj—still holding both bloodied hands away from his body. She asked, "Tell me what happened."

He looked at her, as if seeing her for the first time. "None of us saw him go in. I found her—after she didn't respond to her pages. It was too late, nothing worked."

Nothing worked? Of course nothing worked. "Look at her," she wanted to say, but didn't. Even a millisecond after it happened would have been too late. Kaj was obviously in shock, and Zoe wondered just what he'd tried doing in order to save Connie.

"Why? Why would someone do this?" Kaj seemed to come to attention again. "We should check her patients, see if she had any run-ins—maybe there's a disgruntled patient on record."

Her cell phone sounded.

"Dr. Lawrence here."

"Got what you wanted. Name's Kurt—Kurt Wilson. Expect a text with his info in a second."

"Thanks, I owe you."

"No. But I don't owe you anymore," the woman chuckled.

THE MAN WALKED OVER TO LUCY'S TABLE, smiled, and sat across from her. He pointed to her hamburger and said, "On the house."

"Thanks."

Then he grabbed her half-filled job application, looked at it, tore it in two, and said, "No need for this, Lucy, you've got the job. You can start in back—bussing tables and dishwashing. If you're good, I'll move you up front."

"Thanks."

"What hours can you work?"

"Pretty much any hours, if I can plan ahead."

"You have a place to stay?"

Lucy hesitated—she hadn't thought about this. "No."

"I can help you with that, too."

This was happening too fast, Lucy thought—way too fast. "I think I might have a place for tonight. If I don't, I'll let you know. How do I get hold of you?"

He pointed at the bartender and server. "They know. Through them." He smiled, and so did Lucy. The man seemed to like that, because then he laughed and reached over the table to take her hand in his. Lucy tried not to cringe after seeing what he'd done to the bartender's hand, but instead, with her, he was tender. Lucy realized that if she were really still on the streets, he might have made her feel safe for a moment.

"What's your name?"

He nodded, "My name? It's Kurt."

RAY ARRIVED AFTER THE SQUAD.

"Here's a name and an address. Might be worth a look."

"Why?"

"This guy helped a patient of mine sign out AMA this morning. He was the driver. My patient was supposed to have seen Connie, but it worked out that I saw her instead."

"So?"

"My patient seemed pretty interested in seeing her. I just thought there might be a connection."

"Okay. We'll keep it in mind. First I have to interview all these worthless witnesses. Did you see anything?"

"No. I got here late. Sorry."

He turned to walk away, but Zoe gabbed his arm. "Here, take this, too."

"What is it?"

"A guy jumped me earlier in one of the basement hallways. I head-butted him. He had me from behind—couldn't see his face, but I'm pretty sure I broke his nose. His blood was in my hair," she pointed to the plastic bag in his hand, and wondered if it would turn out to be Kurt Wilson's blood.

"What?"

"Yeah, might be the same guy. Probably is, I suppose."

"Yeah, probably. What the hell happened?"

"Like I said, I head-butted him and he ran off."

Ray stared at her.

"What?"

"Zoe, what the hell? You mean this could have been you?"

"I suppose."

"Why? What did he want?"

"Don't know, crazy I suppose."

"Why didn't you tell anyone?"

Zoe hadn't yet asked herself that same question. Maybe it would've saved Connie. "You know me. I scared him off, I was busy, figured I'd deal with it later."

He still stared.

"Lame, I know."

"God, Zoe."

"I know."

"Take a seat, I'm interviewing you, too."

"Can't it wait? I've got so freaking much to do, and you know where to find me. Besides, I've given you the most important clue you're likely to get," and once again she pointed to the plastic bag, "I really don't know much else. Check it out—and the name, check that out, too."

Ray sucked in a long, hard breath, "Okay. We'll run this and I'll talk to you later, after I finish up with all these people."

ZOE HEARD THE SHOWER STOP and rapped gently on the door to the on-call bathroom.

"Yeah?"

"It's me."

"Come in."

Zoe pushed the door open. Kaj was toweling off—the blood gone, a frustrated, impatient expression left in its place.

"I'm sorry," Zoe said.

"I just don't understand it."

"Neither do I." But even as Zoe said it, she knew that only a day ago she would have liked to see Dr. Fucking Pink dead. "I am sorry," she said again, trying to convince both Kaj and herself.

"... And how did he get in with a knife?"

"They say he copped a scalpel off a cart."

Kaj pulled on a fresh pair of scrubs.

"So that's another thing we need to address." His face reddened, "I'm in charge here and it's my goddamned fault this could happen in the first place. I never anticipated it."

Zoe knew better than to argue. It was partly true. But she did add, "And it's partly security's fault—and partly a lack of everyone's imagination," and maybe even Zoe's fault, she realized. "You've sat through countless meetings where ER security has been addressed, haven't you?"

"Of course, but ..."

"But it's partly your fault. I agree."

He only nodded. In lieu of a comb, he ran his hands through wet hair while a sad smile made its way onto his face. "She was a good person. We lost a very good person today."

"Tell me about her."

"She was a good doc." He ran his hand along her face. "Almost as good as you. Competent, very competent—and caring."

Zoe hadn't detected the caring part. But the competence she didn't doubt. Kaj was a good judge of that quality.

They both looked toward the police, the crime scene tape, and the techs. Kaj kissed her and turned to leave, "The ER needs to keep functioning, and someone has to be in charge of it."

"Angie's."

It was a peppy, carefree, female voice—probably a server. Couldn't be a cook—in Zoe's experience cooks were either morose, depressed, loners or hyperactive, jittery, and ambitious. Certainly wouldn't call them peppy—or carefree.

"Can I speak to the bartender, please?"

"Sure," she heard the peppy voice call out, "Hey, Mike!"

Zoe asked after a woman named Sally Taylor and got no recognition at all. She hung up.

There'd been no time for lunch, and now no time for dinner. Instead she grabbed an Ensure from a nurse's station fridge and dropped a few quarters into a machine for a salted nut roll. From there she rendezvoused with her team in the sign-out room off the CCU. She readied her pen and paper to accept everyone's patients for the night. Taking fast notes, she ate as she listened. And when all the outgoing residents were through describing each patient and their condition, she divvied them up between her two interns and readied to gather in new ones through the ER.

A call came in right away. She grabbed one of the interns and said, "You— with me. You're up first. Let's go see this lady."

"Can you start right now?"

"Yes."

He kept her hand in his as he led her to the back. The cook's head turned from his work. "New help?" He was grinning.

"Shut up." Lucy felt Kurt's hand squeeze a little tighter as he said the words, and saw the cook's grin disappear.

Her feet slid on the greasy floor as they walked and his grasp of Lucy's hand kept her upright. "We'll probably have you work on these floors. Right, Gary?"

Gary—apparently the cook—said, "Yeah, boss."

But Gary wasn't doing much cooking. Instead he was placing a frozen pizza in a small oven.

Kurt shook his head apologetically, "They're not all frozen. We have a few specialties, and if you're smart, they're what you order here. Problem is, we only have two cooks who know how to make them. When Gary, here, covers . . . everything's frozen."

"You're not the cook?" she asked.

Gary grinned, "Not officially, no."

"What are the specialties?"

Gary answered. "Best one is Doyle's Habit. After that, it's a toss-up between Sherry's Last Meal and the Down Low Revenge. But, hey, we do great hamburgers, and anything deep-fried turns out pretty good, too. Mostly we make our drinks strong enough that no one cares."

Kurt hadn't asked her age. But then again, he hadn't wanted her to finish the application form either. Lucy decided that she'd better be interested enough to ask. "How much will I get paid?"

Kurt stopped. He turned her hand over in his, admiring it. "How does five dollars an hour sound to start with?"

"Sounds good."

"Cash."

"Okay. I wouldn't know what to do with anything else."

He smiled and released her hand. "That's what I thought. And if you work out, you'll be getting raises . . . and perks. You know what perks are?"

"No."

"You'll find out. You'll like 'em. Now, let's go downstairs and find you a uniform."

ZOE PUT HER FEET UP ON THE DESK. The nurse sitting next to her only shook her head.

"Ripe, I know. But it's been," she looked at the clock, "only fifteen hours since I put them on. Consider yourself lucky."

The nurse's only acknowledgment was another shake of the head.

Zoe pressed on, "I need to get 'em up, okay?"

"Well, how about the call room? That's what it's for." The nurse emphasized that last point.

There were rumors about Zoe and Kaj in the call rooms, but Zoe didn't bite. "Are you kidding? I'm working, here. And if I do go in there, you'll just call me anyway." Zoe looked up from her notes. "Am I right?"

The nurse grinned.

Zoe reinforced her argument, "Price you pay, bitch."

The nurse's grin grew wider.

LUCY HUNG HER COAT IN THE CLOSET and tried on three different uniforms before she found one that fit—well, sort of. She still had the body of a twelve-year-old boy. The neckline was too low, and she had nothing to hold it in place. She practiced bending forward, and decided that she'd better avoid that if possible.

Kurt waited outside the closet door. When she emerged, he insisted she go first, his hands around her hips, playfully guiding her up the stairs to the kitchen. He paused at the top, saying, "You look nice," and ran his hand along her cheek. "Let me know if you need a place to stay."

Okay." Lucy thought fast. "But what if it's in the middle of the night? What if they're not open here?"

Grinning at the small, sixteen-year-old girl before him, he said, "Okay, here's my number," and held out a card. Pointing to the number that had "fax" next to it, he added, "Use that one. It's my personal cell."

"Thanks."

"I need to get home for a while, but since we need someone right now, tonight—Gary will break you in." He left her standing next to the not-quite cook, but turned before exiting through the greasy curtain. "Maybe I'll see you later."

ALTHOUGH KURT'S HOME WAS A NICE ONE, it was not where he spent most of his time—and still, they'd found him there. A police officer stood at the front door of the home where his wife and kids lived. How and why had they found him? He had to remind himself to think about that later—be pissed later. Not now, not in front of a cop. He didn't need more trouble right now.

But later—trouble was something he could handle, even if it was with a cop. He'd killed one before—ambush-style. A revenge killing that conveniently ridded himself of the dirty cop who thought Kurt could be blackmailed. The problem with something like that was that once you did it, you wanted word to get around—but only to the right people. Then no one would ever think of pulling a stunt like that again. If word got to the wrong people, you'd be dogged. It was a tricky business. And still, he'd managed to pull it off.

He had a reputation—one artfully cultivated. Kurt was badass crazy, capable of anything, and everyone who needed to know it, did. The kind of guy you didn't even look at, let alone know what he was up to. If you knew, you were a potential liability to him—and that just wasn't healthy. If he didn't have a problem killing a cop, then everyone ought to be afraid. And they were—to the point of keeping his secrets, to the point of not knowing him if asked. No one wanted to get involved. And he'd left a trail of murdered witnesses to prove it. The cops wouldn't know, but everyone else would.

Abel was proof. The minute he turned up dead, everyone was aware of Kurt's wrath. He'd left his calling card there, a tag, on a tree—an abstract skeletal head image, probably considered by most to be a gang symbol—something only the right people were aware of.

But for the moment, he had to stuff his anger—and greet the fucking cop. Wrong attitude, Kurt, he told himself. Breathe and everything changes. He did. He took in a deep breath, and opened the door.

"Hello, can I help you with something?"

"Nice neighborhood."

"Yeah, quiet and all. What's up?"

"A lady was murdered today. Just checking out persons of interest."

This didn't look good. What in the hell had he been thinking?—giving a ride to a streetwalker and signing her out AMA from the hospital. If this were a good cop, he'd be asking that very question.

But the cop didn't ask that question; instead he asked where Kurt had been that afternoon—which was easy to answer.

He sized up the cop. Guy was clearly a rookie, probably sent to do the last-on-the-list tasks. Clean up loose ends. No one expected anything from this visit, or they wouldn't have sent this punk. He was too green for Kurt to even bother with altering his demeanor—no need to fit the occasion. Normally, when people see a cop fill their doorframe, even when they haven't done a damn thing wrong in their lives, they still feel like they did. They get scared. They maybe even think back to stupid things they did when they were kids, and get ready to cop to them.

Instead, Kurt simply informed him that he'd been at his place of employment. It was his business, one he owned—Angie's. And the cop didn't even ask for a contact, someone who could verify his story. Instead he simply said, "Been there once. Had some pizza."

"Yeah? What's your favorite?"

"Can't say that I have one."

Kurt couldn't help it—he smiled. It was habit to give anyone identified as a cop the pizza that tasted like cardboard—it tended to keep the riffraff out. "So, why the question? How does my name come up in all this?" It was important to wonder, and in reality, Kurt needed to know.

"Just running down license plates."

"Where did this happen? I mean, I'm wondering why my license plate comes up?"

"At the hospital."

"Oh, that explains it. I helped a friend of a friend get home from the hospital this morning. But I was out of there well before noon."

"Okay, then. That pretty much clears it up. Sorry to bother you."

"No big deal. Hope you find the guy you're looking for."

Kurt closed the door. He didn't have to wonder anymore about how his name had come up—or in association with what crime. There were a few to choose from at the moment, but in this case, it was that bitch doctor—and that bitch Sally.

But the cop was too dumb to ask the question about his visit to the hospital earlier. Or maybe he didn't know about it. Maybe he'd just been given a license plate to track down. In any event, the rookie had been so locked in on the murder that he wasn't connecting the dots—and Kurt figured the nice neighborhood had made his alibi one the cop didn't need to verify. Solid citizens lived in this neighborhood. The cop for one—he'd probably grown up in a neighborhood like this. He probably viewed his people as the standard—the ones you trust. Had to be, because if the cop had grown up around Kurt's childhood haunts, he'd have known not to trust anyone.

It didn't matter anyway. Kurt had people. They were like offshoots of him. They did his dirty work—except for the dirty work that Kurt liked—and they'd lie for him, no questions asked. Every employee at Angie's would swear that he'd been there all day of any day, if asked. Every person, now that Josh was in the river.

As the evening wore on, Lucy noticed that most of the patrons must have figured out who was working the kitchen. Occasionally someone would make the mistake of ordering a pizza—after which Lucy would wind up discarding most of it, uneaten, before she washed the dish. But mostly, Gary was deep-frying things. He would mumble a lot and curse under his breath as each order came through—acting like it was beneath him to cook.

Lucy said nothing to him. She only kept working. Scrubbing floors meant she had to bend over a lot, and she continuously caught Gary's eyes on her chest. But he didn't make a move—which kind of mystified her. From her time on the streets she was familiar with that look, and she'd managed to avoid guys like him at all costs—even to the point of sharing a doghouse with a Newfoundland during a particularly cold stretch one winter. That dog was better than selling her body. Even though the dog slobbered like crazy, he also generated a lot of heat. Right now, Gary looked like a Newfoundland.

The floors weren't coming clean, and probably hadn't been deep cleaned in years. She found herself looking forward to breaks when she could wash dishes. At least she accomplished something there. Finally, Gary asked her if she needed an actual break and offered her some food. He pointed to a stool and poured her a Coke. They sat together at the prep counter and shared an order of deep fried chicken with fries.

"Got sent back. Wrong order," he laughed.

"Oh." And Lucy figured they got at least one wrong order every night around this time. But if she were Gary, she wouldn't want to fuck with Kurt.

She let Gary do all the talking. Thankfully he didn't ask many questions. Instead, Gary liked to complain.

ZOE USED HER NEXT BATHROOM BREAK to make the call again. This time she got the bartender on duty directly. It wasn't Josh. And according to "Mike," Josh didn't work there anymore.

SO, THE PROBLEM WAS FIXED. He'd boiled the rumors down to two doctors and a homeless guy. The homeless guy had been easy to track. The doc who'd come in questioning Josh had led right to him. And according to Josh, that doc was clueless—she didn't know anything. In fact, she was looking for Christie, which meant that she didn't know where Christie was. She knew squat. But she'd been curious enough to require the threats—warning her away.

The second doc was a little harder, but Sally had been a big help there. And as far as she knew, it had just been that doc and the homeless guy. That was the extent of the interference—a doc and a homeless guy. And now they were gone. Kurt was good at keeping things tight. No clutter in his life, or in his business. No loose ends. No more disappearing merchandise.

Still, he wondered about the second doc. The one called Zoe. According to Gary, she'd been scared shitless. But she was a loose end. And if she made one wrong move, even one, he'd forget about her boyfriend or her house. He'd go directly for her. A disappearance, just like he'd considered. But two docs, that was a stretch—one that might attract too much attention. So he was willing to go with the threats . . . for now.

LUCY HEARD MIKE SAY INTO THE PHONE that Josh didn't work there anymore. That made her breathe a little easier. He might have ratted her out if he didn't buy her story. Better this way. Kind of funny though—seeing as how he'd liked working there so much.

JEB GETTING KILLED WAS STILL A MYSTERY to Kurt. Of course it might have been someone dumb enough to think they could compete—but more than likely it was some business of Jeb's. Some shit he got caught up in. Which was to say—they'd saved Kurt the trouble.

Yet in theory, it was still a loose end, too—and everyone who knew Kurt would know he hadn't killed him. Now of course there were pros and cons to that. The upside was that he didn't have any problems with the cops over it—after all, he hadn't killed Jeb and hadn't even been there when it happened.

The downside was, and everyone would know this too, that leaving the body right outside Kurt's business establishment could be interpreted as a message—a warning of some kind. Yet there'd been nothing expected of him in response—no one had come forward with any ultimatums or threats. But since Kurt couldn't let the world know that, he might be perceived as vulnerable.

When Kurt balanced the pros and cons, he decided that Jeb's death was a windfall. If Jeb really had gotten involved in something outside Kurt's sphere of influence then it was simple enough—he needed to die anyway.

JOSH HAD GIVEN IT UP TOO EASY. It hit Lucy like lightning. Sure, they'd worked Josh pretty hard, but from what she'd seen of Kurt, she didn't think Josh's drug history would have offended him all that much. No—it seemed that Josh was afraid. And after seeing this hothead Kurt in action, being afraid was very believable. So why would he want a job working for Kurt? But he had mysteriously wanted the shit job, or so he'd said—so why had he left it?

Something else occurred to her—lightning striking twice. Where was he?

"Gary, is there a phone I can use?"

"Sure, over there." He pointed to a wall phone. Close by—she'd have to whisper.

"Zoe. You got a minute?"

"No, but it's yours anyway." Zoe took long strides down a hallway leading to the dialysis unit.

"Okay, I'll be quick. Remember that bartender? Josh?"

"Yeah. Funny thing. I was just thinking about him."

"Me, too. And you know what? I've got a question about him. He said he'd never been in prison, right?"

"Yep."

"Made me wonder why."

Zoe was silent—she stopped walking. "Shit," was all she could manage to say.

"Yeah, that's what I was thinking, too. I mean, remember, he knew who you were—and Angie's isn't exactly a cop hangout."

"Yeah, it's not." Zoe thought some more, then asked "But how did you know it wasn't a cop hang-out?"

"My time on the streets, Zoe. You underestimate me."

Zoe laughed. "Not anymore. I'll call Ray and see if they had anything going with the guy. That sort of stuff is held pretty close to the vest, though. Usually just the cop working him would know about it. Ray probably won't have a clue. But maybe he can find out. What got you thinking about Josh?"

"Don't know. Just happened."

Zoe called Ray. As predicted he didn't know anything about Josh.

"Can you find out?"

"I'm pretty busy, Zoe. Got a fresh homicide on my hands, as you know."

"Please, for me."

"I'll ask around."

"What about that other name I gave you?"

"Hang on, I'll look."

Zoe heard papers rustling in the background. She continued with her own charting while Ray scanned the reports. Finally he came back on.

"Says here they found him at his home in Edina. He was cooperative. Apparently he was at his place of business during the time in question. Said he had helped a friend of a friend earlier in the day—placing him at the hospital in the morning. But he was at work when the doc was killed."

"And?"

"And what?"

"Did they verify it?"

"Let me see." There was more paper noise. "Well, I don't see here that he made any note of where the guy worked—so I guess not. We'll have to follow up on that."

"Do it now. Call his sorry ass in and teach him the proper way to track down a lead."

"Zoe, do I tell you how to take care of your patients?"

"No. But that's because I do it right. Your guy isn't doing it right."

"It's late. I'll do it myself. Okay with you?"

"Yeah, but if I were you, I'd still want a piece of his ass in the morning."

"Don't worry, that'll happen."

"Call me back, will you?"

"Sure. Later."

GARY CALLED KURT.

"I heard her. She was saying something about Josh."

"What?"

"I couldn't hear most of it, she was like . . . whispering."

"Well what did you hear?"

"Just his name and . . . something about prison."

Kurt ran the possibilities through his head—there were a couple that made sense. In one scenario, the new girl might live—in the other, Lucy wouldn't make it through the damn night.

"All right, you know what to do."

"I'll get everything ready, boss."

"I'll be there in twenty. Don't let her go."

As things wound down, Lucy felt nervous about the hour. "When do I get off?"

"Not yet. Boss says he wants to treat you to dinner. I told him you were one of the best new hires we've had in a long time, so he wants to show his gratitude—only does that with the best. You should be proud."

Lucy looked at the clock. "I am, I guess." But it seemed pretty weird that what she'd done was all that great. "It's just that, you know, if I'm gonna score that place to stay tonight, I'd better get going soon."

"Don't worry. The boss said he'd be here in a few minutes."

"Okay, I suppose."

"Why don't you sit down and get started? He placed a meal and soft drink at a table in the room behind the kitchen. "It's on the house. Boss'll be here in person to thank you. Bet he'll even give you a ride if you need one."

"No. That's okay." Lucy thought about Pushpa's car, waiting for her outside. She couldn't let them see her get into it when she left. It would blow her cover as a homeless kid from the rez—a kid who might need to do awful things in order to survive. And right now, that's what they made her as. "It's not far. I'd rather walk."

He shot her a look, and then said, "Suit yourself, but the boss can be very helpful. Sit. Eat."

Lucy started on the meal—fast, washing down large bites by gulping soda. She had to get home soon or someone might wonder where she was—unless they didn't notice her absence until morning. That was possible, after all—she lived with a bunch of old people who went to bed early. Besides, she'd carved the evening off and okayed it with Sara.

Kurt filled the doorframe—big and smiling. "I see you got my gift. It's one of those perks I told you about. Remember?"

Lucy nodded, but she couldn't find the word to go along with it. Such a simple word—yes—wasn't available to her. Instead "no" kept running through her brain. But she couldn't say that either.

He sat across from her at the table and reached for her hand.

LUCY WOKE UP IN A BEDROOM—no, it wasn't a bedroom. It was just a room with a bed. It was damp and chilly, perhaps the basement—where she'd changed into the uniform. She didn't feel like moving, but her mind was starting to kick in and she tried to recollect the events leading to her presence in this room.

There was a meal, and a man—a man who'd bought her a full meal. She remembered the man—the hothead man, Kurt—sitting down at the table, uninvited, talking about perks. They'd drugged her, she realized—and she could remember nothing else. No, wait. She did. She recalled talking to Zoe—and she remembered the gun. Being in the basement meant it wasn't far. But noises outside the door meant that no matter the distance, at that moment, her gun was too far.

"Damn it!" She'd become part of the experiment again—no longer the observer. "Shit," she scanned the room. There were no windows. And though it was very dark, light through cracks around the doorframe afforded something to see by.

The sounds outside her door became footsteps, and then the door opened.

ZOE GOT THE CALL FROM RAY.

"Your guy? He owns Angie's."

"What?"

"You heard me. Legit businessman. But Josh?—turns out he was an informant, a scared-shit one, and not all that good at it, apparently. Narcotics cut him loose. But you're right about prison. He worked a deal that kept him out. And when he Larry, Moe, and Curly'd everything, his guy in narcotics took pity—let him go. No telling where he's off to."

"But was he at Angie's for a reason? Or was it a legit job?"

"Not sure. But apparently after he took on there his information dried up anyway. He was useless. And he was either going to get himself killed or burn the cover—maybe both. So it was felt best to cut him loose."

"Doesn't it bother you that so much intersects at Angie's? I mean the murder, and this Kurt Wilson guy?"

"Well, yeah, of course. But what do we have, exactly?"

"At least check out Kurt's alibi. Pay a visit to Angie's."

"I was planning on it. Tomorrow."

"Guess it'll have to do."

But Zoe hung up the phone—wondering.

KURT SAT DOWN NEXT TO HER ON THE BED. "You got pretty sick." He petted her forehead. "Since we didn't know where you were staying we took care of you here."

"I'm better now. Ready to go."

"I couldn't possibly let you go in this condition—and it's the middle of the night. No, I'd rather you spend what's left of the night here. We'll look after you."

"It's okay, really. I'm fine now." She tried to move, but her head swam with the effort.

He grabbed her, cradling her next to him. "See what I mean? You're staying here. I'll be with you all night. You're safe here with us."

Lucy said nothing. She breathed in his scent, looked toward the damp walls, and finally asked, "Then can I just go to sleep, please?"

He looked right through her. Lucy was sure he knew exactly what she was doing. It was more than unsettling. Her stomach rock-tumbled, and she hiccupped.

He chuckled. "Is there someone we can call?"

"No. I don't have anyone."

"But Gary said you'd made a call earlier."

"Just a girlfriend. Someone I met."

"Well, then you do have someone who knows where you are."

"No. She doesn't."

"But Gary said you mentioned Josh's name."

So that was it. That's what had brought this on. Her mind was waking up. "Yeah. A few days ago I was in here with her—we saw Josh and thought he was so cute. I called to tell her that he didn't work here anymore. She was pretty disappointed."

"Yeah, too bad he quit. Guy like that brings in the ladies. Did you tell her you got a job here?"

"No."

"What about prison? You mentioned prison. You think that's where Josh is now?" he grinned.

"No. I just told her it was pointless anyway, because they lock guys up in prison for making moves on girls our age."

Kurt only stared.

Lucy added, "It was a joke."

Kurt didn't laugh. But he did smile. "Well, that's a good one. Now, since you have no one to look after you I took the liberty of talking to a doctor and he recommended that we give you this. It's some medicine that will help you feel better."

"I don't really need anything. I'm feeling a lot better already. But if I could just sleep, it would be great. I'd pay you back later, when I feel better."

Kurt smiled again, "Oh, yes. You will indeed. But you'll also take this medication. Look familiar?"

Lucy looked at the small vial—a white top. She wasn't sure what color they were in this neighborhood, but she did recognize its contents. "No. I've never seen anything like that before."

"Gary?" Kurt shouted from the bed. "Come in and help me with this."

***

ZOE KEPT WONDERING, even as she admitted another patient—diabetic coma, so there wasn't anything to talk about, it was all examination and lab results and she could do it in her sleep. There were things that didn't make sense. What had Betty said? She ran the other side of the trade? What did that mean? She'd referred to Angie's as her competition.

Okay, so what did she know about Betty's? It wasn't a cop hangout either. No different than Angie's in that respect. It was a place a cop could find an occasional friendly contact among the working girls. But that was all.

She remembered Josh's statement after he'd said he recognized her—something about cops hanging out at Angie's. Lucy was right—and that was all wrong. She should have latched on to it right away. Josh had already started dancing, making shit up.

But so what? He'd just let something slip, about having contacts with cops, so he was hiding his trail. No big deal there. He was inept, like Ray had said.

Back to Betty—she knew Jeb. She knew he'd been killed, too, even before the cops knew who he was. But that was probably because of the girls who hung out there. Betty had a direct pipeline into their world.

The patient's cardiac monitor alarmed and Zoe refocused everything on his rapid rhythm.

LUCY FELT AMAZING. She'd never felt this way before—this good. She didn't want it to go away. But it was. It was falling away fast.

She shivered under the blanket and thought about her parents. Of course they would come to mind at a time like this—a time when she'd just experienced what they had, what had driven them into crime, into neglect of their daughter, and full-tilt toward their deaths. She'd watched it all, telling herself that she must never, ever try it—because, after all, she might like it. And now she knew.

He was sitting on a chair in the corner and smiled when she looked his way, knowing, too—maybe even expecting gratitude.

But her stare was as cold as the draft along the floor.

Lucy knew a few other things—for certain. It was about control. Drugs were a lazy way to control people, but they were very effective—more so than fear of violence. How else to explain the walking dead? How else to explain the streetwalkers—let loose on the street only to return voluntarily for more? But the two together—violence and drugs—that was a powerful mixture.

She also knew that men like Kurt weren't immune from being controlled themselves—even by people like Lucy, underlings, people without power. All one had to do was to threaten someone they cared about. The problem with this particular guy was—and Lucy was pretty sure about this, too—he didn't care about anyone.

His face came clearly into focus, and she remembered looking at him from across the table at Angie's. His cheeks were pockmarked, his forehead sweaty. He had a nervous habit of touching his thumb to all his other fingers, over and over again—it reminded her of Walt and his obsessive tics. Whenever she looked Walt in the eyes he would look away—it made him uncomfortable. But this guy—when she looked at him it was as if her own face was mirrored back. He was almost like a pattern-changing chameleon, giving her the look she needed, the one she wanted to see.

But it was when she showed fear that he didn't seem to have an answer for her. He seemed to lack all sense of empathy with her terror. And she was showing fear by then—no doubt. Lucy gripped the bed sheet to calm her tremor. But her chin was still shaking.

She involuntarily gasped when the realization hit her—that she needn't fear what was there, but rather, what wasn't. This man would cast no shadow—a shadow depended on light . . . and substance. But he was empty. Perhaps that was what pure evil was.

He stood, walked slowly toward her, grabbed at her uniform—ripping it off in two pieces—and then turned her over, pulling down her underpants. Lucy was momentarily stunned into inaction, but her thoughts were racing even as she let her body follow his lead.

He wanted an excuse to beat her into submission, to demonstrate his power over her, she was sure of it. She'd known people like this—a man like this had killed her parents. One wrong move and she'd be spitting blood and rearranging her nose—and that would only be the least of it.

If she didn't resist, she'd be raped.

No, that was all wrong, too. It wouldn't matter whether she resisted or not, she'd be raped anyway. The only question was—would she have a broken nose and missing teeth afterward?

But by not resisting, at least she still had the use of her hands—he wasn't considering her a threat. Yes, she'd shown fear, as she should. He'd want it that way. It would be how he'd expect to control her. But resisting or not resisting—either choice would end badly.

She was facedown on the bed and still had her hands free—so even as he lifted her hips to his, she made secret use of them. Thank God for the meal, she thought, as she shoved a fist down her throat . . . and vomited.

Kurt shoved her away with an impatient curse. "Bitch!"

Lucy made sure to fall into the vomit, creating a barrier between her and the man. In her attempt to crawl away from him she rolled in it. There wasn't a place she could be touched that wasn't corrupted by the return of a "perk."

THE PATIENT WAS TUCKED IN AND STABLE. After a brief code induced by the man's electrolyte imbalance, all was well. She made her way down the stairwell, ready to pick up another patient. Kaj was just leaving.

"Long day," she said.

"Yes, and I'm still not done. There's a lot to deal with after what happened down here. None of us have had even a moment to grieve her loss."

Zoe reached around him and he pulled her into his arms.

"I'm sorry," Zoe said.

He pulled back, looked at her face, and said, "And you're a beautiful sight for these tired eyes."

"I'm on all night. Wish I could be with you."

"Likewise. Until tomorrow night, then?"

They kissed—his hands wrapped in her hair, hers resting at his waist.

LUCY REMAINED WHERE SHE'D FALLEN, shivering in her own vomit.

"I could kill you." He walked around the bed, smiling at her attempt to keep the vomit between them. "No one will miss you."

"Yes, yes they will. I lied. There are people who'll miss me. If I'm not back by morning, they'll come looking."

His smile didn't fade. In fact he seemed even more amused. "No. If that were the case, you wouldn't have come here in the first place. You're desperate, on the street, and you have no one."

"No, I do! You can check."

"Babe, you knew exactly what you were walking into. You wanted it. You wanted a way off the street. I won't be wasting time on any of your lies."

"No. I was lying before. But not now."

"Let me see … which lie makes more sense?" He weighed his hands, palms up. "A lie that gave up a good life in exchange for this," he looked around the room, "or the one you think is going to save your ass right now?"

Lucy said nothing. It was clear.

"Right. You see my situation, here, don't you?"

Lucy nodded—and started lying like crazy. "Yeah, I figured I might get work with you. But I would've been willing. Why'd you have to go and do that to me?"

He grinned. "Okay, so now we're getting somewhere."

He walked back to his chair and sat down—staring at her.

Lucy shivered. She was naked and cold—the liquid part of her vomit evaporating. She angled to pull a blanket over her and he shifted in his seat. His eyebrows went up and he shook his head slowly from side to side—only once.

Pam Leonard

Lucy dropped the blanket and let her head fall back on the pillow. When he didn't move, she closed her eyes, thinking, and waiting—for him to move or to say something. But neither happened, and she willed herself to take deep breaths and stay calm. The gun, she thought—and Pushpa's keys.

CHAPTER NINE

I T WAS 4:00 A.M., THE TIME WHEN ZOE'S BODY STARTED doing strange things—like shiver uncontrollably, and nod off. But there were still new admits she hadn't even seen yet. Her interns were babysitting until she could get around to them. She jogged down the quiet hallway, her sneakers squeaking, and came to a stop at the next patient. The man was asleep, so she ran through everything with the intern, looked at the notes and lab results, and then signed off on a job well done.

The next patient was one floor up, the other intern waiting for her. He looked impatient.

Zoe shot him a look. "What? You think you're getting some sleep tonight?"

"Yeah."

"Idiot."

"Well anyway, this idiot just admitted a train wreck. You can thank me now, or put my name in for a medal later. Both would be good, actually."

"How bad?"

"Exacerbation of chronic liver disease."

Zoe scanned the notes, and then looked up in admiration. "Maybe you do deserve a medal after all. Nice work. I guess I'm finally getting through to you guys."

He liked getting stroked. In fact, to hell with sleep, it looked like he might just prefer to stand there all night—if only she'd keep telling him how great he was.

But that wasn't going to happen.

"We'll go over what you fucked up on tomorrow—but it's not too bad. Definitely could have been worse. Now go get some sleep. 8:00 A.M.—be done with breakfast and meet me in the conference room. That is, unless we get another admit between now and then. And if so, you will be perkier than hell and show up in a fucking good mood."

"But . . ."

"You don't want to know right now. I said you didn't fuck up too bad—overall, a pretty good job. Save it for tomorrow. And I promise not to embarrass you in front of the attending."

He didn't move.

"Bed."

He left. Zoe stayed to sign off on the patient and change a few orders.

As Zoe wrote her brief note, her mind played one of its early morning tricks. An imaginative leap she might not have made had she been more focused.

Betty had a pipeline. Yeah, okay, so what? She got info from the girls. So what? To what end? And why should she feel threatened at all? Why should someone threaten her? Information. She knew something. Something she still hadn't shared. And it had to do with Angie's.

Okay. The other side of the trade—it had to mean the girls felt safe with her. Which meant they didn't feel safe at Angie's. Which meant . . .

"Shit."

"I COULD KILL YOU. Make sense now?"

Lucy nodded.

"What do you think I should do with you?"

"Let me work."

"How hard?"

"Hard as hell. I'm young. They like 'em that way."

"Sounds like you've had experience."

"No."

"No?"

"I've never done it before."

"You mean never whored, or never had sex?"

"Both."

He seemed to consider this, then pointed at the vomit. "That just might have been our lucky break."

Lucy said nothing.

"And you might be worth a lot more to me than I thought." He got up and went to the door, "Gary, get in here. Clean her up," he looked back at Lucy, "then we'll get her seen."

Gary came in holding a towel, soap, and shampoo.

"Watch her—closely."

"That's not a problem, boss," he grinned.

A Newfoundland, Lucy thought, again—slobber and all.

"Watch, only. Do not touch. She's worth a lot the way she is."

"Got it, boss." But he looked at Lucy and said, "Still gonna be fun."

ZOE CALLED BETTY.

"What the hell, Zoe? It's too early for this shit!"

"Do you know a doctor named Connie Sayre?"

"Why?"

"Just answer the fucking question!"

"Maybe I've heard of her. Yeah, I think she was in the diner once or twice."

"Why? Why was she in the diner?"

"How the hell should I know?"

"Well, then, tell me what she did when she was there?"

"She ate!"

"Wiseass. Did she talk to anyone? Or meet anyone?"

"Aw, fuck. She talked to Sally, okay?"

"Sally Taylor?"

"None other."

"That's a lie."

"She did!"

"I mean the 'none other' part."

"Okay, so maybe she talked to Christie, too."

"How long has she been doing this?"

"Maybe a couple months."

"Who did it before her?"

"I don't know if anyone did. I just don't know, okay?"

"What did they talk about?"

"What do you think? Their STDs, their injuries, the unwanted pregnancies—that kind of stuff."

"What about drugs?"

"Yeah, she delivered on that. Sometimes it was antibiotics, sometimes pain meds, but I think some of them were scamming her for painkillers—at the direction of certain individuals, if you know what I mean. These girls get used in more ways than one."

"The girls—so they're cleaned up and get a clean bill of health?"

"I suppose you could say that—as much as possible, anyway. Some of them have pretty nasty diseases, though. A couple girls showed proof of HIV and Hepatitis C—never saw them again. But some of the others, they disappear, too."

"Betty, Connie's dead."

GARY, STIFF AS HE WAS, DIDN'T MAKE A MOVE—except to jack off in front of her. Even so, Lucy ignored him—just as she'd ignored more flashers than she could remember. What she needed was time to think, to plan for contingencies—with a gun, and without, because she had no idea if she could get it back. It was in the basement—the closet where she'd changed clothes. But would they let her anywhere near the closet, let alone allow her to keep her coat?

SO CONNIE HAD BEEN INVOLVED. But how—whose side was she on? Was she on retainer with the pimps? Was she just a bleeding heart asshole who actually thought she could make a difference—take pity on the working girls and put Band-Aids on their owies?

She works them up for communicable diseases, after which the girls disappear? What in the hell was with that?

. . . And fucking Betty—she'd known more.

But Jeb was dead. And still people were dying. There was another character at work in all of this—connected to the guy who'd threatened her. A guy she couldn't make—hadn't seen. And the only tangible lead she had was this Kurt Wilson dude—a guy with an alibi. A name she'd already given to the cops, but maybe shouldn't have—a guy who might have been the one who wanted her warned off. Once again she worried about Kaj, and about what in the hell she could do about any of this.

GARY WRAPPED HER IN A TOWEL when she was done. He made sure to cop several feels in the process.

"Fuck you. Should I tell Kurt?"

He just laughed. *Yeah, prove it,* she thought.

Kurt walked back in. "I'll get her dressed. There's an exam scheduled in an hour. You go clean up the bedroom. Throw out all the sheets. And when you're done, bring the car around back. There was a cop snooping around here earlier. We need to move her anyway."

Zoe apologized for the early hour, "Charles, sorry to wake you, but I've got something I'm curious about. You know the owner at Angie's? A guy named Kurt Wilson?"

"Sure do. Not personally, but I know who he is. In fact he's wound up in more than one of my novels. Great character. Lot's of inspiration from him."

"Tell me about him."

"You could read my first novel, the villain gives you a pretty good overview."

"Oh, I will, believe me. But right now, I don't have time, and I need to know."

"Okay, well, he's what I'd call a bully. He's got everyone under his thumb around there. His employees are all afraid of him, but they stick it out anyway. Except for Josh, that new bartender. He's gone—didn't show up one day is what I overheard. One of the servers was laughing about it—said he didn't have the balls to work there."

"But what goes on there? I mean, how is it that a boss can bully everyone around and nothing happens?"

"It's kind of hard to explain."

"You're a writer—so try."

"Hey, now, it's not that simple. But he's one of those guys that runs hot and cold. One moment, he's berating someone, and the next he's giving them shit— I mean shit like free tickets to some pro game, or extra money. And I think, but do not quote me on this, that he gets them fixed, too. He's a source."

"Fixed? As in drugs?"

"I think so. Everyone around there's using. Makes the place interesting as hell for a writer. I get half my material just sitting, watching, and jotting it all down."

"Don't they care?"

"You think they read?" He laughed. "Besides, I buy food and drinks. That's all they care about."

"Do you feel safe there?"

"Aw, it's not that bad. In fact your little friend was in there last night."

"My little friend?"

"The kid you were with when you spoke with Josh. Now that was funny. I don't know what you guys were saying to him, but you had him all worked up."

"The kid?"

"Yeah, the girl."

"What was she doing there?"

"Filling out a job application, I think."

"Then what?"

"Maybe she got hired. I left about then."

"CAN I GET MY OLD CLOTHES ON?"

Kurt looked around, and nodded. "Yeah, we're going outside."

"Okay, I'll get my coat, too. It's all in that little closet."

"Wait." He grabbed her arm. "I'll go with you. Give me the towel."

Kurt grabbed it from her and pulled her in the chill as he led Lucy to the closet. He held on to the door, keeping it open.

Lucy waited for him to shut it.

He didn't. "Hurry up!"

She dressed quickly and put the down coat on, trying to make it look light. "Where are we going?"

"Ever been examined down there?" He patted her butt.

"No."

"Well, we're going to get you checked out."

"Why?"

"Make sure you're a virgin. There's big money in that rarity."

"Yeah, but after the first time, I'd be worth a lot less. So I don't get it."

"Oh, you won't be working for me anymore. You'll be working for one guy and one guy only. But he'll take good care of you—nothing but the best, kid. And that prime shit I gave you last night?—you'll have all you want. Best quality. Meanwhile, I just keep getting richer." He grinned at her, "You're going to help me further enhance my business reputation."

But Lucy got a vibe off him—a distaste for the fact that her continued existence was at all instrumental to his continued success. That she mattered at all to him, that he needed her in any way, Lucy guessed, was what bothered him—and that needing to keep her in virginal shape gave her at least a temporary advantage.

RAY CALLED FOR THE OFFICER WHO'D made the trip to Kurt Wilson's home—had him stand in front of his desk, then said, "I went to his business early this morning. Some janitor said he wasn't in yet. So, tell me about the guy."

"He was legit. Had a really nice house in Edina—that hilly spot with all the mansions?

"Really? What do you guess it's worth?"

"At least a couple mill, maybe more."

"Is that so? Know anything about his business?"

"Ah, not really. Just that he owns Angie's. It's a diner, sort of—or a bar. I'm not sure what to call it."

"I know the place. It's over Northeast—a dive with stiff drinks and pizzas that taste like cardboard A rat's nest otherwise."

The young officer looked at him quizzically.

"So, what does that tell you?"

The cop was trying, but he was so nervous that his brain wasn't working anymore. He had nothing, Ray could tell.

"Kid, it should tell you that something doesn't add up."

Still nothing but a blank look from the officer.

"Oh, for God's sake, where in the hell did he get the money for that house? Unless his wife's independently wealthy or he hit the right lotto numbers, Angie's isn't good for that."

"So, you're saying that you don't buy his alibi?"

"Officer—that is exactly what I'm saying. And you shouldn't have let him off so easily. Bet you spent exactly two minutes with him."

The young cop didn't argue that point.

"Get back out there. Go to Angie's and find the guy. Talk to him again. Verify his damn alibi! Look around at Angie's—see what you can find. Then come back to me with something useful."

"GET IN THE BACK, KID. Gary, you drive. I'm back here with her."

"Where are we going?" Lucy dared to ask.

"I told you."

"But where is it?"

"You'll see. It's a ways—so get comfortable. Lie down and put your head in my lap."

Lucy watched the top of the buildings speed by. They were going out toward the edge of the city. She tried to glance past Gary's elbow, at the speedometer—hoping—but he was keeping it under the limit.

"Is it a clinic? Or a hospital?"

Gary laughed.

"Shut up." Kurt caught his eyes in the rearview. "Keep your eyes on the road." He looked down at Lucy, "No, it isn't."

Lucy had to know that would be the answer—but at least she wouldn't be busted by one of those metal detectors. And in the meantime she had to hide the fact of the two gun components hidden in the lining of her down coat until she had an opportunity to connect them.

"KIM, YOU'VE GOT TO COVER FOR ME. It's important, or I wouldn't ask—you know that. My interns are good and they have everyone tucked in, it's all taken care of. I'll page them and let them know to take over and bug you only if they really need to. Honest, it's important."

"Quit groveling. But you owe me, okay?"

"Understood. Thanks, bye."

Zoe was out the door, paging her interns as she ran—and planning on ringing Lucy's neck at some point later that day. She filled the interns in as she jumped through the gears of her Jeep, heading for Angie's. The first thing she would do when she got there would be to give them Lucy's resignation—that is, if she'd been hired, and she imagined the talk she'd have later with Lucy. It was not going to be pleasant.

Angie's was closed up tight—too early. She saw a janitor inside, cleaning up around the bar, and so she knocked. He glanced at her but didn't break from his cleaning, and she knocked louder.

This time he looked irritated, but came over. Cracking the door, he said, "We're closed. Come back at eleven."

When he tried to close the door, Zoe slipped her foot in to block it.

"Hey! I told you we're closed!"

"I just need to see the owner. It's important."

"He's not here. There's no one but me right now."

The squad pulled up as she was debating whether or not to believe the guy.

A young officer approached the stalemated couple, and this time the janitor opened the door. Zoe slipped in with him.

THE DOCTOR WAS OUT IN THE COUNTRY—or suburbs, or something. She wasn't sure what to call it. It was sort of like the snooty neighborhoods she used to steal from, but a slightly lower-class version with a lot of homes for sale. A good place to squat, she thought, if she ever needed to again. There was a strip mall across the highway, but they didn't head there. Instead they went to one of the houses.

The doctor welcomed her in, and asked Kurt, "So this is your daughter, then?"

"Yes. She had a difficult experience last night, and I just want to make sure she's intact, if you know what I mean?"

"Absolutely. As any father would."

Lucy considered it worth waiting until she was in the room alone with the doctor. Then she could tell him what was what—that she'd been brought there against her will, under threat of harm, and then he would call the police. In fact she marveled at how stupid Kurt must be. Just wait, she told herself. Just wait.

The doctor waved his arm in the direction of the exam room door—which, from the outside, looked like just another bedroom. "Come in," he said—but not just to her. He said it to Kurt as well.

"No! I'm not his daughter!"

The doctor simply smiled. He said nothing in reply, and only held the door for them to pass through.

THE YOUNG COP WAS GETTING NOWHERE. Zoe wished she were authorized to do the interrogation herself, but every time she tried to wade in, the cop stopped her—getting way too authoritarian.

Zoe pulled out her cellphone and punched in the number at Sara's.

"Can I talk to Lucy?"

It was Pushpa. "Let me go find her."

Zoe waited, rolling her eyes at the incompetent cop. What was Ray thinking?—sending a guy like this to do the job? He reminded her of some interns she'd had on occasion.

Zoe heard a crackling on the phone, it sounded like someone had dropped it.

"Sorry, Zoe. She's not in her room, and no one's seen her yet this morning. I looked out back and my car is gone as well. She must have gone somewhere."

"Did she come back last night?"

"Well, I assume she did. But I guess I'm not sure. You want me to ask?"

"Yes, Pushpa. Please hurry."

"Okay."

Zoe waited again, longer this time.

Finally Pushpa came back on the line. "I can't say for sure, but no one saw her, so I don't know."

"Thanks."

Zoe dialed Ray's number.

"Ray, I'm standing here with your piece-of-shit, punk officer. Lucy's missing—last known whereabouts was last night at Angie's. Put an alert out on the owner's car." Zoe poked her head out the door and looked down the block in both directions. Then she came back inside. "Pushpa's car is parked near here. It's what Lucy came in."

The young cop was staring at her, his mouth hanging off its hinge.

She nodded through Ray's response.

"Okay. But first I'll see if he can redeem himself."

She handed her phone to the cop—who listened, went pale, nodded, and then handed it back to Zoe.

She closed it and asked. "Where do the Traceurs hang out?"

"The what?"

"You know, like free runners, the ones who do all the trick jumps off buildings."

"Oh."

"Think fast and you might save your ass."

He looked rattled.

"Don't be nervous. Think!"

"Well, I guess I've seen them over at the library, there're stairs they do tricks on. And . . . hmm, let me see, I've chased some away from the Army Surplus buildings. They buy clothes there, but when they're not open they use their ramps and rooftops."

"Where else? Where do they hang out when they're not doing their shit?"

"Guess I'm not sure about that. Nowhere that I go, anyway."

Zoe wondered. "Okay, that's good enough," and she left.

THE EXAM WASN'T SO BAD—except that they ogled and talked about her like she was some sort of show animal. But she'd been through worse. And she hadn't lied—she was a virgin. Lucy didn't want to think about what Kurt might have done to her if the doctor had discovered otherwise.

But the doctor was gentle with her, and didn't go too far. She guessed that was the whole idea.

He took some samples from her, and drew some blood.

When they were done, she asked, "Can I go to the bathroom?"

"Sure," the doctor said. "It's right outside the door and to your left."

"Wait!" Kurt grabbed her hand. He called for Gary again. "Go with her."

Gary grinned. "Guess it's you and me again, kid."

Lucy made her self go, even though it was in front of Gary. Then she worried about the coat, which was still in the examination room. She had to get back there before they moved to leave, or Kurt might pick it up.

ZOE WENT BY THE LIBRARY FIRST. It wasn't open—too early for that. And no one was hanging around. The Army Surplus Store was closed, too, so she hoped to find at least one of them messing around—a contact, a starting point. Maybe a kid she could scare the life out of until he gave up a name. But all she saw when she climbed to the roof were some old soda bottles and some crumpled food bags. One was from McDonalds. She made a mental note to swing by there; at least they were open for breakfast. But she was beginning to think these kids weren't in the habit of getting up this early.

There was also an Arby's bag. Her search was getting tougher. Another bag moved on the breeze, turning over at her feet. At first glance it was a plain brown bag, but as it turned she saw Betty's insignia on the up righted side.

"Damn her!"

WHEN LUCY ENTERED THE EXAMINATION room, her eyes went immediately to the coat. It looked like it hadn't been moved, but she couldn't be sure. She looked quickly away from it to see Kurt's eyes follow hers. His went back to the coat.

"You're not going anywhere, if that's what you were thinking."

"You mean we're staying here?"

"For a little while." He turned to Gary. "You know what to do."

Gary walked out holding the samples, the tube of blood, and some documents.

"Do I get my own bedroom?"

Kurt laughed. The doctor merely smiled and looked at his notes.

"We're not staying that long. Just long enough to get a little documentation done. A lot of money's riding on this—and the potential for future business is worth even more. Right, Doc?"

The doctor nodded.

"Doc, here, wouldn't have this particular house, or a wife, or anything if it weren't for me? Isn't that right?"

The doctor nodded again, but his smile went away.

"That's not very enthusiastic," Kurt took the doctor's face in one hand and turned it toward his. "You know what's riding on this, don't you?"

"Yes." But he still didn't smile.

"There are other documents, Doc. Remember those? I hold them. You mess, you're in prison. That's my promise to you."

Lucy thought the doctor was going to lose it. She'd almost have recommended vomiting, if only to get Kurt's hand off him. Clearly Kurt held power over this guy. And by the way they were talking, she'd have bet Pushpa's car that he had gotten his wife through just such an exchange.

Kurt continued to hold his face. Waiting.

Finally the doc said through his distorted mouth held in Kurt's grip, "It's just that I'm a little nervous about this one. She's not foreign."

"Might as well be. She's from up on the damn rez. It's a different world."

Kurt let the doc's face go. "So, that's all that's bothering you?"

"Yes."

"Well—then we have nothing to worry about."

Chapter Ten

Zoe looked through the windows and didn't see anyone resembling a Traceur. There were neighborhood couples, and a few tired-looking women—probably streetwalkers. She pushed through the front door, not caring about her promise to use the phone. "In back!" she yelled at Betty, and then walked ahead into Betty's office.

When Betty followed, Zoe pushed her shoulders up against the wall. "A kid, a Traceur—you know, a free runner. He's white, hangs out here, or at least gets food here. He's about my height, dark hair, wears an Army Surplus jacket and a Rasta hat. I need a name! Now!"

"I don't know what you're ..."

"Now!" Zoe pushed her harder against the wall. "Someone's life may depend on your answer, so make it a good one."

"Probably Marie's son. Jason."

"Where?"

"They live above the dry cleaners. One block south, take a right. It's on the next corner."

Zoe let her go.

"Not in the living room. My wife ..."

"Your wife came through here just like Lucy. It was part of the deal, I gave you the pick of the litter—and now I own you. You think she cares?"

The doctor looked as if he was deciding.

Finally he said, "No. She won't mind."

"That's right. She's had a good life, hasn't she?"

The doctor nodded again.

"How old was she when you took her in?"

"I can't remember."

"That's a lie. How old? It seemed to matter very much to you at the time."

"Twelve."

Lucy gasped.

"Bet you'd like this one, too." He pulled at Lucy's hair. "…And how about your wife? Bet she's getting too old for you anyway. Thought about an upgrade?"

The doctor looked at her with eyes that Lucy couldn't make.

Kurt was nodding. "We can make another deal down the road. You'll trade your current model in. In my line of work, I've got use for the certified, pre-owned ones."

The doctor looked like he was thinking about it. Lucy guessed that he was in so deep already he'd be making the calculation about how to get everything out of it he could. But trading in his wife?

"Okay, let's go into the living room. I'll have my wife make us something to eat while we wait for Gary to return."

It was the longest sentence she'd heard the doctor say since they arrived. He'd certainly perked up.

ZOE JUMPED THE STAIRS AND KNOCKED ON THE DOOR—but not too harshly, she didn't want to spook anyone.

The kid answered and, after seeing her, tried to shut the door in her face. Zoe kicked it in, running toward him as he made for the window. After all, this was a Traceur—a quick exit out the third floor window was certainly possible—and Zoe didn't have time for that kind of chase.

Instead she tackled him at the windowsill.

He made a lame attempt at shoving her off, but she pinned him and grabbed his crotch. This was a weak link, she thought, and shouldn't take much time.

"Want to go for a testicular rupture?"

His voice strained, "No."

"Then settle down. I just have a couple questions. You answer correctly—this never happened."

He nodded.

"Where's your mom?"

"Out."

"Okay, obviously. Where?"

"At work."

"This early?"

"She hasn't come home yet."

"Then we'll make this quick, unless you want me to grill her about what you've been up to?"

"No. Hurry."

"Who hired you?"

"For what?"

"You know what. The job at Angie's."

"That was the homeless dude."

"Did he raid the till?"

He hesitated. Zoe gave his sac a little squeeze.

"No! I did. It was too good to pass up."

"Then what did he pay you to do?"

"Just distract everyone."

"When did he hire you?"

"About two minutes before I walked in."

"How much?"

"A twenty."

"A homeless dude? Quit lying."

"I'm not. I swear, he pulled it out of a wad of bills."

Zoe considered it. Why would he lie about that? Why would he lie about anything—she had his balls in her hand.

"Did you see who killed the guy?"

"No. I grabbed the goods and ran."

"Out the back door?"

"Yeah."

"Did you see the dead guy?"

"Yeah. I bumped him when I ran by."

"You mean tripped over him?"

"No, bumped him. He was still alive."

"Was he with anyone?"

"Yeah, a lady with a kid. He had her in a grip and the lady had the kid in a grip. He told me to go fuck off when I bumped him. Lady—he was very much alive."

"That's all you saw?"

"Yeah, I ran. That dude meant it, and I'd just fuckin' ripped the place off—not much to stick around for."

"Okay—I'm going to let you go. You stay right here until I'm gone. And kid?"

"Yeah?"

"Get your act together. What you can do with Parkour?—quit wasting it on snatch-and-grab shit. You could be somebody."

He didn't look too sure about that.

"Like I said, get it together."

THE DOCTOR'S WIFE LOOKED ASIAN, and young. What was with this "too old" shit?

Lucy guessed at why the doc had an underground practice, and reminded herself of what Zoe had said . . . What's there to be afraid of?

When the woman—or rather, girl—brought the tray of food, she bowed submissively to both her husband and to Kurt, with something like confusion on her face. Then, after getting a good look at Lucy, her face turned to anger. Black, silky hair whipped across her face as she spun her neck to confront the doc with an accusatory look.

"Not now. It's not the time."

She slapped him.

Which seemed to amuse Kurt. "I've got a good man for her. She'll be perfectly placed—in just the right home. We'll call it a rescue. But I'm not sure which one I'm rescuing, Doc—her, or you."

The doctor didn't react, instead he calmed her, "This is just business. It's not about us."

She looked back and forth between Lucy and a grinning Kurt then spun on her heels to vanish into another room.

Lucy remained quiet and still, her coat lying beside her on the sofa—the two pieces that could save her, not yet connected.

"WOLF! DAMN IT ALL!" Zoe had nearly forgotten about him—filed him away. If Wolf hadn't paid the Traceur for a distraction in order to rob the till himself, then maybe, just maybe, his focus had been on killing Jeb. Zoe dialed Ray's number again as she started up her car.

"Ray, what kind of car? And the plate number, give me that too."

Ray shuffled a paper or two and came up with the information.

"So no luck yet?" Zoe already knew the answer. "Can you give me anything else?"

"No, but just because she was seen there last night, doesn't necessarily have anything to do with this Kurt Wilson guy."

"In your imagination it doesn't, but mine is telling me otherwise. Meanwhile, I need to look. Let me know if you come up with anything."

"Will do. Jack is talking to Sara right now. He'll get everything pertinent."

"Yeah, Jack I trust. That other guy though—what a piece of work he is."

"He's new."

"Great, just don't trust him with anything important yet."

Zoe gasped as she had a near miss with a bus.

"Damn bus drivers!"

"You're not at work?"

"No, driving. Looking for Lucy."

"I'll call you if Jack comes up with anything. Both hands on the wheel."

LUCY DIDN'T EAT. SHE WAS TOO NERVOUS and didn't even want to move on the sofa for fear she might disrupt the coat causing the metal pieces to come together and make noise. As long as they were separated in the down lining on either side of the coat, they were silent. But there were two things she worried about. First, if the two sides of the coat were in proximity when she was handling it, the metal pieces might bump and make noise. Second, and an even greater worry, was that Kurt might pick up the coat and feel its weight. Miraculously, up until now, she'd been able to prevent that from happening. These two things were just about all she concentrated on at the moment, because so much depended on them.

"Where will I go from here?" Lucy finally dared to ask.

Kurt, still making sure the doctor was firmly in his place, said, "A place much nicer than this one. The man you'll be going with can actually afford you. The doc, here, can't. His missus was a gift—in fact, I'd call it more of a charitable donation."

The doctor's eyes closed momentarily. Long enough for Lucy to believe what Kurt said.

"Where are we?" she asked.

Kurt only looked impatient.

"I mean, roughly speaking."

Kurt smiled. "Too bad I can't afford to keep you myself." He reached out to touch Lucy's breast. She recoiled but then stopped, thinking of her coat—and the gun—and forced herself to wait, unmoving, seemingly unperturbed, while Kurt tortured the doctor with his groping. Then he turned toward him and said, "See? Very cooperative, if that's what you want—and I have a buyer who does. Willing to pay top dollar. But personally, I like 'em a little more feisty."

Well that was good information to have, Lucy thought, reminding herself not to get feisty—whatever the hell that meant.

Lucy heard a car return.

ZOE NAVIGATED THE TRAFFIC WITH EASE. There wasn't much at this hour—midmorning was normally calm. With a turn of the radio dial she had passengers, the Rolling Stones rode with her.

Ooh, see the fire is sweepin'
Our very street today
Burns like a red coal carpet
Mad bull lost its way

By the time she turned down Wolf's driveway she no longer cared about keeping his secrets.

It's just a shot away

She didn't care about giving away his location.

Rape, murder!
It's just a shot away
It's just a shot away

She didn't care about her oath of confidentiality.

The floods is threat'ning
My very life today

She drove fast, making tracks, and continued on—past the rotting house into the tilled field.

Shadowland

Gimme, gimme shelter
Or I'm gonna fade away

Her Jeep bounced and kicked, but she was over it and into the woods without getting stuck.

It's just a kiss away

She had to slow for the woods, the passage through was narrow in spots and Zoe found herself navigating between trees that were too close. They scratched and caught on her mirrors, eventually giving way to snap back. At one point, forward progress required a hairpin turn, which led to another hairpin turn, and then she was back on track, headed for the pole barn.

Zoe accelerated out of the woods, and slammed on the brakes at the barn's door, jumping out of the Jeep. She ran to the large hanging door and pulled on it as she had before, then shimmied her slender body through the narrow opening. The dog was barking, and the front door to Wolf's cottage opened. Once again, he had a gun.

LUCY HEARD ANOTHER CAR COME TO A STOP outside. A car door slammed, and Gary came in with documents—and another man.

The new man was a greasy-looking, slack-jawed, bottom feeder. But he was a greasy, slack-jawed, bottom feeder with ties to a lab. Lucy wondered what it took to get that. He was also a greasy, slack-jawed, bottom feeder with a habit. And it looked like this exchange would be dusted with a "perk."

Lucy watched and listened as the four men discussed her. She was a virgin, free of all diseases. They had the lab results and the examination notes from the doctor spread out on the table. The doctor signed off, and then Kurt said to the new arrival, "Get lost." But in addition to peeling off some bills, he handed him a vial—meth, she thought, but wasn't sure.

After the front door closed and they heard the lab guy's car speed off—clearly anxious to open his present—Lucy asked, "What now?" She was hoping for information that would enable her to plan, to anticipate an opportunity for reuniting the two components of the gun.

"Now? We call your new owner. See when he wants to meet."

"You're staying here?' the doctor asked.

Pam Leonard

This time Kurt reached out and grabbed the doctor by his collar, surprising the man, and disrupting the big couch they all three sat on. Lucy reached out to settle the coat.

"Doc, you don't seem to get it—I own you! Now if you can manage to understand that, I'll let you keep on going with this very nice life of yours. You might even qualify for an upgrade. You see, I'm really a very nice guy—in fact a very cooperative guy, generous to a fault. But, Doc, if you cross me in any way whatsoever, it won't just be prison—and believe me, guys like you don't do well there. It'll be much worse. Now, if I need a place to wait for a call, what would your idea be?"

"I'd offer you my place—to wait for your call." The doctor was sweating. He dry swallowed and made no attempt to remove Kurt's hand from his collar.

"Now see? It's nice when I don't have to come up with all the good ideas. Got any more?"

The doctor looked perplexed.

"Gary here hasn't had much lately."

Kurt grinned at Gary, who looked a combination of embarrassed and hopeful. "Where should I send him—that is, while you and I wait?"

The doctor closed his eyes again, pointed, and said, down that hallway, second door on the right.

Kurt nodded, and Gary nearly tripped over himself trying to get down the hall. He stood before the closed door and unbuckled his belt. After freeing it from the loops, he unzipped his pants and opened the door. The woman screamed, the belt found skin, the doctor flinched, and Kurt finally let go of his collar—watching him the whole time. In fact he continued to watch the unmoving doctor as all three of them sat on the couch and listened to the doctor's wife being raped.

THE GUN WASN'T RAISED, and Zoe recalculated her approach. She smiled at him, and moved forward. He still didn't lift it.

Instead he asked, "What in the hell are you doing out here again?"

"Visiting. Okay if I come in?" It was hard to be civil, and she had no illusions that she was hiding her anger successfully.

"I suppose."

Zoe walked past him as he held open the door. She turned once inside and said, "Mind putting that gun away? It makes me kind of nervous."

"That's what guns are for," he said, deadpan. But he opened a closet door and leaned it against the back wall.

Once the door was closed, Zoe asked, "Why'd you do it?"

"Do what?"

"You know what. Pay the kid to distract everyone at Angie's."

WHEN GARY WAS FINISHED, the door opened again to the sound of a woman sobbing. Lucy's stomach threatened. She had a gun—and goddamn wished she could use it.

Kurt said to the doctor, "Might want to work extra hard, qualify for that upgrade," and then grinned at the doctor's lack of response.

Kurt's cellphone chirped. "Yeah?" He listened and replied, "We'll be there—with everything."

Then he turned to the doctor and told him to get his car out of the garage.

The doctor's only question was, "Where do you want me to put it?"

"Up your ass! Just get it out of the garage. I need to move mine in there." He turned to Gary, who was already moving.

The doctor could have thought of a better question, Lucy thought. And she wondered just how easy it was to get a doctor's license.

He turned back to Lucy, "Get your coat on, it's cold in the trunk. I need to deliver you in good shape, and he'll be checking. I plan on getting paid."

When the doctor returned, Kurt unfolded a wad of bills, counted off several—it looked like hundreds, and then stood.

Lucy was already in her coat.

"PAY THE KID? WHAT ARE YOU TALKING ABOUT? Where'd you get an idea like that?"

"There's a witness."

"To what?"

"Saw you give the kid money."

"So what?"

"As if you have any to give."

"I'm a generous guy. As you can see, I don't need much. If I can do a good turn..."

"Cut the bullshit." By now Zoe had moved herself between Wolf and the closet. "You were overheard. About two minutes before it all went down. Starting to sound familiar?"

"That's not possible..." but he stopped.

Zoe grinned. "And just why is that not possible, Wolf? Because there were no witnesses around you?"

Wolf didn't respond. He was thinking, calculating, Zoe knew.

Finally Zoe asked, "Why'd you kill him?"

"I didn't!" But then he looked away from her—at what, Zoe couldn't tell—as if reconsidering.

"Then who did?"

"I don't know."

"Where is she?"

"Who?"

"Lucy."

"Who the hell is Lucy?"

"My friend. And she's been missing ever since she showed up at Angie's last night."

Wolf's look of resignation changed in a heartbeat. Gone was his concern over being caught in a lie. Instead he asked, "Tell me about her."

"Good kid. And you'd better produce her. If you've got something going with Kurt Wilson, so help me God, I'll see you rot in prison."

"Tell me about her!"

"IN THE TRUNK."

Lucy was grateful beyond belief for the opportunity, but didn't want to act too enthusiastic about getting in a trunk. She balked, just a little. "In the trunk? Do I have to?"

"Yes, you have to. We'll be collecting our money before we produce you. But you'll have company." He turned to Gary, "In there—with her."

Gary beamed.

At which Kurt responded, "Don't get any ideas, you've had enough for one day." But Gary was still smiling.

In order to fit in the trunk they'd have to spoon—he'd have his arms around her, and might feel the gun. No, not might—would, for certain.

Lucy did a quick reassessment—and decided. Though she couldn't yet use the gun, maybe she could still keep them from finding it. After all, she would need it after the transfer. Then, presumably, it would just be Lucy against one man—the rich dude who could "afford" her. So she asked, "Okay if I use my coat as a pillow?"

"I don't give a shit, kid. Whatever floats your boat."

Lucy removed her coat and carefully curled it on itself, trying desperately not to let the metal pieces clang together.

"Gary, you first, then the girl."

"My pleasure, boss." Absolutely nothing would wipe the smile off his face, not even getting into the trunk of a car in freezing weather ––and once again, Lucy recalled the Newfoundland, giving off heat.

"As if you didn't know."

He made a move toward her and she put up a hand. "I'm a lot stronger than I look. You really don't want to do that."

"Then goddammit, tell me about her! Is she clean?"

"Clean?"

"As in no STDs?"

"I sure as hell hope so! She's only sixteen. What does that have to do with anything?"

"It matters! It matters where she'll go. Only sixteen? Is she a virgin?"

"I'm pretty sure." Zoe decided to go with it, he was leading her somewhere, even if it all sounded like nonsense—the guy had info. "Why?"

"Quiet! Let me think!"

Gary's hands were all over her. Thank God she'd managed to roll the coat below her head—if not, he'd have discovered the gun by now.

Their car ride didn't last long—she estimated only a few minutes on some sort of hard-surfaced road, and then they were crunching gravel. One of Gary's hands kept wandering off her breast, bracing against the bumps. She found herself silently praying that he wouldn't accidentally come across her coat and the hard metal within.

Finally the car slowed, made a wide turn, and came to a stop.

She heard Kurt get out and slam the door behind him.

Another voice, presumably the man who would purchase her, said, "Good to see you. You've got the documentation?"

"Everything I promised."

Lucy guessed that an exchange of money was taking place. Both were silent. Then the buyer said, "Okay, where is she?"

Kurt was all over it, "She's one of the best I've ever netted. No doubt about her. She checks out perfect. And she's real cooperative. She'll do whatever you ask—worth every penny."

"Let me see her."

"WHAT DOES SHE LOOK LIKE?" Wolf shouted.

"About five-feet, black hair, half-Ojib, skinny—like me."

"She might be at the farmhouse. He knows the place is deserted—that's where we think he makes the high-end exchanges. Maybe we can catch her before they leave."

"What do you mean, 'high-end exchanges'?" Zoe asked.

"Big money involved. We think they're usually foreign, from what we can tell, but the main thing is they have to be virgins—and young. No diseases, and easily manipulated."

"Who buys?"

"We're still working that out—not sure yet. But we think there're several contacts—maybe more. There always are in his business."

"We?"

He ignored the question. "All we've been able to do so far is to get some of the streetwalkers out—the ones who want out."

"So why would these high-end exchanges be here?"

"He's connected to this land. He knows it's deserted—it's a perfect meeting place, no chance of being seen."

"Except by you."

"Yep, except by me, now that I'm home. But it was still random luck that I saw it go down. Didn't know what to make of it at first. But after talking it over, we figured it out. We think so, anyway."

"But why didn't you just report it to the police?"

Wolf ignored that one too, except to say, "There're other reasons this location is perfect—but we'd better hurry."

"WAIT, MY COAT!" Lucy protested.

"You won't need that anymore. Don't worry about it." The buyer looked her up and down, then turned to Kurt, "I'll take her from here."

"Like I said, very cooperative."

That was when Lucy made her stand.

"WHERE?" ZOE SHOUTED AT HIM.

"Behind the farmhouse. When I saw them they met in the middle of all the buildings—hidden from view." He added, almost in disbelief, "But maybe it's not happening."

Zoe didn't wait to hear more. She was already outside and in her car, retracing her path through the woods, banging against tree limbs—one mirror already sacrificed in exchange for speed. She opened her window, to listen.

As she emerged from the trees she cursed herself for not grabbing Wolf's rifle on the way out but continued across the tilled field at speeds that sent her flying in her seat, untethered by the seatbelt she hadn't taken time to fasten. With each large bump, her foot slipped off the pedal and she lost speed. When she reached for her cellphone, the Jeep jumped and it slipped out of her hand, falling somewhere outside of her opened window. Hard to shift a manual transmission, maintain a firm grip on a jerking wheel, and dial 911 all at the same time.

"Dammit! She kept adjusting the stick shift and tried to hold top speed. There were outbuildings between her and Lucy, so she had no visual and only hoped they were still there.

"IT'S ON!" LUCY YELLED AND THEN TRIED making a run for it. But Gary was too quick. He had her by the elbows, her arms pulled back.

The buyer hadn't budged, and only remarked, "Cooperative, eh?"

"Trust me, just a little cold feet. She'll be fine."

"Just what did she cooperate with?"

"A little something. Nothing much."

"Something? I wanted her pristine."

"I was talking about the exam—and the whole idea of this. She's okay with it. Just give her time to adjust."

The buyer watched as Lucy attempted to free herself from Gary's grasp. "Go easy, I'm sure she'll work out just fine."

Lucy yelled at them again, loudly, "It ends here! I'm not going anywhere with anyone." Then she kicked down on Gary's instep, causing him to drop her.

This time when she ran, it was the buyer who caught her. He grabbed her, but less roughly than either Kurt or Gary had—there was enough of a difference to make her pause and wonder if she'd have an easier time getting away from this new guy. Apparently he did indeed want her pristine.

But instead of relaxing, Lucy looked up into his eyes and said—although softly this time, "I'll die first."

He looked pained and said to her, while looking back at Kurt. "It would be best if you cooperated."

"Then I'll kill you!"

Kurt said to the buyer, "You gonna let her get away with that?"

Lucy screamed, and the buyer's hand went over her mouth. She tried to bite but couldn't get hold of anything. It felt like she couldn't breathe, so she stopped her struggling.

"There now, that's better, isn't it?"

Better? All she knew was that this relationship was not destined for domestic bliss.

ZOE ACCELERATED AROUND THE BARN, hoping for the element of surprise, and stopped within the ring of buildings. She jumped out of the Jeep, running toward the group.

Gary drew a weapon, raising it sideways. It was aimed at Zoe, and she slid to a stop, arms raised.

"Do it! What are you waiting for?" Kurt shouted at him.

She had nothing to hide behind but there had to be at least thirty feet between her and the group of men, maybe fifteen feet between her and the Jeep. Based on the way he held the gun, Zoe knew, with a guy like that?—he'd miss. She angled her body sideways just as he pulled the trigger, and noticed the buyer start moving Lucy behind his vehicle.

The first bullet pulled at her coat, but it missed her flesh and she dodged back—increasing the distance between them, then she angled sideways again. The odds still favored her, as this guy was definitely not practiced—his stupid sideways hold on the gun was proof enough. And by moving, she'd prevented him from working off his last miss—he'd have to start all over again.

He pulled the trigger.

Nothing. The gun failed to fire. *Better yet*, Zoe thought. He'd managed to jam his weapon with the stupid perp draw. That, too, was a function of holding the gun sideways—the bullet wouldn't fall properly into place. It happened far too often, and if he'd known what he was doing, he'd have known that. Zoe moved forward this time.

"Shoot!" Kurt urged.

"I can't! The gun jammed!" Gary was banging on it.

Zoe ran straight toward Lucy—who, in the commotion had been dragged behind the buyer's car. By this time, the buyer had produced his own weapon and stood from behind the car—gun rising.

In that moment, Lucy began struggling again, jerking both the man and his weapon—her instincts gave Zoe the opportunity to cover ground between them. She lunged as the man threw Lucy down and tried to redirect his weapon toward the group.

But the shot caught him between the eyes. A direct t-zone hit. It had come out of the trees, and Zoe didn't have to look back toward Wolf's hideout to know it had come from the gun with the Leupold scope.

Everyone scrambled. Gary limped behind Kurt's car while Kurt ran toward the old farmhouse, and Zoe grabbed Lucy's hand, pulling her toward the Jeep.

But instead Lucy broke free and ran toward Kurt's car.

"Lucy! What the fuck? This way!" Zoe ran toward her, saying, "That was friendly. We've got help!"

"My coat!"

"Not now, Lucy, come on!"

But Lucy was too quick. She dodged Zoe and ran toward the open trunk. Reaching inside, she grabbed her coat and turned toward Zoe. "Got it!"

Zoe grabbed Lucy's hand and yanked on it. "Run!"

Within seconds they'd covered the distance to Zoe's Jeep. Both hopped in and Zoe turned over the engine just as Gary rose from behind Kurt's car and fired four rapid shots at them. Apparently he'd fixed the jammed gun.

Her Jeep stalled, and Zoe shouted at Lucy. "Fucking lucky shot! Get out! On the other side of the car!" Zoe ran around to join her. "And keep down!"

Gary had dropped again—behind his car. No chance for Wolf to set his sights. Zoe imagined Wolf's predicament. Which end of the car would he surface from next? Wolf might have to guess if he were going to take a quick and accurate shot.

Zoe recalled the Traceur—redirecting attention. "Let's flush him out," she whispered to Lucy, "and give Wolf a chance at him."

Lucy only said, "Wolf?" as she fumbled with her coat.

Zoe looked at the ground around her. She picked up a small rock and threw it at the ground near the front end of Kurt's car. Gary moved in response—she could hear him, but he didn't make himself visible.

Instead he hollered, "Good try, bitch."

Lucy was still doing something with her coat.

"Lucy, what are you doing? Just stay down and stay still."

"Here," Lucy handed Zoe the gun—in one piece now, united.

"Th' fuck? How'd you get this?"

"It was hidden in my coat," Lucy said, as if it should have been obvious to Zoe. "Get Gary."

"We'll talk later," Zoe's smile betrayed her serious tone. "Gary, eh? Okay, let's get Gary." Then she fired under Kurt's car, wondering why Gary hadn't thought of that yet.

He jumped up, dancing, and ran toward the house. Wolf now had all the time in the world for an accurate shot—and Gary fell, a few feet from the farmhouse.

He was dead before he hit the ground.

Shadowland

ZOE STOOD AND LOOKED OVER HER JEEP at the carnage in front of them.

Then she turned Lucy away from it and aimed her toward Wolf's hideout. "Let's go." The two started their jog toward the woods. Lucy carried her coat, while the gun swung low in Zoe's hand. "Come on, let's hurry. I want you safe before I do anything else. We don't know for sure if that other guy kept running." She was scanning the ground as they ran, hoping to see the cellphone—without results.

"Kurt."

"What?"

"That's his name—the other guy."

"I know. Save your breath, let's hurry."

A TIMBER MIST WAS FORMING as they came across Wolf at the trees' edge. "Any longer and I wouldn't have had visibility."

"Nice enough shot," Zoe acknowledged, though she had a lot of questions for him. "Let's all get inside, there might be another guy out there. We don't know for sure."

KURT WAITED UNTIL HE HEARD THE GROUP CONNECT. They were talking and running, communicating in that high-pitched, out-of-breath way. Only then did he emerge from the farmhouse. The first thing he did was to pick up Gary's gun, then his buyer's gun, and then retrieve his own weapon from the car. He reached into the glove box and gathered all the ammunition he had. He may be outnumbered, but he sure as hell wasn't going to be outgunned.

So this is the way it was going to be. He wondered why he hadn't seen it coming. That bothered him—seriously bothered him. His stupid relatives were like shadows on the wall—always there, but you didn't notice them. Grace's presence, for a while, had been irritating—as if purposefully taunting him. But eventually she disappeared into the background, along with all the other drunks at the bar. She was either there, drinking, or she wasn't. And what she did with herself when she wasn't . . . didn't concern him. She could rot in hell for all he cared.

And Wolf—a shot like that, it had to be Wolf, the former sniper. Who else would be on this land? Ah, of course . . . a homeless dude. Why hadn't he seen that before? Then again, why should he? Wolf was a drunk, just like his mom, incapable of anything. But apparently Kurt had killed the wrong homeless guy— and it was that bitch doctor's fault.

This land had always been a good place to use for his swaps. It was deserted, and always would be. Grace would never let herself actually sell the place, and Kurt knew it. He was pretty sure he knew why, too.

This place had always felt haunted.

WOLF OPENED THE POLE BARN DOOR and then closed it again after the three had entered. Zoe noticed that it didn't lock. Then they entered the cottage, which did have a lock on the door. Thor was waiting for them inside.

All three sat down and simply breathed—their run over the field and through the woods had taxed them all. Finally Zoe said, "You don't have a phone, do you?"

"No."

"I was afraid of that."

"What are we going to do?"

"I have to go back out there. Take a chance, I guess. Either find the phone, or circle around and find a house to call from."

Wolf said, "Or we can just wait him out here. That is, if he's even out there."

"You're crazy. We'd be sitting ducks, eventually."

"No. Even if he got in here, he'd never know we were here."

"What?" Zoe and Lucy said in unison.

"Come with me."

Wolf led them down the hallway toward his bedroom. He reached into the bookcase on the back wall and—in Lucy's terms, "Holy shit!"—the entire wall moved.

And there was Christie.

KURT FOLLOWED AT A DISTANCE. He started by following their voices, and then tracked them the rest of the way. It wasn't hard. They weren't being careful, only fast.

The pole barn was unexpected. He hadn't even been aware that it existed on this property. He and his stepbrother had never been close.

He stayed back in the woods, and circled it at a distance—looking for entrances, and conversely, any way they could get a shot off at him. There appeared to be no way in, except through the front door, and no openings from which to fire on him—creating a bit of a stalemate.

He sat down, leaned against a tree, and thought.

So THEY'D BEEN RIGHT—the homeless camp guys. They'd known all along. They just didn't know where.

"Christie! Are you all right?" Zoe rushed to her side.

"She's fine! Leave her alone!" Wolf's weapon remained in his hand.

"I'm okay," Christie said. "Really."

Zoe looked around at the room they were in—windowless, a bedroom of some sort, with another room attached to it. A room that Christie's son emerged from—cautiously.

Christie scooped him up into her arms and said, "It's okay."

Zoe looked into the room the boy had come from—a bathroom.

She turned to Wolf, "What the hell is this?"

"Security."

Zoe actually laughed, "The only real security is in having no enemies." She looked at Christie, then at Lucy, and then considered the man who might or might not be outside, "Guess none of us can relax."

"Laugh if you want, but this is all gonna come in handy. You just watch."

"Nope. I'm not waiting around. I'm going back out there and get help."

"I wish you wouldn't do that."

"Why not?"

"It'll bring the police down on me."

"Well then, just what do you suggest we do with all the bodies out there in the farmyard?"

"Bury them, like the rest."

HE COULD LEAVE, RIGHT NOW. JUST RUN. He had a family, but that didn't matter. He could start all over again. In his mind, he'd already left his family anyway. In fact, they'd never had him in the first place. It had been up to his wife to do the raising. When it came to little kids—he didn't know how to play.

But there was the house—a damn nice one—and that would be harder to regain. Still, it could be done.

No—because if he ran, he'd leave witnesses, and have to keep running. Settling down again wouldn't be easy. He might wind up no better off than Wolf and his homeless crowd.

On the other hand, if he finished it all here, no one would have to know. The land was in Grace's name, and he was pretty sure she never came out here. He was pretty sure she'd never want to see the place again—but neither could she sell it. He could finish them off, and get rid of the evidence, right here on the farmstead—like some sacred burial ground. Just three easy kills away from security.

"LUCY, STAY IN HERE WITH CHRISTIE. Make sure she's okay." Then Zoe grabbed Wolf's sleeve and yanked him out to the living room. "What do you mean, 'bury them, like the rest'?"

"The other pieces."

"What other pieces?" She watched his hand on the weapon—attentively.

"It had to be done." He looked distant, disconnected—not entirely present anymore.

"What had to be done?"

"My mom."

He was drifting into the past, a good time to ask, "Your mom what?"

"She saved me. I didn't see all of it. But others did."

"Others?"

"Yeah, the neighbors. They came roaring up in their cars when they heard the screaming. Guess that was a time when people helped each other out."

"Screaming?"

"At first it was me—I remember that—and then it was my mom. He never screamed, though—he didn't have a chance to that night. But mostly, he always just yelled anyway."

"Who?"

"My dad."

"The one who disappeared?"

Wolf smiled slightly. "Yep."

"Wolf, where did he disappear to?"

"I don't know," and he really did look puzzled. "My mom came out with the baseball bat. He dropped me and she swung—and swung, and kept swinging, even after he was on the ground, not moving anymore. When blood sprayed in my eyes, that's when I quit looking. Then I remember that she dropped the bat, scooped me up, and ran me into the house."

"And? What happened next?"

"She put me to bed."

"What happened to the neighbors? And to your dad?"

"I don't know. She took me upstairs, wiped the blood off my face, and put me to bed. Right after she kissed me goodnight, I looked out the window and they were all gone."

"What about the body? I assume he was dead, right?"

"Yeah, I didn't know it for sure then, but after what I saw in Iraq—he was dead, no doubt."

"So what happened to him?"

"Good question, really. I always figured the neighbors must have helped, because he disappeared while Mom was putting me to bed." He was quiet a moment. "After that, I used to roam this neighborhood and imagine that he was in pieces underground—you know, like a piece in each neighbor's yard. I even wondered which ones—you know, as in what body part belonged to which neighbor. But now I realize that he's probably buried somewhere here on the farm. I don't know where ... and I haven't tried to look."

"Why'd your mom do it?"

He looked at her as if it was the silliest question he'd ever heard. "Doing right sometimes means turning bad. Don't you know that by now? She had no choice—at least not if she was going to save me. It's only for limp people—who've never been tested—to say otherwise."

Zoe looked up, Lucy was in the hallway, listening.

"Okay, Wolf. That's enough. I get it." She directed her question to Lucy, "How's Christie?"

"She says that she'd be dead if it weren't for Wolf ... and his mom."

"I see." Zoe recalled the postmortem beating the assailant had laid on Jeb. She leaned close to Wolf, still caught in his memories, and whispered, "Was it your mom?"

"What?"

"Your mom—she killed Jeb?"

He nodded.

Zoe wanted time to think this through, figure out the best way to deal with this while not involving Wolf—or his mom—anymore than was required. But she didn't have a clue as to how. Right now, all she knew was that they all needed help.

Chapter Eleven

SOMETIMES THE ANSWERS COME TOO EASILY—or at least you jump on them that way—and Kurt knew that. What Kurt couldn't decide was whether it was the right answer, or an impulse. When he was young, the teachers told his mom that he had poor impulse control. They'd recommended strict discipline. It's where he'd learned all about intimidation, terror, and revenge—and how one maintains enough discipline to wait until the right moment.

So was this the right moment? He couldn't see running—that just didn't compute on any level. It didn't work in his gut, and it didn't work as a rational solution. Either he'd be found out, or he'd be on the run for the rest of his life. So this had to be the answer—the right one. And one he should move on—immediately.

"WOLF, WHY DID YOU BUILD this room in here?"

"My mom owns the property."

"Okay, I get that, but why this kind of place? Why all the security?"

"You just think I'm paranoid, don't you?"

"No. Just asking why."

"Because we had a plan. We've been saving some of the girls."

"How?"

"They need to see the doctor once in a while, right?"

"Yes."

"Especially his girls."

"Kurt?"

"Yep. He's my uncle. We've helped a lot of his girls get out. Mom fixed it that they should get a special number to call if they wanted out—like an Underground Railroad sort of thing. We got to them through the doc."

Zoe persisted, "Connie?"

"Yes. But Kurt has some special deals going, and Mom found out about it—by hanging around at Angie's. I just happened to see one of the deals go down—out here. Pure luck, I say, but mom says God works in mysterious ways. I don't know what to believe anymore and I guess I don't much care, seeing as how people believe in the wrong stuff all the time—just as long as we can help. It's what we do that matters. Mom's pretty jazzed up about the idea that she owes it to them. I guess I agree."

"Owes it to them?"

"Yeah. We may have stopped my dad, but we never stopped Kurt."

"Why . . ." but Zoe stopped—she got it.

"Because we'd committed murder, and the neighbors had helped. We couldn't exactly go to the police, could we?"

"Okay. I get it, Wolf. But why does Kurt trade them out here?"

"Because he thinks it's deserted. This is where the really young ones are sold."

"Like Lucy?"

"Yes. That's why I wanted to know about her. We didn't know about Lucy."

Zoe paced the living room, scratching her head and grimacing with mental effort. "So, let me get this straight. Your mom, and several neighbors, were all involved in a killing many years ago. Now your mom killed Jeb—for basically the same reason."

"Yes, but we hadn't intended to kill Jeb. He just got in the way when Christie was about to make her escape with Mom. I saw what was happening, and I tried to make it possible for them to slip out without going through Jeb by hiring that diversion—but it didn't work."

"And all those neighbors, the ones who helped your mom before, they still live around here?"

"Most."

"And they have families, and homes, and lives that are good?"

"Most do."

"And you've all been living with this secret?"

"Yep."

"Have you ever talked about it?"

"Not once."

"How about your mom?"

"Not once. No one talks about it. It just had to be done. Someone had to do it—and someone had to help her. They all knew that."

KURT MADE HIS MOVE. He crouched low and quietly made his way to the corner of the barn. He'd gotten a good look at the door on his way. It wasn't open, not even a crack, so he moved right up next to it and listened.

There were muffled noises from within—sounding distant. At least it meant they weren't right up next to the door. Of that he felt certain. But he had no idea about what might be inside. There could be places to hide and shoot from before he could take cover or get a shot off himself. Though he was armed to the teeth, they had at least two guns and could shoot at him from more than one angle. He had to count on being able to outlast both them and their ammunition.

... And what if there was plenty of ammo inside the barn? What then?

An answer did occur to him, one that would require going back to the car for some gasoline. He could burn them out. But that would attract attention. Gunshots on farmland never alarmed anyone. But a fire would bring everyone here fast.

No, he had to keep this place as it was. Deserted, marked against trespassing, for sale—but not really for sale. A burial ground—with a few more bodies. He'd already progressed in his mind to the part about getting the doc's Jeep and the buyer's vehicle into the pole barn and locking it up tight. He'd have all the time in the world to make sure he left no prints and no trace of his presence there. There'd be no witnesses, and the bodies could be buried inside the pole barn's dirt floor. That way no dogs or other critters would get to them and drag a bone back to someone's house—because people love their five minutes on the news.

No, if someone did find them, it would take years—time and failing memories would protect him. And when they were discovered, most likely, it would be by Grace—spooky Grace. Haunted, drunk Grace. The fact that she owned the property made his use of it all the safer. If there were any questions, she'd seem harmless—and of course she was truly clueless.

He pulled on the door and it creaked loudly. He waited a moment, and only heard a muffled barking from within. But it sounded so far off. He risked pulling some more, just enough to get a peek inside, and lowered himself nearly to the ground before looking in.

"QUIET!" WOLF COMMANDED THE DOG, sternly, but quietly. When Thor immediately stopped barking, he praised him, "Good dog, quiet, good dog."

Thor sat, his tail brushing back and forth across the floor, attending to Wolf. "Listen," he said.

He and Zoe remained quiet. They heard nothing.

Finally Zoe said, "I'm going to look."

"No!"

"I've got my weapon. You stay here with the rest and look after them. I'll be right back with the cavalry," she smiled reassuringly at him.

"Don't chance it. The room—he'll never find us there. At least not if he doesn't know there's someone in here. He'll give up looking."

"But he would have to know we're in here."

"Why would he?"

Zoe thought about it. Maybe that was true. "But how long could we wait until we were sure he was gone?"

"We wouldn't have to wait long. Come with me. There's another way out."

THEY LEFT THOR IN THE MAIN LIVING AREA. "He might bark," was all Wolf said.

"He'll be fine on his own," Zoe responded, recognizing Wolf's dilemma.

They all crowded into the sheltered room at the back of the house and Zoe whispered, "You know, I bet you're right, it'd be hard to recognize that there was more to this house. When you look out the windows, all you see is the same view of the inside of a pole barn. There're no landmarks to get your bearings—no external cues."

"Exactly. And it's a narrow room. It juts up to the back of the pole barn wall, so you don't expect any windows on that side. And the bookcase doesn't seem out of place either—along that wall in my bedroom."

"Have you ever had to test it?"

"Only when you were in here snooping around," he smiled.

"Really? Christie and her son were here the whole time?"

Christie nodded, then stroked her son's hair and cautioned him, "Quiet."

"Let's all be quiet, and listen."

There was a faint sound as if the pole barn door was being opened, but it was hard to tell. In any event, there were noises.

HE STOOD THERE, ALONE, EXCEPT FOR THE SMALL HOUSE built within the pole barn. It took a moment to register in his brain—that this was a house, for God's sake—and when it did, he ran toward it and crouched, flattening himself next to its siding under one of the windows. Two weapons remained in his pockets, along with extra ammo, while one was held ready. Out of the thickening fog, a soft light poured in through the barn door—just enough for him to see his way around.

He waited a long time before scooting along below window level around the perimeter of the house. It ended in the back wall of the barn, but he knew there were no windows or doors there, only the large sliding one in front. The interior of the cottage was dark, no sign of life except for the occasional short bark from a dog. He examined the edges of the pole barn floor—no egress routes.

Finally he stood, and looked in the first window.

"HE'S OUT THERE, SOMEWHERE CLOSE. Thor's trying to obey, but he can't help himself. He hears him."

"So what do we do?"

"First, just sit tight. There's another way out, but if we exit when he's outside, he might see us. So we wait until he's in the house proper."

Zoe nodded. She heard Thor bark again—a brief, interrupted bark. He was trying. "Where's the exit? Let's at least get ready."

"Okay, but we can't all go out there at once. We'll attract his attention."

"Okay, I'll go," Zoe said.

"It would be better if it was me," Wolf countered.

"Okay, you go and take Christie and her son with you. You've got a weapon. So do I. Lucy and I will wait until we think it's safe. Then we'll catch up. But I think we shouldn't go back toward the farmhouse. That's what he'll be expecting; he'll be trying to watch for that. Instead we should go straight down the back toward the river bank."

"That makes sense."

Before he moved to open the exit door, Zoe couldn't help but say, "Wolf, you and your mom should have just reported Kurt's activities to the police."

Wolf looked at her as though it was the stupidest thing he'd ever heard. "My mom."

"… Killed two people," she said, answering her own question.

He only nodded.

"And other innocent neighbors helped her." Zoe looked at Lucy, then back toward Wolf. "They're all involved—and none of them are innocent anymore."

"But you can't deny that the world is a better place." It was said with confidence. "We're living the best we can. It's not great, but it's better than when he was around. My mom put up with the abuse, but she wouldn't let him start in on me. Some might call her weak, but I know better—and at least we're trying to do something."

"There'll be questions about the dead bodies in the farmyard."

Wolf grimaced, and he nodded.

"Why did your mom seem so afraid to see you in Angie's that day?"

"Because she doesn't like that I'm involved. Says I went through too much already and she doesn't want me exposed to any more risk. But I am involved. It's my choice."

"So this place didn't start out as a safe house for the girls?"

"No, it was my own hideaway. I just feel better out here—safer. But I added this room after we hatched our plan."

"So, if your mom doesn't like involving you, why were you even there that day—in Angie's?"

"Because of Jeb. Mom was going to meet up with Christie behind Angie's and then take her away. It should have been simple—like the others. But Christie wasn't just another one of Kurt's girls, she was also Jeb's girlfriend—and that made everything harder. I was watching from across the street, I saw through the window that Jeb was about to get in the way. I just had to do something—you know, try to create a diversion so we could still pull it off."

Zoe only nodded, and recalled Christie's son doing the very same thing.

He continued. "I think when Mom saw me she worried that I was going to have a go at him myself. But look at me—that would have been pretty pointless, don't you think? So instead I just let it all play out. You know—the diversion, and then Mom slipping out back ahead of Christie. She hid behind the dumpster, hoping like hell that Christie would follow—just like they'd planned. But then Jeb came out after Christie."

Wolf paused, appearing deep in thought.

"I think my mom must have felt kind of like I did. It brought things to mind, if you know what I mean. Mom and I are a lot alike that way. I get flashbacks—I admit—but so does she. When she saw the tug of war between Jeb and Christie's son, with Christie caught in the middle and her son watching Jeb lay a beating on her, I think Mom kind of snapped. It was like she still is in my memory—running at him, swinging away. Only this time it was with a tire iron—and she didn't scream."

Zoe didn't know what to say.

He brightened. "We'd gotten others off the street, though. A couple times the girls wanted a clean break so Dr. Sayre faked a document saying they had HIV and then Kurt had to let them go. With a few others, we just got word that they wanted out so we used her money to set them up somewhere else. That way Dr. Sayre didn't have to go out on such a long limb. It was almost too easy. Gotta say, Mom and I felt pretty good about that—outsmarting Kurt at his own game. We were planning on setting Christie up in Fargo. She was going to go back to school."

"Whose money?"

"The doc's."

"Connie?" Zoe's throat tightened around the word. Apparently some shadows weren't so evil after all. "That's where you got the money to pay the kid?"

"Yep. She'd fronted us a lot of money—and I only used it to help the girls get free, I promise."

"I believe you—but what about Betty? How was she involved?"

"She could get word to the girls—and Connie used her place to meet with a couple of them."

"That's all?"

"Pretty much."

"Did Betty know what was going on?"

"Not the details. Only the gist."

Zoe recalled Betty's address. "Was she one of the neighbors? You know, from back when your mom interrupted your beating—and abduction?"

He nodded.

"How about Connie? What did she know?"

"Only that we had a sort of Underground Railroad thing going, helping the ones who wanted out. She was willing to help, even if it wasn't exactly on the up and up."

"Okay, let me think." Zoe paced the small room while the others watched. Everyone was quiet, listening. But there were sounds of glass breaking in the house and Zoe snapped to attention, "Wolf, you saved my life out there—and I'm the one who owes you this time. So I'll think of something. I don't know what yet, but I will. Please don't worry. No one needs to be a hero today."

"STUPID DOG!" ONCE INSIDE, Kurt picked Thor up by the scruff, went to unlock the front door, and then tossed him outside. He closed the door and turned around in the room. The dog was barking at him from outside the window now, making one hell of a racket. He aimed his gun out the window and fired. The dog yelped and ran out of the pole barn.

Kurt decided that his aim needed work.

"HE HAS A GUN, AND HE'S INSIDE. IT'S TIME." Zoe turned to Wolf, "Take care of them."

Wolf patted his rifle. "No doubt."

Wolf reached down to pull up a section of carpet. Beneath it was a trap door. It squeaked when he opened it, and he stopped to listen.

There was movement in the bedroom beyond the false wall. Everyone was silent. Wolf, holding the trap door open at a forty-five degree angle, Christie and her son, waiting at the threshold, Zoe and Lucy looking at the false wall, waiting—a standoff. Zoe imagined the man on the other side doing the exact same thing they were—waiting, and listening.

Then Thor appeared at the bottom of the tunnel, barking to get in.

"WHAT THE FUCK?" THE DOG SOUNDED like it was inside the house. Kurt ran out of the house and then around its perimeter—still inside the pole barn, looking for the dog. Nothing.

Next he ran out of the pole barn and around it, looking for the dog, but all was quiet again. There was no more barking.

"Weird." He stood at the back of the pole barn, just looking around.

THEY HEARD HIM CURSE, AND RUN THROUGH THE FRONT DOOR. It slammed on his way out.

Wolf opened the tunnel door fully and reached down, grabbing Thor, "Quiet!" he said forcefully, but quietly. Thor was quiet, except for a low-pitched involuntary whining. He was injured.

"Put him in the bathroom," Zoe whispered, "An extra layer of wall might make him harder to hear. You got any pain pills in there?"

"Yep. Some Motrin."

"Crush one up and give it to him in some water."

"I'll do that," Lucy offered. She grabbed Thor and went into the bathroom, shutting the door behind them. The dog's whining was now barely audible.

"How fast will it work?"

"Probably not fast enough, but it's worth a try."

"Where is he now?" Christie asked.

Wolf listened, "I can't hear anything. But we don't dare move until we know. If we crawl out of that tunnel while he's out there, we'll be sitting ducks. Right now, we're safe. He doesn't know where we are. Why mess with that?"

Zoe thought—it was true. They needed to be patient. All of them waited, still, and listening. The only sound was Lucy's soft and gentle cooing from behind the bathroom door, trying to calm the dog—keeping him quiet.

She poked her head out. "He's bleeding pretty bad."

"Shit." Zoe looked at Wolf. His expression echoed hers.

"We have to get him away from the tunnel entrance. He might discover it if he sees a blood trail."

Zoe considered their options. "We need to get him moving again. So we can place him—know where he is." She looked at the group. "Wolf, will Thor bark on command?"

"Yep."

"Can you get him to bark once and then stop right away?"

"Sure." He opened the door to the bathroom.

"Wait." Zoe held up her hand, and whispered. "Do it inside the bathroom, don't bring him out here. It will be harder for him to place where the sound came from."

Wolf closed the bathroom door behind him, urged softly, "Speak," and waited for one loud bark. Then he said, "Quiet!"

"Good dog," Lucy said softly as Wolf exited the bathroom. And they all waited again, silently.

"FUCKING DOG!" IT SOUNDED LIKE THE MUTT was back inside somewhere.

Kurt ran back into the pole barn and looked around the outside of house itself. There was no dog, and the door to the house was closed. So if the dog was inside, how in the hell did he get there? No way that little mutt could jump in through the window—it was too high. He circled the perimeter of the cottage once more, but there was no obvious entry.

Maybe this place was haunted after all, he considered. Grace might be crazy, but that didn't necessarily make her wrong on that point.

He opened the front door and walked inside again. Starting at the front and working his way toward the back, he looked into every nook and cranny of the house. Maybe there were two dogs?

"HE'S BACK INSIDE. GO. NOW! We might not have another chance. Don't turn around, just keep going—no matter what. We'll be right behind you as soon as we can."

Wolf jumped down into the tunnel, and then reached back up to help Christie. Zoe stood ready to hand Christie's son down to him, but first, she whispered, "I'll think of something, I promise, don't say a word about this to anyone. Like you guys were never here, okay?"

"You're sure?"

"Yes. That's how we're going to work it. You guys weren't here—and as far as you know, this never happened. We all in agreement?"

She got nods all around and handed the boy down, thinking about the secret he now had to keep—not unlike the one Wolf had been carrying all these years. Then she looked at Lucy and tried to rehearse their eventual exit in her mind.

KURT HEARD SOMETHING. It wasn't a dog sound though; it was more like muted conversation. Maybe a radio on somewhere, turned way down. He ran back through the house, looking, but found only one radio—and it was turned off.

Sometimes the wind sounds like people talking, he thought, but it was foggy outside, so there couldn't be wind. Once, when he lived in St. Paul, they were doing a big underground dig to replace some huge sewer pipes, and he could hear the vibration from inside his house. But out here, there'd be nothing like that happening.

Then he smiled, and said, "Come out, come out, wherever you are!" That's when he started shooting. He fired into the ceiling, even though he saw no attic access, because maybe they were hiding on the roof. He fired into closets, into cupboards, into the floor, and even into the mattress in the bedroom.

———

"NOW, LUCY! GO! I'll be right behind you. He's in the house, and he's on to us—now's the time! Go! Run! And don't look back!"

Lucy jumped into the tunnel and Zoe said, "Wait! Take this, and handed Lucy the gun. Lucy nodded and disappeared.

Zoe stood at the threshold, ready to jump in behind Lucy, when two bullets were fired through the bookcase and lodged in the far wall behind her. The bedroom on the other side was darkened, which meant that if he were looking, he'd see light shining out at him from the hidden room.

Zoe froze, and saw his eye look through one of the holes—he looked right at her. Zoe would have given just about anything for the gun that was now in Lucy's hand.

———

"WHAT THE FUCK?" He shot several more rounds through the wall, aiming at the woman he'd seen on the other side. He ducked and dodged as he fired, expecting a return of fire, but there was none. By then he'd created a bigger opening, and cautiously went back for one more look—a better look. The woman was gone—presumably through the fucking hole in the floor!

Kurt ran out of the cottage, out of the pole barn, and around to the back.

———

ZOE PEEKED ABOVE THE RIM OF THE TUNNEL as it surfaced just inside the perimeter of trees. In one direction, Lucy was gone—Zoe caught a glimpse of her at a distance, circling toward the river. From the other direction, Kurt was coming toward her—but he jogged cautiously, looking at the ground as he did. Zoe gathered herself under the vegetation and remained absolutely still—low to the ground. Part of her was hidden in the tunnel, while her upper half was supine under branches and leaves. In her hand she held what Lucy had decided to leave for her at the tunnel's edge.

Kurt's approach slowed, and Zoe figured he'd caught sight of the dog's blood trail. She watched him kneel down to touch something, look ahead along his path, then lift off his knees and advance a short distance. Once again he knelt, and then confidently moved forward again. He was close, maybe twenty feet away. Closing in.

Zoe could have told him to drop his weapon, that she had him good to rights—that it was over. But she didn't. Instead she said "I could kill you right now," which in her mind meant basically the same thing.

He spun around, looking for the voice's source, and raised his gun.

Precisely the wrong thing to do, Zoe smiled inwardly—especially when his opponent was less than a foot off the ground.

The instinct to protect oneself is normally translated into pulsing hormones and physical response a fraction of a second before being consciously aware of the need for action—that is, unless it unfolds as it did with Kurt. Instead of the normal fight or flight response, Kurt had to get past an initial competing emotion, one that even a sociopath wasn't immune from—and Zoe recognized the exact moment when it happened, because she'd been looking directly into his eyes.

His face reflected the mistake as a feeling of being creeped out mixed with disbelief. Zoe saw his upper lip curl in disgust and form around the words "What the?" It was only momentary, but long enough to delay the panic-point he should have reached immediately. Because in that first moment, the buffer moment, he would have been looking at nothing but vegetation, leaves, twigs, branches, until suddenly locking on to the two eyes looking out at him from the ground—nothing but the whites of two eyes, everything else camouflaged.

Allowing Zoe to fire first.

He fell to the ground, his gun dropping, useless, from his hand—and again, Zoe could have run. But she didn't. Instead she kicked the gun away and stood over him, asking, "Where's Sally?"

He moaned and grabbed at his stomach. The ground around him was pooling red.

"Where?" Zoe yelled.

"You're the doctor?" he managed to ask.

"Yes. Now where is she?"

"You'll save me? You have to."

"Only if you tell me where she is."

"Our warehouse—Central Avenue. The bartender knows where it is," his mouth bubbled with blood.

Zoe knelt, and methodically searched his pockets as Kurt moaned and begged her for help. In them she found the other weapons, more ammo . . . and some medical documents. She quickly scanned them, trying to stay calm, then stuffed them in her pocket.

It was to her great relief that she had a simple tool for accomplishing her next task—the gun Lucy had left her at the edge of the tunnel.

Zoe raised the weapon and said, "The first one was for Christie. This one's for Lucy," then she aimed and shot him through the heart.

Zoe turned away, easily, and ran toward her group hiding at the river's edge. She thought as she ran—working out what needed to be done. Zoe always thought best when she ran.

KNOWING THERE WAS AN ALERT OUT ON KURT'S CAR, instead they risked using the buyer's vehicle to transport Lucy back to Pushpa's car and Christie and her son back to Grace's. But not before a little swing through the surrounding neighborhoods so that Lucy could identify the doctor's house. Along the way, they helped Lucy compose a good story that explained her brief absence—a simple miscommunication was all, and Zoe was confident in Lucy's ability to sell it.

Zoe timed the drive and asked Lucy to ring her cell exactly twenty-five minutes after they dropped her off at Pushpa's car—it would give her enough time to get back to the area where she'd lost her cell. Then, twenty-five minutes later, after hearing the ringtone and locating the cell, she thanked Lucy and immediately called Kaj to say that she would be working through the night.

All that done, Zoe and Wolf returned to the carnage. First they used the buyer's SUV to tow Zoe's Jeep into the pole barn. Wolf steered the Jeep while Zoe drove the SUV. Then Zoe told him to go.

"Where?"

"Take the bus and go back to your mother's place. Stay with her for a while. But Wolf, you have to talk to her about this land. Make sure she never sells it. I'll send you both some money to help continue paying the taxes—but whatever you do, don't sell this place. Keep it posted—keep people away. That's the way it has to be—for a good, long time. Do you understand? Don't draw any attention to this place."

"Yes. Nothing's really changed, has it?"

"Everything's changed! There're more people involved now, and I don't like that. You can't use this place any more, either. Not for anything. You have to keep it shut tight, no trespassers, nothing. Get it?"

"Yes," he paused "Thanks."

ZOE WAITED UNTIL 1:00 A.M. TO PULL KURT'S CAR into the driveway of the snake-oil doctor's house. She'd watched the lights go out in his home at about eleven, and waited until she was sure he was asleep. She'd also waited for every other light on the street to go out. One by one, she'd waited for the houses to darken. And even then, she'd let another hour go by before acting.

After she parked it, Zoe softly closed the car door behind her—leaving two dead bodies locked in the trunk, and another in the backseat.

Zoe had considered leaving the guns with the bodies, but that left too much to chance—and besides, in the tale she hoped the police would invent, it would be plausible that the doctor would have already started to cover his ass and gotten rid of the guns.

So the guns were now at the bottom of the river—even the expensive Leupold scope.

The only loose end was her car. She'd have to make it up that she'd sold hers, and then quickly buy a new one. Her license plates now accompanied all the guns along the bottom of the river. But she had no way to get her Jeep out of Wolf's pole barn—not for a long time. Not without the help of a third party—and not without attracting attention to the burial ground. And so it was sacrificed.

Pam Leonard

Zoe ran from the doc's house back to the farm and retrieved the buyer's SUV—then she drove it to the doctor's house and parked it directly behind Kurt's car, boxing it in. She took both sets of keys and made her way back to the farm at a jog. She was getting tired.

At the farm, she ran some more—down to the river to toss in the keys—and then she used Wolf's bike to make her way back to the hospital. She cleaned up there, while her thoughts were with Kaj.

It hadn't surprised him—her staying to work the night. With her, nothing surprised him anymore. He'd only asked how she was feeling.

"Great," she'd lied. "Just great," and Zoe only hoped like hell that another generation could keep this secret.

Chapter Twelve

ZOE ALLOWED HERSELF TO SINK BACK INTO the heated leather seat of his SUV. As he downshifted the powerful machine to navigate the steep descent into Duluth, she was treated to a beautiful view of Lake Superior.

"Scenic route," he said. "Glad you decided to take everyone's advice. A little vacation was definitely in order."

She spotted the old lift bridge that everyone thought of when they pictured Duluth, connecting the main city with a thin sliver of land known as Park Point—a place that existed here in defiance of the lake and its power. Park Point seemed more like a giant sand dune populated by hardy, but probably crazy, people. The small weather-beaten cottages lined up on Minnesota Avenue facing the lake like sentries.

She turned to scan Duluth itself, and the variety of structures built into and up the hillside. The whole thing reminded her of a smaller version of San Francisco. She watched as an ore ship made its way toward the lift bridge until Kaj turned east along the main drag and it was lost to sight.

"I know how much you like architecture, so enjoy the view."

The old buildings had been put to the oddest assortment of modern uses, from strip clubs to upscale hotels, condos, and art galleries.

"Place sure has character."

The gentrification was obvious, but you could still feel the city's original sin. Along with its charm was the sass and swagger of a mining town and sailors' port.

She noticed several art galleries. "Artist's enclave?"

"Yes. I've a few of my own works on display up here."

Her jaw dropped, and he smiled. She suddenly realized how little she actually knew about him, even after a year.

"Quick, look to your right and you can see Canal Park. I have a few pieces in a gallery down there."

"Are we talking about art as an investment, or art that you've created?" She caught a brief glimpse of the town-within-a-town known as Canal Park, the lift bridge still up.

"They're my creations. Not my favorites though. Those are at my residences." He turned to grin at her, "I've never hidden the fact that I'm a selfish man."

"Are there any paintings at your cabin?"

"Yes, including the one I'm happiest with." His smile had her wondering. There was mischief in it. He risked a long look away from the road, at her, and seemed to consider his words carefully.

"You know, in the end, it's the paintings that go through what I call a 'wrecked' phase that I wind up liking the most. I've learned from experience that when I feel as though I've ruined one, to the point of being ready to throw it out, that I shouldn't. With that level of frustration, as though there's nothing left to lose, a painting becomes more accepting of risks—and I'm willing to take more risks with it."

He checked her face once more, then returned his gaze to the road and continued. "Once I allow that in myself, I discover things. And I never fail to be surprised by what happens with those paintings. Something that starts out as very intentional, and ends that way, gets there by way of a reckless, explorational energy."

"Kaj, I've seen some of your paintings. It's the imperfections that make them so interesting...and beautiful. Besides, if you insisted on perfection, you'd never finish them," she laughed. "Nothing would ever get done."

She watched him smile as his hand reached out for her shoulder, and from there, wandered toward her neck. He ran his fingers along her scar.

"You're right, beauty is in the disorder. It's proof that we exist—that we matter."

"It's what I should have told Lucy, that humans are unpredictable—like vibrating strings."

"I think she's got that one figured out by now. She's a smart one."

Zoe shifted uncomfortably in her seat—it was the topic—and redirected it back, "So why not approach them all that way? Wreck them? Then see what happens?"

He laughed. "I wish it were that simple. But it's nothing like that. It's not something I can force. And you've no idea how stressful the process becomes when I have to give up control, even for a little while. Normally it doesn't matter whether I'm working on an abstract or a nude, the process is *very* intentional. It evolves, yes, but still it's ultimately my creation.

"And yet the 'wrecked' pieces, well, it's as if they fight me. Fight for control. So much so that in the end I almost feel as though I can't take full credit for them.

Honestly, I can only stand so many of those. They're exhausting. And one in particular has given me more trouble than any other," he shook his head, "but just wait till you see it." He reached over to take her hand.

"It's up here? At the cabin?"

"It is. I just had it moved here."

"Can't wait," she smiled at him.

As they pulled out the other end of Duluth and headed up the North Shore, he chose the scenic Lake Drive over the expressway. The day was uncharacteristically calm, a fog moving in.

"Should we stop somewhere for supplies?"

"I called ahead and asked Marc to do it—he's the caretaker when I'm not around. He stocked the refrigerator and got everything set up—including the painting."

"So is this where you take all your lovers?" she asked, grinning.

He smiled. "There've been a few."

Zoe laughed. "That's what I thought. But I also think I can make you forget them."

She felt him speed up, and had to tell him to watch the road, not her.

"I guess I have some work to do on that front myself—and I promise to spoil you."

Zoe smiled at his profile, and then let her head fall to the right, watching the lake through a luxurious half-sleep. Just as she was about to doze off, she felt him brake and turn onto a narrow driveway that meandered toward the lake. It wound around trees before opening to a clearing where they parked. The cabin perched at the edge of a cliff, with sharp, fallen rocks in tangles below. To one side of the rocks was a small sandy beach shared by a fire pit and boathouse. The shoreline was barely visible in the fog as they made their way around the cantilevered walkway to the entry.

She stopped in her tracks as they approached the doorway. It was so abrupt that he bumped into her as she pulled up. He wrapped his arms around her.

"Well, you *are* full of surprises aren't you?" She stood still, taking it all in.

"Thought you'd like it."

"Yes, very much!" Then she twisted in his arms to face him. "Is this a Frank Lloyd Wright?"

"It was designed by one of his apprentices. Let's go inside. I know you'll appreciate it."

They made their way to a front door constructed of wood and stained glass. In the opalescent window she saw an abstract pattern representing something of nature—from this place, she thought. Looking at it closely, she asked, "This place have a name?"

He smiled proudly, "The architect christened it *Splashing Rock*."

"Fits. And this?" She pointed to the glass design. "You, or the architect?"

"He designed it. Beautiful, isn't it?"

She touched the iridescent glass reverently before opening the door. As expected, the foyer was intimate, the ceiling low. It felt safe and sheltering, an entry that didn't reveal everything right away. As you walked beyond it, the ceiling vaulted. Again, not too capacious, it was still grounded in the intimacy of the human scale. There was nothing to contribute to any sense of unease.

And though it was stimulating visually, it was also a retreat, a place of relaxation. There was no competition between the structure and its view of the lake. Instead the many windows brought it in—as if art on the wall.

"I love it." She swept the room with an appreciative eye. The great room was dominated by the lake view and a charming fireplace around which were comfortable chairs and a small sofa. The same room contained a dining area off of which branched a galley kitchen. The table and chairs appeared to have been handcrafted to reflect the design of the house. She pointed to them. "Custom made?"

"Yes, to the architect's specifications. You can see how I enjoy coming here, can't you?" He stepped over to his sound system and pushed a button. Bill Withers' "Lovely Day" came on.

"Absolutely. It's amazing. Why haven't we been here before?"

When the day that lies ahead of me
Seems impossible to face

"Circumstances have conspired."

When someone else instead of me
Always seems to know the way

She looked around, noticing several pieces of artwork on the walls. "Which one is it? The one you said you were happiest with? Your favorite piece?"

"My new addition." He smiled. "It's not out here."

"Where is it?"

"In here." He led her toward the bedroom.

Then I look at you

And the world's all right with me

"You're not serious are you? Getting me into the sack on the premise of seeing your *etchings* or some such thing?" she teased.

Just one look at you

"Trust me darling, I'd do anything to get you in the sack. But in this case, it's no ruse."

And I know it's gonna be

"If it's your favorite piece, why would you hide it? Why not place it out here? Or display it at one of those galleries?"

"From now on, it's private," he said as he stepped aside to allow her a view of the painting.

A lovely day . . .

Lovely day, lovely day

"Oh, my." It brought her up short—and breathless. "I'm . . . I mean . . . it's . . . beautiful."

"Yes, you are." He stared at her—the living, breathing Zoe.

She looked closely at the painting, and then walked over to the full-length mirror leaning against a wall. Staring at the woman she saw reflected back, she turned to face him. "It's me, but it's not. I'm not beautiful in that way."

Without thinking, she reached a hand to touch the scar at her neck, the one her abductor had given her so long ago—her talisman. She had others, plenty of small scars as reminders of bike crashes and hockey, not to mention her work as a cop. But it was this one she reached for. The one she defiantly refused to hide, yet the one that reminded her of a more profound damage every time she looked at it.

It had always felt uncomfortable to stare at her image in a mirror, yet she was strangely drawn to it in the *painting*—and though it was out of character to admit, seeming vain even, she actually liked it.

"Is this the way you see me?"

"Almost. It comes close, but after all, it's only a painting. My frustration with not being able to truly capture the way I see you was one of the things that led this work through its 'wrecked' stage."

"What else?" She continued to stare at the painting as she spoke.

His eyes were still on her. "That, and the illumination."

"Oh, but that's what draws me into this painting. It's as if I'm lit by . . . what . . . candlelight? No. Neon? A sunset maybe?"

Lovely day, lovely day

She turned to look at him, expecting a response, but he only smiled.

Returning her gaze back toward the painting, she continued to study it. As she walked back and forth, drawing closer, then backing up, the painting began to feel much more complicated.

"No, it's as if there's a fire somewhere. The light reflected off my skin looks like it comes from a fire." She could almost feel heat off the painting.

"You see it then, don't you?"

It suddenly dawned. "It's you, isn't it?" She swung her head to face him. "You put *yourself* in that painting, didn't you? You're the light—the fire."

He nodded and kept his eyes on her, not the painting.

"There's more to it, though. There's something I can't quite . . . you painted me as a reclining nude, and yet it's kinetic, there's energy in it. It's unexpected in this painting, unless," she looked back toward the canvas, staring at it, and then gasped, "you made love to me in that painting." This time it was a statement, not a question. She turned to face him, and his smile—that smile.

"It was indeed an act of lovemaking." As he pulled her onto the bed, he added, "And it wasn't easy."

"Well I'll make *this* easy for you," and she took charge until morning.

"YOU'LL FIND OUT SOONER OR LATER, so I'd might as well fess up."

Zoe opened her eyes. His arms encircled her from behind. Both were still in bed, the sun already arcing overhead. "Fess up to what?"

"That painting?—it was the one at the fundraiser, the one everyone came to see."

"What? Everyone saw me like that?"

"Yes. And you were right."

"Right about what?"

"About Connie. But only partially right."

"How so?"

"She was after me—made it pretty clear that night."

"Yeah, I sort of noticed that. But I wasn't right about her," and Zoe only wished she could tell him what she knew—about how heroic and generous Connie had been.

"No, you were right. But after she saw that painting . . . well, anyway . . . she backed off."

"How do you know? I don't mean to speak ill of the dead, but really, how do you know?"

"She told me. Said she could never compete with you—and with what we have."

"Well, I knew she was smart."

"Zoe."

"But I never gave her credit for being so kind and caring. Not to mention brave."

"Brave?"

Zoe's cellphone rang. "Shit."

"Don't answer it."

She looked at it, "I have to—it's Ray." She spoke into the phone, "Hey, Ray. What's up?"

"That anonymous call about the doctor and the dead bodies?"

"Yeah, it was all over the news. What about it?"

"Well, the doc's in a spot o' trouble, for sure—but so are you. Remember that DNA you gave me to run?"

Zoe's heart was in her throat. "Yeah," she said warily.

"It matches one of the vics."

"So?"

"So . . . your DNA also showed up, too—not only in the bloody hair sample you gave me, but in the vehicle."

"Well, maybe one of my hairs was still stuck on his jacket from when he nabbed me."

"Wrong car, Zoe. They found it in the SUV—in fact they found it all over." He waited to let it sink in. "You'd better get back down here."

"Yeah . . . guess I should." She hung up. So she'd fucked up, in more ways than one. Zoe was sure she'd wiped down all the prints, but she must have dropped some hair. And sadly, it shouldn't have mattered—after all, the other participants wouldn't have their DNA on record—but after turning in that bloody hair sample, they had hers. What she should have done was to simply bury the bodies, like the neighbors had done so long ago—make it a simple disappearance—and then stash all the cars in the pole barn. But no, instead she'd needed to to make the doctor pay—had to implicate him somehow.

"What was that all about?"

"Nothing." She looked at Kaj—looked as deeply as she could. Took him in completely, trying to create an image she would never forget. He might be better off, but oh ... oh, how she would miss him.

SHE KNEW HER RIGHTS, REFUSING TO SAY ANYTHING—either in her defense, or to implicate anyone else—got herself a lawyer, and posted bail. No other names were mentioned, either by her, or by the questioning cops. It meant they didn't know.

Kaj was supportive—irritatingly so. It would make everything else she had to do that much harder, especially the part about keeping everything from him. The not knowing would be hard on him. But he'd get over it—and be better off.

She spoke to Lucy, apologizing like crazy for involving her and for being such a piss-poor role model, then reminded her to pay attention—as a means of survival, as a form of prayer, even as an answer to prayer. Then Zoe made promises to her, promises she was pretty sure she couldn't keep—but promises that Lucy needed to hear.

She emptied her bank account and deliberated over the amounts. In one envelope she put enough for Wolf and his mother to continue paying taxes on the property for a good long while. In another she put enough for Kelly to pay expenses on her house and added a note that read, "Live in it, if you want." She sealed both envelopes, addressing Kelly's care of the hospital and Wolf's care of his mother's apartment, then put more than enough postage on each and dropped them in the outgoing mail.

Next, Zoe opened a medium-sized backpack and assembled a small set of supplies that included the rest of her money and the ladies wallet she'd taken off the Traceur—having almost forgotten about it. She walked the distance from her home to the Amtrak depot and used some of her money to buy four tickets.

The first two tickets were purchased under Christie's name. They were for the Empire Builder headed for Seattle in two days. The third ticket was to board the Chicago-bound Empire Builder scheduled to leave in thirty minutes, and the fourth was a connecting ticket aboard the Lake Shore Limited bound for New York City. Zoe bought those under the name of the woman whose wallet had been stolen. Then she took the two Seattle-bound tickets, sealed them up in another envelope addressed to Wolf, care of his mother, and dropped it in the mail. Included in the envelope was more money and a note, "For Christie and her son, if she wants to go—tell her to get off wherever she likes."

Zoe looked out at the morning sun. It carried the shadows of window mullions across her feet. She'd caused the deaths of Abel, Josh, and Connie—maybe not directly, but she'd played a pretty big, fucking role. Now she was alone with the knowledge of having dragged Lucy into the whole mess and filling her head with all kinds of things she didn't even understand herself—encouraging her to take stupid risks.

Zoe reached out, her hand stopped by the hard surface of a windowpane—and wondered how big or small the nearest universe really was? She pulled her hand back, rotating it in empty space—in stuff that she couldn't sense. Zoe hadn't yet told Lucy that many scientists believe there are more than four dimensions of space and time.. She thought it was eleven. Could they be that close? What were they like? Zoe watched her hand rotate in front of her, in what she was only capable of sensing as empty space. Were they as near as the sex trade that Lucy had ventured into?—or as intimate as the brief, but privileged glimpse one gets of homeless camps through the window of a train?

There was no escaping it. In another universe, maybe—one with a better outcome, one in which she'd made better decisions—but not in this one. In this one, she'd put Wolf in the position of having to kill a cop. She owned that.

Zoe fingered the detective's shield in her pocket—the one she'd found on the buyer's body. It would have to be up to someone else to decide if he'd been under cover—trying to solve the same mystery they'd been after. Or was he dirty?—using his position to procure underage girls for fun and profit. It wasn't that Zoe didn't care anymore—but to protect others, certain sacrifices had to be made, and quite a few people would be better off.

Zoe threw the policeman's badge into a garbage can before stepping out the door and into the sun. It was early, her shadow long—it traveled the distance between who she was and the person she was expected to be, until disappearing under the train as she stepped aboard.